P9-DDU-243

The Girl with the Long Back

Also by Bill James in the Harpur and Iles series:
You'd Better Believe It
The Lolita Man
Halo Parade
Protection (TV tie-in version, *Harpur and Iles*)
Come Clean
Take
Club
Astride a Grave
Gospel
Roses, Roses
In Good Hands
The Detective is Dead
Top Banana
Panicking Ralph
Eton Crop
Lovely Mover
Kill Me
Pay Days
Naked at the Window

Other novels by Bill James:
The Last Enemy

By the same author writing as David Craig:
The Brade and Jenkins series:
Forget It
The Tattooed Detective
Torch
Bay City

Other novels by David Craig:
The Alias Man
Message Ends
Contact Lost
Young Men May Die
A Walk at Night
Up from the Grave
Double Take
Bolthole
Whose Little Girl Are You?
(filmed as *The Squeeze*)
A Dead Liberty
The Albion Case
Faith, Hope and Death

Writing as James Tucker:
Equal Partners
The Right Hand Man
Burster
Blaze of Riot
The King's Friends (reissued as by Bill James)

Non-fiction:
Honourable Estates
The Novels of Anthony Powell

THE GIRL WITH THE LONG BACK

Bill James

W. W. Norton & Company
New York London

First American Edition 2004

Printed in the United States of America

For information about permission to reproduce selections from this book, write to Permissions, W. W. Norton & Company, Inc. 500 Fifth Avenue, New York, NY 10110

Manufacturing by Quebecor Fairfield

ISBN 0-393-05855-7

W. W. Norton & Company, Inc.
500 Fifth Avenue, New York, N.Y. 10110
www.wwnorton.com

W. W. Norton & Company Ltd.
Castle House, 75/76 Wells Street, London W1T 3QT

1 2 3 4 5 6 7 8 9 0

Acknowledgement

Part of Chapter Two, in slightly different form, appears as 'Like An Arrangement' in the short story collection edited by John Harvey, *Men from Boys* (Heinemann).

Chapter One

Harpur detested running undercover jobs. In any case, Desmond Iles, the Assistant Chief, had put his own absolute ban on these operations. Now and then, though, Harpur decided to ignore that. Of course, it could be dangerous to ignore Iles, and not just career dangerous: physically dangerous, limb and/or eye dangerous, life-expectancy dangerous. But Harpur had always realized policing was a risk game.

Most of his inner-city, hardened officers were too well known to trick their way into a gang. So, it usually meant finding someone from an outlying station, preferably someone young and new to the Service: no big, publicized cases in their CV. That is, they were novice cops, and normally might still need some lumps of guidance from a venerable Detective Chief Superintendent like Harpur. Not always possible, once they began to play crooked. They had to live a role, like an actor, and contact with them might smash their cover. A good undercover man or woman infiltrated the highest and most secret corners of a villain firm and had to be faultless in their part. In those highest and most secret corners a rumbled snoop could be most secretly tortured and done to death. It had happened a while ago to a detective called Raymond Street. For ever this darkened Iles's soul. And so, the ban.

At present, Harpur had a youngster into one of the drug outfits on the west side of the city. Or half in. Don't rush. Infiltration always took a while and sometimes went catastrophic even after slow, slow months – even after a year plus. Louise Machin came from one of those rural outposts. He had asked for her secondment, allegedly to help with youth club liaison. Yes, allegedly. If Iles got a whiff of that he'd know the real ploy instantly and come looking. There was a bit of a tale around that the ACC's power could be on the slide. This might make him even rougher. His claws would dig deeper, to help him hang on.

A minimum connection with Louise had to be kept. Harpur met her at pre-fixed times to talk method and information, if she had any, not at her place or his place or headquarters or any of the supposedly safe but predictable rendezvous sites such as supermarkets, art galleries, swimming baths, cinemas, the opera. Instead, he liked to use the rippling turmoil of Parents Evenings at a school somewhere. This would not be his own children's school, naturally. At the start of every term, the local paper printed a schedule for Parents Evenings, and he settled dates and places with Louise then. He reasoned they could blend with the parent crowd and nobody would realize they had no offspring there.

Tonight, talking at the back of a geography room, Harpur said: 'Listen, Louise, at every meeting I tell undercover officers that if they get the smallest sense of something wrong ditch it. Leave.' His voice always took on a terrible thinness and frailty when he briefed undercover people. Dread of what he was asking almost silenced him.

'Don't I know you tell them – us – at every meeting?' she said.

'Yes, leave, go fast to headquarters or any nick or my house or, at a pinch, Mr Iles's house. He might not be there but his wife and child probably would be. Even if Mr Iles himself were at home, I don't think he'd try anything sexual when you were distressed after baling out, especially with his family about. He can be surprisingly sensitive.'

'He's at Idylls, Rougement Place?'

'That's it. I'm 126 Arthur Street. No hesitation. Abort the whole thing immediately. Don't return for belongings.'

'You sound like a fire drill, sir.'

It *was* a fucking fire drill. In theory, infiltrating drugs operations rated as one of the easier undercover jobs, because the trade had a long, complicated chain – supplier, wholesaler, pusher, client – and a talented detective should be able to penetrate it somewhere and take a role. Yes, in theory. 'Just textbook procedures,' Harpur said.

'Right setting for a textbook.'

Stop smartarsing, you smug tit. 'Anyone would go over these basics with you, Louise.' Meteorological maps heavy with wind arrows crowded the walls. He liked a classroom to smell of chalk, make you sneeze through chalk. But it was all whiteboards and felt markers here.

' "The smallest sense of something wrong" meaning I feel they've spotted me?' she asked.

At once Harpur said: 'There's been something like that?', his voice even frailer.

'Don't get het up, sir. No.'

He stared at Louise, trying to read her eyes and face, in case she were being offhand and brave and fucking loony. But one reason he'd picked her was she could thesp and do deadpan. 'I say this to everyone, every time,' he told her.

'Yes, you mentioned.'

'Routine. I don't want you to feel alarmed.'

'No, right,' she replied.

Her detachment, even jauntiness, scared him. She gazed about the room, apparently more interested in the maps and chatter than Harpur's warnings. Another reason he had picked her was she did seem calm and full of self-belief. 'Or if you can't get out, ring the urgent assistance number. Always a help team there. They'll come and get you. You've memorized the number?'

'Haven't I poll-parroted it often enough for you?'

'Standard check, that's all.'

'Routine,' she said.

He'd have liked to ask her to repeat the number once again, but decided she might be right and he was into hyper-fret. No might. But did she realize how fast memory crumbled when you were screwed by fear? Did British Telecom realize, loading us with all those fucking digits? 'So, is there anything?' he asked.

'I think they may be going to clip someone,' she replied.

Harpur didn't mind Americanisms. All languages searched for softer ways of saying kill: a kind of woe-begone, daft delicacy. 'Going to?'

'Either going to or they've done it by now.'

'We've no unexplained deads reported.'

'Just the same, that's what I'm picking up. They could lose a body, couldn't they – sink it, concrete it, burn it?' she said. 'Or take it to some other part of the country?'

Where did she get her seen-it-all worldliness from, this kid? TV drama? Yes, they could sink it, concrete it, burn it, freight it. He did not say this. He wanted the silence so she would work aloud at justifying her guess to him. At the other end of the room, two teachers talked to parents, with a good-sized queue on chairs waiting. A whiteboard still showed part of its rainfall lesson, with the words DO NOT ERASE big in the bottom right-hand corner. Harpur liked schools, at least as an adult. They were well intentioned. Even with the lost-looking people ambling about here tonight, schools did suggest some underlying organization. They spoke of continuity. There would always be weather and weather maps bringing it to a kind of order. DO NOT ERASE. He gazed at Louise. Schools made him feel things might be long-term OK. Stupid, and he knew it.

'I can't work out who,' she said. 'Not yet.'

'One of their own people? Or the competition?'

'Are you expecting something like that?'

'Like what?' he replied.

'Warfare.'

'What warfare?' he asked. This was unquestionably a

smart child. At other Parents Evenings ten years ago teachers probably told her parents they'd produced a flyer. Now, she was in Harpur's care and he had better make sure she did not get shot down. She was clever, so he had chosen cleverly. And idiotically? Did she see too much, and did this flair make her barmy-blasé?

'Warfare,' she replied chattily. 'Oh, you know what warfare is, Mr Harpur. Is that why I've been put into Dubal's? You sensed something might be starting?'

Along those lines. 'What starting?' he asked.

'Warfare. Either civil warfare inside Dubal's outfit, or general warfare between the firms.'

'You're getting melodramatic twice,' Harpur replied.

'We've had nice peace on the streets for so long, haven't we, but is it ending?'

'What's it based on?' Time for the head-on questions.

'What?'

'Your . . . your feeling's someone's dead.'

'Based on a feeling,' she said.

'Something heard? Something seen?'

'Based on a feeling.'

'Yes, but –'

'A feeling,' she replied.

'Or maybe not heard, but do people go suddenly quiet when you're around? In that case, get out now. Now.'

'I'm only middle rank in the firm, so far. If they've killed they might want it kept boardroom, so when they clam it needn't mean they've sussed me.'

'Is it top people who go quiet when you're around? You get close to them?' Harpur asked.

'What the job's about, yes – reaching the chiefs? No good infiltrating flunkeys.'

God, she was so magnificently assured, the dodgy, arrogant young cow. She could look like a teenager but talked like a veteran. Harpur knew he could not have selected better, unless she finished slaughtered. When their talk paused he caught occasional fragments of conversation between parents and teachers: '. . . been all over the main rivers in Africa with Celia, Mr Green.' Chuckles followed. 'When I say "been over" I don't mean like in a canoe, but at home, learning . . . Nile, Congo, Limpopo. Celia will never sell rivers short.' Harpur was afraid the queue would run out soon, and then the teachers might call Louise or him for a consultation about their supposed schoolchildren.

'If you're that near to getting something big, we should have an earlier meeting than our schedule says,' Harpur suggested. 'As soon as you've found a name and possible location for the body we'll close you down. A three weeks' wait after this is too long.'

'I'd prefer things as planned. I'm used to the pattern. I don't want to feel hurried.'

'No, but –'

'Best as it is, sir.'

She was offering a cold lesson in how not to panic. All the same, he felt panicky for her. She was a biggish, wide-faced girl of twenty-three, not pretty, not especially bright in appearance, though damn bright. At least, he hoped damn bright, however awkward this might make her questions and guesses – above all, bright enough to spot the difference between being treated as a run-of-the-mill exec in Ferdy Dubal's organization, and being lulled up towards extinction as a spy. She was dressed to suit her supposed job as ranker in the Dubal firm: jeans, brown leather bomber jacket, trainers. Her fair/mousy hair had been chop-cut, tufted all directions.

As route into Dubal's firm, she bought from one of his dealers for a time, then offered to sell to pals. Dubal's people gave her small amounts at first and, when she came back with the loot, increased her stock. She disposed of this, too, and religiously brought them the full takings, without turning junky herself. Main folk in the firm might want to meet her soon, even Dubal personally.

She didn't actually sell to pals, but to anyone. What she couldn't sell she stashed and made up the money with some Harpur provided from his informant fund. Supervision of that was woolly, the accounting blissfully approximate. The ACC knew Harpur would never disclose pay scales for his grasses, and stuff the rule saying superiors must be briefed. This money went where it helped – where Harpur decided it would help, and that was private and would stay private. He had heard the European Union Court of Human Rights wanted to get its worthy, legalistic grip on the British informant system. Fuck the EU.

'This will upset Mr Iles, won't it, sir?'

'What?'

'Dubal murdering, or Dubal's minions, on his say-so? Isn't there a kind of deal?'

'Deal?' Harpur replied. He made it sound true puzzlement.

'Dubal, Mansel Shale, Ralphy Ember can do their drugs business as long as they guarantee peace on the streets, and especially no deaths. Isn't that Mr Iles's arrangement, in defiance of the Chief and even the Chief's wife?'

A brilliant summary. It left out only that the deal might start to fade soon, if the rumours stood up and Iles himself was fading. This girl really did have good ears. Thank God ears were not sexy. He could do without that kind of interest in her, to make his worries even worse.

Perhaps the headquarters rumours about change had reached Dubal and the rest, too. The speculation was not just that Iles might slip. It said Mark Lane, the Chief Constable, might be promoted away from here to the Inspectorate of Constabulary, with someone new from outside taking the post. Iles would not get it: he had reached ceiling. And there were too many tales in circulation about him. In fact, a new, vigorous Chief would most likely want some of Iles's present filched powers cut. And, if Iles did have his influence chopped, and the peace arrangement collapsed as a result, there would be big violence again. Major commodity folk like Manse Shale and Panicking Ralph Ember, and smaller teams such as Dubal's, would suddenly feel they must start protecting themselves and their trade positions once more. Pre-empting would be the fashion – the bloody and rough fashion. It was why Harpur wanted this girl in one of the firms to read any signs. And it was why, more than during any other undercover ploy, her role had to be secret from Iles. It was actually *about* Iles.

Harpur laughed for a while and managed to get his tone satirical: 'A deal? An arrangement? Policing could never function like that, Louise.'

'I don't think I understand Mr Iles – his mind – what I've heard of him, it.'

'No great problem,' Harpur replied, giving this another fragment of laughter. Oh, no? Christ, Harpur would love to understand the ACC's mind himself. Much of it stayed a mystery, although they had worked with and against each other for so long, and at one time shared a woman. Iles's competing spells of highest calibre brutality, highest calibre tenderness, his adoration of his wife and infant daughter, his lust for teenage girls – on the game or not – his uncrackable loyalty to Mark Lane, the Chief, his gross subversiveness of Mark Lane, the Chief, his radiant brain, his interludes of screaming mania – these made the ACC quite tricky to profile, possibly a little more than other Assistant Chiefs. Using a special, large voice from somewhere central in him, Iles had once recited a line of his favourite poet, Tennyson, to Harpur: 'Trust me all in all or not at all.' Harpur did not read much Tennyson, nor poetry in general, and decided it was better to give Iles a bit of trust, but only a bit. In fact, when it came to the sexual safety of Harpur's fifteen-year-old daughter, Hazel, he trusted Iles that 'not at all' option, or less.

'The Chief would never permit deals with people like Dubal,' Harpur told Louise.

'But the Chief doesn't control things, does he? Mr Iles does. This is what I gather.'

Another brilliant summary, at least to date. 'Policing can't function like that,' he replied. 'Mark Lane commands here, believe me.' Harpur had always thought that people only said 'believe me' when they were lying at full throttle and feared it was obvious. He still thought so.

'Is that why you put me into Dubal's team?' Louise said.

'Is what?'

'You had an idea he'd started to stray from the agreement – getting stroppy? Is there some sort of revolution imminent or under way? You think there've been earlier killings?'

A third brilliant summary. Harpur had never fully accepted Iles's doctrine of controlled trading in exchange for urban tranquillity. Always he feared the fixed peace would disintegrate. Perhaps it was happening. Now, Harpur wanted evidence of what Louise called warfare to push in front of the ACC and force a change. Louise might find it. Very occasionally, Iles could be reached by reason, even from an underling.

'Perhaps Ferdy Dubal isn't in favour of the arrangement,' Louise said. 'He might want to destroy it because he considers others are favoured more than himself. The way to destroy it is by clipping someone, maybe more than one. So, peace is kaput.'

He had not turned out here for a policy discussion with some detective sergeant, but that's what he was getting. This girl had come from the accelerated promotion course at Bramshill. And he could see how she'd got there. Harpur said: 'Suppose – suppose . . . Suppose it was true Mr Iles has what you call an arrangement, a peace arrangement, with –'

'I do suppose it, sir.' She obviously thought she could be as insolent as she liked as long as she stuck a 'sir' on the end. Harpur often used the same technique with Iles. Louise was a true find.

'. . . so, suppose a peace arrangement with the drugs firms,' Harpur said. 'Surely the –'

'You're going to say Dubal is a drugs firm so, *surely,* the sensible thing for him to do is preserve the peace, not smash it, because he needs settled conditions to trade in as much as others.'

Yes, he *had* been going to say that. This girl was a bright pain. God, she would need some looking after. He went back to all-out attack-from-defence: 'Of course, the whole notion of an arrangement is crap. How could it be implemented?'

'By . . . by arrangement. It's nice for Mr Iles – and for you, perhaps. People don't get killed on the streets or in the clubs, like London or Manchester. Good for your statistics. Law and order rule, except, naturally, for the comfortable trade in substances. And that's nice for Panicking Ralph Ember and Manse Shale, also.'

'And, if your analysis were right – which it never could be – but, if it were – nice for Dubal, also.'

'No. Too much of the business had been shared out before he arrived. Panicking and Manse are drawing – are drawing what, half a Big One from trade every year? Say even £600,000?'

Yes, say £600,000.

'Dubal's at low point gain. Possibly only eighty, ninety thousand a year. Only possibly. He's a late incomer. It's amazing he's got so far, but he doesn't think it's far enough. They never do. This lad has major ambitions. Why he moved in here from Liverpool.'

'You sound like his PR.'

'He can't go higher because of the established, holy arrangement. The trinity against one. Three very powerful and settled outfits against his.'

'Two as far as I know – Shale, Ember.'

'Shale, Ember, Iles.'

'That's crap.'

'Yes, you said.'

'Crap,' Harpur replied.

'Ferdy Dubal's heard about the future.'

'Which?'

'Mark Lane to be promoted out of here. New strong

Chief. Iles's power hacked to what it officially should be, or less.'

'Some story,' Harpur said.

'Ferdy wants to be sure that, when Lane does go, Mr Iles and the arrangement have no chance to hang on. Or not an arrangement favouring Shale and Ember. Iles is a toughie. He's smart. He has smart and influential mates. Ferdy knows it. So he'll try to wreck or even get rid of Iles every way he knows – now, before the switch-over.'

'Mr Iles a target? An Assistant Chief? Oh, come on, Louise.'

'And Ferdy will do everything to blast the peace. Probably he'll look around for ways of doing both at the same time.'

'Kill Iles?'

'Or someone close to him.'

'Kill Mr Iles personally?' Harpur kept on at it because for a couple of moments at least the idea of the ACC removed did not seem unbearable. Would Hazel grieve? She could grieve if she wished, but she'd be safe from him.

Louise said: 'Personally, maybe. Plus other ways to weaken him, crack his mind. He's got associates, pals. He's got a family there in Rougement Place. His address isn't secret. The place is wide open, no fortress.'

'*I'm* a sort of pal.'

'Sure. *Your* address is even in the phone book, for God's sake. And that's no fortress, either. You think I need a lot of protection, don't you, sir? What about you and yours? Dubal's young, perhaps a bit mad, undoubtedly fixated by estimates of Panicking's and Manse's profits. It's almost a mystical thing with Ferdy, an identity thing. And generational. He has to win the succession. Anything in the way gets annihilated, or at least flattened. You might be in the way. Iles and some of his other buddies certainly are. Ferdy's thinking could be that, if he gets a war going and Mr Iles negated here, he – that's Ferdy – will come out victor and be able to run those two profit accounts together, plus his own, which means another nought on the end and a plumper figure at the beginning. Then he's powerful enough to take on any new firebrand Chief. And they're sure to put a firebrand in after the soft Lane years.'

'Mr Lane has always tried to –'

'Oh, I know he longed to be strict, a cleanser. But there was Desmond Iles. As they'll see it in the Home Office, someone who can't control an assistant is feeble.' She spoke as if she had daily Westminster briefings. At the Bramshill selection interview she must have been titanic.

Harpur said: 'You've met Dubal? He talks to you about strategy?' Was this the most talented undercover detective he had ever known? Could there be bigger justification for having put her into the firm?

'I told you, it's what I feel,' Louise replied.

'Oh, *feel*. That's all?'

'I feel it. Got a better explanation for what's happening, sir?'

'Nothing's happening, not that we know of.'

'It is. It will,' she replied.

'Scenarios. Projections.'

'That's right,' she said.

'Not right enough.' But probably as good as was going to show, to date, anyway. Even if the rumours about Lane's move and Iles's possible decline were wrong and the warfare never started, or started for other reasons, Harpur still needed to keep tabs. He might be able to put what he found in front of the ACC and convince him that the peace policy was tottering. Yes, occasionally Iles would listen to a point of view from Harpur.

That depended on the ACC's moods, though. Iles had two supreme obsessions. To understand *him* you had to understand *these*. The first brought very tricky problems and, when Iles was gripped by it, Harpur had no hope of getting any argument through to him. The ACC never forgot, and never let others forget, that there had been a time when, to use Iles's own brisk phrase, Harpur was 'giving it in the backs and fronts of cars, by-the-hour hotels and similar' to the ACC's wife, Sarah. Occasionally, Iles would still yell unhinged, near-frothing condemnation at Harpur, and to everyone else around. In headquarters, people loitered about the corridors when they saw the ACC speaking to Harpur at any length, in case the Assistant Chief suddenly soared to one of his gorgeous, noisy fits of rejuvenated jealousy. If Harpur wished to be heard about the safety-on-the-street pact he would obviously avoid discussing it at these kinds of encounters –supposing he were allowed to open his mouth and discuss anything then. Once in a while, Harpur met people from other police forces who had bumped into Iles at some conference or seminar and who'd describe him as aloof, impassive, cool verging on cold. And he *could* be like that. But not always. Oh, God, not always.

Harpur pushed these uncomfortable notions under. It was time to get out of the school. Louise had no more for him now. 'Look, I know we've been over and over this, but just recite the assistance number again, will you?' he asked. 'Another routine.

She groaned but did it.

'And watch your substance intake,' he said. 'Only enough for credibility. Too much and you'll get daring and slack.'

'Is that what happened to Ray Street?'

'I don't want Street darkening everything all the time, like a threat,' Harpur replied.

'He does, though, doesn't he?'

He did, mostly because of Iles. Overwhelmingly because of Iles. The second of the Assistant Chief's ruling impulses concerned Street's death. This Harpur preferred to regard as Iles's truly crucial fixation. It dated from when the ACC allowed Harpur to put Street undercover in a drugs syndicate, where he was eventually exposed as a cop, beaten and murdered. Harpur and everyone else at headquarters knew this terrible dark memory never left the Assistant Chief: the regret and sick guilt. Iles was even more famed for this than for his dementia spells over Harpur and the ACC's wife. Iles specialized in guilt, most particularly the guilt of others, but also his own when it came to Street. Although the two heavies reasonably regarded by the ACC as responsible for Street's death escaped conviction when sent to trial, they were soon afterwards found dead, one shot, the other very picturesquely garrotted.* Harpur and others felt it might have been Iles who personally brought this off. He possessed many deep, interesting skills, enough to keep him secure, at least until these recent whisperings. There had never been charges against him: Iles knew about evidence, and how not to leave much, or any. But even those neat vengeance killings failed to quell the ACC's self-blame. Consequently, his eternal embargo on undercover work. Harpur knew Iles saw himself as the caring guardian of all his people. When he failed one of them, the humiliation and pain were so appalling and permanent he could not load the risk on others or himself again.

A couple of weeks after his school meeting with Louise, Harpur took to walking late in the evenings around the Valencia Esplanade district, where most of the city's drugs dealing happened. He needed to see her. Only that: see Louise. It would be crazy to approach or talk to her here. They were certain to be noticed by someone in touch with Dubal. It might be crazy for Harpur even to walk here alone. Everyone recognized him. Trading stopped as soon as he left his car – club trading, shop-doorway trading, alley trading. Mobile phones spat his name across the Valencia. Dubal would hear he was about and might wonder why. Pushers in these designated streets were supposed to be left alone, as long as they stayed there: part of Iles's non-violence bargain with Dubal and the rest. In any case, Harpur was too big a rank to start chasing pushers. Dubal would suspect these walks were policy walks.

* *Halo Parade.*

Just the same, Harpur felt he had to come here. He needed to check Louise was alive. Yes, only that – inventory her. But although he had been down to the Valencia three times lately, he never saw Louise. He did not see her tonight, either, and went home. The phone rang as he was taking a couple of nightcap gin and cider mixes.

'Col?' Harpur knew the voice immediately. He gave no answer, waited. 'Col, I pick up a buzz about one of your troupe.'

'What buzz?'

'This is grave, Col.'

'Who?'

'We need to act.'

'We?'

'I mean immediately. They've been leading her on, setting her up. Well, she's set up now. You'll need my help. I don't suppose you're carrying anything.'

'What sort of thing?' Harpur asked.

'The ordinary sort – muzzle, trigger, full magazine.'

'I've heard of them.'

'Louise. That's the name I get in the buzz.'

Jack Lamb heard a lot of buzzes, had a lot of knowledge. He was possibly the greatest informant in the world. He talked confidentially to Harpur and only to Harpur. He belonged to Harpur. Or, likewise, Harpur belonged to him. Harpur thought the EU Court of Human Rights might not like this. Very sad, that. Security worries would normally stop Jack opening up so fully by phone. Things must be . . . must be, as he said, *grave*. 'What buzz?' Harpur asked. He felt the same tremor as when Louise revealed how much she knew: if Lamb had heard it Dubal and those around him could have heard it. That's where this buzz might have begun.

'This is all part of the general disturbance in the patch, isn't it, Col?'

'What disturbance?'

'Mark Lane possibly translated to make room for some leader capable of getting a for-ever arm lock on dear Ilesy.

Outcome? Panic in the firms. Naturally, as a gifted detective, you want to know about all this dangerous unease. To find out, you risk a young girl.'

'You do collect some tales, Jack.' Yes, he fucking did. 'Who's been filling you with dream stuff?'

'She's installed, right?' Lamb asked.

Harpur said: 'Usually, when it comes to information, you can sort out so brilliantly the shit from the champagne, Jack.'

'Louise Machin,' Lamb replied.

'Installed?' Harpur said.

'Wars and rumours of wars, Col.'

'What?' Christ, did Jack have to echo Louise?

'You're a Scriptures man, aren't you? And I hear you've turned night street walker.'

'Just strolling our ground.'

'You won't find her,' Lamb replied.

'Just strolling our ground. Routine.' Harpur hated to be seen through.

'When I say immediately, I mean tonight. Within the next half-hour. They've been keeping her in, but tonight they –'

'Right,' Harpur replied. There always came a stage when he would stop trying to fend off Lamb, give up pretending his material didn't rate. When Jack told you something you'd better believe it, especially if you already knew most of it as truth.

'I suppose you were keen to get to bed,' Lamb said.

'Don't let it trouble you.'

'Is the sweet, undergrad girlfriend there, waiting for you after your Valencia stroll?'

'I like Denise to be in the house with the children when I'm out at night,' Harpur replied.

'I bet.'

'I'm a one-parent family, Jack. Denise is a help.'

'I bet. Is she the only one these days and nights, Col?'

'They're still just thirteen and fifteen, you know, Jack. They need someone here.'

'Oh, the pains of widowerhood.'

'Don't let it trouble you,' Harpur said.

'This operation tonight might be dicey. But you can't bring help, can you?' He sounded joyful. 'Louise Machin is not supposed to be there, is she? There's still the Iles block on, I gather.'

'Oh, yes, I can bring help, if it's bad.'

'Of course it's bad,' Lamb snarled. 'Would I ring otherwise? But, no, don't bring help. We can manage it, Col.' Lamb liked that: Harpur's dependence on him alone, Harpur's gratitude to him alone, if things worked all right, whatever they were. Harpur thought he knew what they were. Jack adored the word 'we' when applied to him and Harpur. The link, the bond. 'Are you carrying something?' Lamb said.

'You asked me that.'

'Meaning, no.'

'Right,' Harpur replied. Naturally, Lamb was correct and Harpur could not look around for aid. If he did, Iles would hear, and know there had been a breach of his ban and sense undercover. Although Harpur shared Iles's horror at Street's death, he could not let this paralyse an entire category of work. Harpur thought he lacked Iles's knack for looking at one incident and seeing universal and eternal lessons there. Maybe it was an aptitude in officers of staff rank only, and Harpur had not yet reached staff rank, as Iles often reminded him – usually adding that Harpur with his prole features, friends, home, hairstyle, trousers and fashion standards altogether, never would.

Harpur felt a double need to keep the Assistant Chief ignorant of Louise's present job. First came the special element of Iles's possible personal involvement in the situation: rumours of his possible shrinkage might have destabilized the drugs firms – Shale, Ember, Dubal. Second, loomed the ACC's abiding, manic dread that the Street tragedy would be repeated. To conceal things from Iles was not easy: he had his own hidden network of tipsters and whisperers, his own magical intuitions. And his own way with reprisals. Yes, those.

Yes, those . . . Harpur wondered if he was beginning to exaggerate, to fantasize, even. Had he been knocked more than he realized by Jack Lamb's call? Perhaps. At any rate, Harpur found himself now accepting as probable that, if another undercover officer were lost, Iles might . . . yes, Harpur did believe this feasible, didn't he: Iles might, in the madness of grief, wipe out Harpur for flouting orders. The ACC's undimmed rages about Harpur and Sarah Iles sharpened the possibility, plus his rabid frustration at finding Hazel successfully corralled off from him by Harpur: or successfully as far as Harpur could tell. Nobody really knew altogether how the Assistant Chief's thinking functioned, nor what replenished stocks of violence lay heaped in him, ready for use.

Harpur felt Iles might well prefer garrotting above all other methods of killing enemies, although one of the men acquitted of Street's death had in fact been shot. The ACC would revel in the physicality and necessary nearness to the victim, and probably still regretted having to pamper that man with a bullet. Most likely, Iles considered garrotting proclaimed with elegance his endless contempt for anyone involved in Street's murder. And Iles did prize elegance of statement. It was obvious in his fine suits and blazers, in his heartily polished, custom-made shoes, and in the careful checking and rechecking via mirrors that his face was at its imperturbable best, and not compromised for the moment, anyway, by his Adam's apple. Because of his Adam's apple, Iles refused to believe in any kind of decent God running the universe and felt he should look out for himself. This might explain so much about the ACC's everlastingly unmild character. It could be that, because of his Adam's apple, Iles had a special loathing for necks and throats, and so the garrotting speciality. Harpur lacked the ACC's focus on Adam's apples, but he'd always thought of garrotting as probably his most dreaded form of death, and supremely most dreaded if Iles in one of his great suits were doing it to him.

As Harpur was leaving to meet Lamb, his younger daughter, Jill, came downstairs alert and frowning, school blazer buttoned up over her pyjamas. 'I heard the phone, dad.'

'I have to go out.'

'Oh?'

'Work.'

'Is it?'

'Yes, of course. Work,' he replied.

'Is it?'

'Go back to bed now, love.'

'Will Denise be upset? I mean, again?'

'Why?'

'You going out. I mean, again.'

'It's work,' he said.

'Is it?'

'Of course.'

'Will she believe it?'

'What else would it be?' Harpur asked.

'Well –'

'Work.'

'A phone call so late.'

'Policemen get late phone calls.'

'I'll tell her it's work. I mean, if she gets jealous again, makes a fuss.'

'It *is* work.'

'I quite believe you, dad, honestly.'

'Thanks, Jill.'

'But Denise –'

'I'll be back soon.'

'If you're not and she makes a fuss, thinking another woman, like intrigue and uncontrollable pash – all that – I'll definitely say it's work – that I really asked you and asked you and you said work every time.'

'Denise is asleep, anyway.'

'But if she wakes up and you're not in the bed – then she could get edgy, that way of hers, and make a fuss.'

'An emergency,' he said.

'Dangerous?'

'An emergency.'

'Are you tooled up?'

'Don't talk tellydrama.'

'Are you? I'll say you went out tooled up which shows it's truly work, not some woman.'

'Thanks, Jill.'

'I really think Denise thinks a lot of you, despite your . . . your everything – your haircut and behaviour.'

'I don't have behaviour.'

'I'll tell her that, dad, I really will. It would be terrible if you lost her – if she went back to sleeping in that student place, Jonson Court without an h, there being two Jonsons in lit, this one called Ben and the other Sam, *with* an h. She told me that. It's bound to come in useful. You're really lucky to get her at your age and so on. Beautiful, knowing all about where the h goes, youngish, clever. Her, I mean. And boobs, no implants. Her, I mean.'

Harpur walked to the gates of a park not far from his house and Jack Lamb picked him up in a van. Once before Harpur had been in this vehicle at Lamb's invitation. He used it to carry pictures to or from customers. Lamb ran a toweringly successful art dealership, and when Harpur last entered the van it was to look at some canvases: good stuff, apparently, by people with names Harpur certainly half knew, and still half remembered – Tissot, Hunt, Mellais or Millais or Molière. He never asked Lamb where or how he came by his rare items. This was the essence of their relationship: Lamb brought Harpur brilliant insider stuff – but not art insider stuff – while Harpur did nothing to shatter the picture business, discouraged moves to have it probed. To entangle Harpur more thoroughly, Lamb liked to show him valuable paintings now and then. Harpur comforted himself with the thought he was helping to keep art and culture hale in the area.

Jack drove hard out of the city. 'The shits,' he said.

'Who?'

'Do you know where they've taken her?'

'Who?'

'Dubal's people.'

'Taken who?'

Lamb didn't think this worth a reply.

'Where?' Harpur asked.

'To Rendezvous One. To our fucking Rendezvous One, Col. Yours and mine. It's a message.'

Normally, when Lamb had something to tell Harpur they met at one of four, listed, pre-arranged rendezvous spots, the same sort of system as with Louise. Rendezvous One was what had been a World War II anti-aircraft gun site on a wooded hill above the city. Concrete emplacements remained and metal rails for ammunition trucks. It was remote and atmospheric: Jack adored old military installations and sometimes dressed in army surplus gear for these meetings. The site had always seemed safe. But was it known about by villains like Dubal all the time? This would be what Jack meant when he spoke of a message. Was Dubal saying: 'We've rumbled your undercover girl, Machin, as you see from her corpse, and we know where you meet your grass. So how do you feel now, Harpur?' But did they also know that Jack, in his bonny way, knew they knew and knew they were out there with Louise now? If they did not, there was a chance of saving her.

'How did you find out about this, Jack – Lane's possible move, Iles, Louise?' Harpur asked. It was the kind of yokel question he always put to Lamb as a formality, and which never got answered. Grasses did not identify sources, particularly sources as infallible as Jack's. These folk might be needed again, but would be unavailable if they found he blurted names.

'I'm not an all-round mouth, Colin,' Lamb said. 'I grass only when I'm nauseated, and to hear they'd terrorize and waste a kid like Louise Machin from the sticks nauseates me.'

Always Jack stressed he did not inform for the sake of it or for favours. Find the moral factor. Even with this choosiness, Lamb was still the best in the world. 'You've got a leaker at the top of Dubal's outfit?' Harpur asked.

'Oh, but what agony among the firms that Iles and all Iles means might be squashed,' Lamb replied.

'Think he will be? Who squashes Iles?'

'A point,' Lamb said.

They left Jack's van well down the hill and began to walk quickly up through trees towards the former gun positions. It was very dark. Harpur found himself hoping the people with Louise would knock her about before the finish, to make her talk. He and Jack needed time. Harpur felt she would hold out for at least a while, and this might keep her alive. The arrogance should help. What could she tell them, anyway? They knew it all. He climbed faster. Thank God the ground was familiar. Jack led. Although about 260 pounds and standing six feet five inches he moved nimbly, swiftly, silently. He was wearing what might be a replica General Rommel, Afrika Korps grey uniform, necklaced Iron Cross, black ankle boots, and peaked grey cap forced into a high, all-conquering V. Now and then when Harpur came up with him for a few yards he could see that Lamb held some sort of semi-automatic in his right hand, perhaps a Glock 9 mm. Good taste: light and easy to strip. Police used these, especially armed response car crews.

Harpur thought he heard voices, or a voice, male. It was distant and no words carried but he sensed a question, a question repeated. Interrogation. Lamb seemed to have heard it, too, and slowed a little, grew even more careful about where he trod, and crouched, now like a jungle soldier, instead. Harpur did the same. He loathed firearms yet wished *he* held a Glock as well. The trees began to thin and there was slightly more light. Nice for locating targets, nice for being located. He heard the male voice again. This time he made out one word, 'Harpur.' Or 'Harpur?' – another question. For a second it dazed him. Then came a female voice, too faint for clarity, and very brief, the tone suggesting a bland denial. She could still hold them off, then, still say she wasn't run by Harpur. Holding them off mentally, that is. He heard something else: what could be a blow, a heavy fist blow, even a pistol whip blow, not a slap. No cry of pain. Perhaps he had it wrong and she had not been struck. But perhaps, also, that's how Louise was: not someone who yelled, that wide face deliberately blank. Or perhaps she had been dropped unconscious.

Jack Lamb turned for a second and pointed forward and to his left. Harpur took it to mean he could see the anti-aircraft emplacement and possibly a vehicle and people. Harpur nodded and put on a bit more speed. Suddenly, though, Lamb began to run very fast, despite the gradient, opening more space between him and Harpur, his pistol out in front. It was as if he had noticed some change in behaviour and decided to ditch stalking and subtlety. Possibly someone was about to end it for Louise.

Lamb bellowed: 'Stop! Armed fink! Stop!' still galloping hard. Harpur rushed to get with him. He heard a shot from the emplacement and a bullet banged into a tree near him. Lamb abruptly stopped and went to a sniper's attitude, on one knee, a two-handed grip on the Glock. He fired four rapid rounds. As far as Harpur could recall, the Glock would give him seventeen if full.

Mark Lane, the Chief, liked to look at the scene of any crime he considered significant not just as itself but as symbol of the general state of law and order. Harpur drove him and Iles out to the hillside. The two bodies had been cleared from there by now, naturally, but Lane wished to see the setting. A concrete road laid for troop supplies in the war was still there, and Harpur took the car the whole distance and parked.

Iles went forward on foot and said: 'Here and here,

wasn't it, Col?' He stepped from where he'd been standing between the truck rails to a place four or five yards on the right. 'Well, the blood's still visible.'

'Yes,' Harpur replied.

Lane said: 'And their status you say, Desmond, is . . .?'

'Oh, Dubal thugs, sir. Enforcers. Percy Kellow, Jerry Henschall, almost always known as Mildly Sedated. Percy's from the Travelling People originally. It's a traditional name with them.'

Lane climbed on to an earth wall surrounding the emplacements. From here he could gaze down at the city. He would probably think of it as *his* city, though he might be moved on soon. 'This place was constructed to protect people,' he said. 'And now? Now, it is foully tainted. Oh, a decline, Desmond, Colin. Could we ever fight an international war again?'

'I rather like it, sir,' Iles replied.

'Like? Like?'

'Two bits of rubbish removed,' Iles said.

'But what does it mean, what does it signify?' Lane cried.

'Oh, this was house-cleaning, that's all, sir,' Iles replied.

'We're talking of two deaths, two murders, for God's sake, Desmond,' Lane said. 'That's what I mean by taint. What does it signify? What does it darkly promise?'

Iles said: 'It signifies Percy and Mildly Sedated had offended somehow and were brought up here and done by colleagues. Most likely they've been skimming. Or they said something about Dubal's looks. He's sensitive. I can sympathize with that. Or they possibly niggled about his failure to catch up with Shale and Panicking Ralph Ember. The deaths are tidy. Hygienic. Self-contained. No wider implications. None. This is protocol. We don't want such barbarism among ordinary folk, sir. These two will do less tainting dead.'

Lane waved an arm towards where the bodies had been found. 'But why? Who?' he said.

'I don't think we're getting very far with that, sir, as yet,' Iles replied.

Harpur said: 'As Mr Iles suggests, we assume some sort of gang battle or a disciplinary episode within the Dubal firm. We're working on both possibilities.' Louise had to be kept out of this.

'I will not accept such contempt for legality,' Lane said. 'It could spread, become uncontainable.' Always the Chief feared that chaos might start on his ground and from there canter out and corrupt at least the cosmos, with himself glaringly to blame. This debilitating dread had brought him to breakdown not long ago. Now, perhaps, it put him in line for the move up and away from the solemn pressures of command, and the interminable jolly hellishness of Desmond Iles. 'I cannot, will not, rest until –'

'Quite nice shooting, I gather,' the ACC said. 'Two bullets in each heart, and not half an inch between either pair of them.'

'And found, how?' Lane asked.

'A New York Bronx-accented anon call from a public box, sir,' Iles replied. 'The usual sort of dubious carry-on.'

Lane groaned: 'Usual? My God, Desmond, do you realize what you say? That this kind of incident has become a standard part of life now? Is this the beginning of –'

'Of Armageddon, sir? Oh, Col here has it all in hand. He often knows a fucking sight more than he lets on to you and me.'

'Colin?' Lane said.

'We're really working on it, sir,' Harpur replied. 'No substantial progress yet.'

'Meaning none.' The Chief walked away along the top of the earth wall, perhaps for a better view of the city, in case there were visual signs of implosion. He went slowly out of sight.

Iles said quietly: 'Do you know, Harpur, when Sarah was struggling one day to think what the hell ever made her see anything in you – desperately, bewilderedly searching her memory – I recall her lighting on some almost witty fragment of your repertoire and telling me you could do an amusing Bronx accent. This was the only small plus she could salvage now.'

'My own feeling, sir, is there'll be terrible problems resolving this case,' Harpur replied. 'Perhaps insurmountable. As the Chief obviously fears.'

'I smell woman. This kid girl I heard you brought in from one of the border stations – was she involved in it somehow here?' Iles said. 'And then the tale's around that you were looking out for her down the Valencia? That it?'

'Kid girl, sir?' Harpur replied.

'Have you been playing some fancy undercover game?' Iles said. 'You're bullshitting me and Mr Lane? Not that bullshitting Lane matters, but bullshitting *me*, Col? Your brain's on holiday?'

'In a way, I sympathize with the Chief's feelings about this place,' Harpur replied. 'It's –'

'Did she tell you that Dubal or his people could be thinking bloodshed? What I hear. We'd better look at that. Things might not be so contained after all.'

'You hear a lot, sir.'

'At Staff College I was known as Listening Desmond.'

Harpur said: 'So, perhaps these two were eliminated in some sort of vengeance thing, a settlement, if Dubal or Dubal's boys have been killing.'

'Fuck off, Col. You know how they died. I also heard of this kid girl – Munching? Machin? Moocher? – this kid girl, chatting with you in a Parents Evening, a Parents Evening at a school your children don't go to. Wouldn't I know very well the school Hazel attends – oh, that enticing uniform? And now I'm told this kid girl – Munching? Machin? Moocher? – is off sick with head and facial wounds but nothing irreparable. Were they going to kill her, Col? A Ray Street reprise? You defied me, in your style?'

'Sir, it –'

Iles said: 'These two, Perce and Mildly, knocked over by rounds from one of our Service's very favourite pistols, the Glock. Were you out here the other night being gallant and ballistic on her behalf? You? But you could never shoot like that. Some gifted chum with you?'

Harpur would have liked to keep pace with the mind of the ACC but knew he would never get very near. Also, he might have wished to ask whether the Chief would soon fly away, and whether his ACC was sure to be curtailed, as Lamb said, by someone new. On top of that, Harpur would have appreciated a line on Iles's gifted sources: perhaps not in the Jack Lamb league, but 20/20 vision, the sods, in Parents Evenings, down the Valencia, and God knew where else. Harpur said: 'I –'

'Two down, Perce and Mildly Sedated. Great. Possibly I can forgive, Col, if the kid girl is really all right. At Staff College I was also known as Desmond the Merciful. And I take it you were up here banging away at these two, or watching a chum bang away at them, and then you go home and bang the student. Was she waiting, all anxious and open, because you'd been out on a noble mission? Does she worship you, Col? Do you ever tell her about other women you've riotously befouled?' Up here among the trees and vistas, Iles's enraged cry could really give itself wings, screech-owl wings. Pain and rage rattled into the sky like anti-aircraft shells. 'Possibly, for instance, my wife. You recall, do you, when by some filthy fluke you were able to –'

'Ah, here's the Chief now,' Harpur replied. Lane approached. He looked appallingly haggard. He looked unsavably ex.

Iles called out to him: 'That's totally right for you, sir, if I may say – the stark prominence on a wall. Eloquent. Something sort of elemental, grand, marvellously reassuring. Don't you glimpse a happy emblem of leadership in the Chief's position there, Col?'

Chapter Two

And then things turned worse – worse above all for Iles. Harpur would have liked to place an arm around his shoulders and mutter solace, but, obviously, you never willingly put yourself into direct, intimate bodily touch with the ACC, nor said anything to suggest he might be down and going lower fast. Iles did not spend all that money on clothes, shoes, hairdressing and deep collars for his Adam's apple, to be told he seemed down and needed comforting. Downness he brought others. He put them down, never himself got put down.

Just the same, Harpur saw he was ravaged. Not long after those bodies at the anti-aircraft emplacement, there came another terrible death on the patch. A lad called Wayne Ridout was found much broken up in the street having apparently been hit by a car: having apparently been hit at least three times by a car, or, possibly, cars, according to the first medical assessment. Harpur had the idea that at one period, or even right up until his death, Ridout was a major voice in the ACC's personal sly web of informants. Such a relationship could never be totally clear to those not part of it. Think of Harpur and Jack Lamb. Clarity would kill the service. But lies had certainly helped set up special favours for Ridout. And now, hearing of his untidy death, Iles seemed almost as devastated as he had been by that long-ago killing of Street.

Harpur could understand this. Wayne Ridout's death was an especially terrible setback for the ACC. Only a few days before the killing by car, or cars, Iles had actually saved Ridout's life from a blatant hit operation. Now, the reclaimed Wayne was dead, anyway.

The first attack on Ridout had happened at the admittedly strange setting of a school prize-giving – a very different kind of school from the one where Harpur met Louise. Perhaps it was odd, symbolic in some way he did not understand, that he should have visited two schools lately, at a time when all the things he usually attributed to schools – continuity, hope, system, or at least the show of system . . . when all these seemed to have grown suddenly so fragile.

Harpur saw a message in what had happened to Ridout, just as he had seen earlier a message in the freighting of Louise to the anti-aircraft gun emplacement. Through Wayne's death so soon after that first thwarted attempt on him, someone seemed to be telling the ACC, *All right, Iles, so you preserved him once, but take a glance at your wrecked fucking whisperer now.* Hadn't Louise Machin said those close to Iles might be targets as much as the ACC himself? The closeness of a police officer and his grass was absolute. Marriage did not compare. So, was Ridout's execution the start of destroying Iles, the first move to make totally sure that, when the Chiefs changed, Iles could not stand up to the new leadership and still keep his special powers? The loss of a major grass did crucial damage. Possibly Wayne had been passing on to the ACC what he knew about how the firms would run their campaigns if the street war opened up again when Lane left. Louise's forecast about targeting might not be the only relevant one. Possibly the predictions from Jack Lamb and the Chief made frightening sense, too, and things were on their way to deepest, all-round calamity.

'I'll visit Wayne's wife and daughter, Harpur,' the ACC said immediately he heard of Ridout's annihilation.

'They're fond of you, sir.'

'Nora, a fine wife. And then, of course, Fay-Alice, the daughter. Eighteen?'

'That's it, sir.'

'Fay-Alice, if you remember, Harpur, has a wonderful . . . well . . .'

'Wonderful long back, sir,' Harpur said.

'Yes, a wonderful long back. Some awkwardness arose between her and me last time we met.'

'Is that so, sir?' Harpur replied.

'You were there, weren't you, you dim prick? That prize-giving afternoon at Taldamon school. Less than a week ago.' It had been here that Iles prevented a gunman from killing Wayne Ridout, only for Wayne to be done in what looked like a road accident so soon afterwards, but only looked like.

'Well, yes, sir, I *was* with you at the school.'

'Didn't you see some awkwardness?'

'Yes, perhaps some little what one might call awkwardness.'

'I think it will be all right with the girl now – I mean, civil – don't you, Col? After all, this is a father very much dead and cut about. That changes things, especially a good and gifted father like Wayne.'

'It will be fine, I'm sure, sir. Do you want me to come with you to their home?'

'You? To their home? Why the fuck would I want that, Harpur?'

'Quite, sir.'

'This is private between me and the family, Harpur.'

'Right, sir.'

'Yes, come, Col,' Iles replied. He waved an arm, as though on second thoughts to encompass Harpur, the way a vacuum cleaner would finally pick up a bolshy bit of muck. Perhaps Iles suddenly felt weakened by the loss of Wayne. Had the ACC decided he would after all be better with Harpur's support? The idea of Iles needing support was monstrous, hellish. Yes, universal calamity might be near.

Harpur had to restore him somehow, and picked what he thought the most likely route. He said: 'I agree with you, a girl with a back like that, sir – it would be very negative to let things remain soured between you.' They were in Harpur's room at headquarters. Ridout's death had just been confirmed.

The ACC paced. Trauma seemed near. 'I have an unquenchable need to be loved,' he stated. 'Few recognize this.'

'When do you want to go to see Mrs Ridout and the daughter, sir?' Harpur replied.

'Did you appreciate it, Harpur?'

'What, sir?'

'My need to be loved.'

Harpur thought he probably *did* appreciate it: one of his blackest anxieties was that this need might get directed deviously and unstoppably at his underage daughter. 'We probably won't be able to go to Wayne Ridout's funeral, sir,' Harpur replied. 'It would proclaim the connection.'

'I think I'm certainly entitled to be loved, Harpur.' Iles stroked his grey hair. It was worn a little longer now than when he had it cut hard back to mimic the style of French actor, Jean Gabin, following a revival season of his films in town.

'But we might be able to do some of the coffin costs from our general grass fund, sir,' Harpur replied, 'in view of Ridout's status.'

'*Was* he a grass?' Iles said. 'Whose? Yours?' Like any detective with a treasured informant, the ACC knew how to go radiantly opaque. Possibly 'Iles the Unreadable' was another of his nicknames at Staff College.

'Always when a grass is killed there's some special malevolence,' Harpur replied. 'A car used like a cosh, for God's sake. Sadism.'

Iles paced on, silent now. Harpur watched. Among those who did spot the ACC's unflagging quest for love, of course, a good number refused to respond and instead muttered privately, very privately, 'Go fuck yourself, Iles.' On the other hand, there was certainly a young ethnic whore in the docks who worshipped the ACC unstintingly, and he would have been appallingly hurt if anyone said it was because he paid well. Once, the ACC had told Harpur he despised love that could be accounted for and reckoned up. Harpur felt happy the ACC received from his docks friend, Honorée, and from Fanny, his infant daughter, the differing but complete affection he craved.

Also, Iles's wife, Sarah, had some true fondness for him quite often at least. She had mentioned it to Harpur unprompted in one of their quiet moments. To Harpur, it seemed that a lot of Iles's unpredictable general behaviour could be explained by this need for free-flowing devotion. What sickened the ACC was when people came to esteem him merely because he helped them in some way: say a piece of grand, wild violence carried out by Iles against one of their enemies. He dismissed such 'measly reciprocity' as he called it. It was this, in fact, that had led to the strain Iles mentioned between himself and Wayne Ridout's long-backed daughter, Fay-Alice, recently.

Although Iles would regard the kind of physical savagery he was forced into at the Taldamon prize-giving as merely routine for him, it had caused Fay-Alice to switch abruptly from fending the ACC off sexually to offering an urgent come-on. This had enraged Iles, as Harpur at once knew it would. The ACC had been doing all he could to attract the girl, probably as stand-by in case Honorée were working away sometime at a World Cup or Church of England Synod. Utterly no go. And then, within minutes, Fay-Alice suddenly changed and clearly grew interested in Iles, simply because he had felled some bastard who wanted to kill her father in the stately school assembly hall, and kicked this intruder a few times absolutely unfatally about the head and neck when he lay on the floor between chair rows.

The Assistant Chief was sure to regard such a turnaround by the girl as contemptible: as grossly unperceptive about Iles, as Iles. That is, the essence of Ilesness, not simply his rabbit punching and undeniable kicking flairs, which could be viewed as superficial: as attractive, perhaps, but mere accessories to his core self. Harpur had seen at Taldamon that the ACC wished to get away immediately from the girl and return to Honorée for pure, unconditional adoration, even if necessary on waste ground.

In Iles's office at present, and stricken with the news about Wayne, the ACC said: 'I owe Nora and the girl a consolatory call, regardless, Harpur.'

'They'll value it, sir.'

'I'll forget the prize-giving episode with the girl.'

'Negligible, sir.'

But it was hard to forget Taldamon. On their visit last week, Harpur had found it a really chic place – private, of course, and residential, and right up there with Eton and Harrow for fees. In fact, it cost somewhere near the national average wage to keep a child at Taldamon for a year, and this without the geology trip to Iceland, the horse-riding and extra coaching in lacrosse and timpani. Harpur and Iles – Iles particularly – were interested in Taldamon because the police funded one of its pupils during her entire school career. This was an idea picked up from France. Over there, it was long established police practice to meet the education expenses for the child or children of a valuable and regular informant, as one way of paying for tip-offs. The scheme convinced Iles and others. It was considered less obvious – less dangerous – than to give a grass cash, which he/she might spend in a stupid, ostentatious way, drawing attention to his/her special income. That could mean the informant was no longer able to get close to villains' secrets because the villains would have her/him identified as a leak. It could also mean his/her life was endangered. A child out of sight at a pricey school in North Wales would be less noticeable. Or, this was the thinking.

Five years ago they put Wayne Ridout's thirteen-year-old daughter, Fay-Alice, into Taldamon, and last Friday Iles and Harpur had gone to see her collect her prizes as sixth former, head prefect, captain of lacrosse, captain of swimming and water polo, central to the school orchestra, destined for Oxford, slim, straight-nosed, fine-skinned, and able to hold Iles off with cold, foul-mouthed ease until . . until she decided she did not want to hold him off, following a gross rush of disgusting gratitude: disgusting, that is, as Harpur guessed the ACC would regard it.

Iles and Harpur would not normally attend this kind of function. The presence of police might be a give-away, as much as at a funeral. But Wayne had pleaded with Iles to come, and pleaded a little less fervently with Harpur, also. It was not just that Wayne wanted them to see the glorious results of their grass-related investment in Fay-Alice. Harpur knew from a few recent conversations with Wayne that he had felt depressed lately. Because of her education and the social status of Taldamon, Wayne sensed his daughter might be growing away from him and Nora. This grieved both, but especially Wayne. His wife seemed to regard the change in Fay-Alice as normal. Harpur imagined she probably saw it on behalf of the girl like this: when your father's main career had been informant and general crook rather than archbishop or TV game show host, there was only one way for the next generation to go socially – up and away. Regrettable but inevitable.

Wayne could not accept such distancing. He must reason that, if he were seen at this important school function accompanied by an Assistant Chief Constable, who had on the kind of a magnificent suit and shoes Iles favoured, and who behaved in his well-known, lofty Shah of Persia style, it was bound to restore Fay-Alice's respect for her parents. And it would impress the girl's friends and teachers. For these possible gains, Wayne had evidently decided to put up with the security risk in this one-off event. Harpur had doubted Fay-Alice would see things as her father did and thought the visit mad, particularly after what Louise had said about hazards. But Iles decided they could go and addressed Harpur for a while about 'overriding obligations to those who sporadically assist law and order, even a fat, villainous, ugly, dim sod like Wayne'. The ACC loved to get among teenage schoolgirls if they looked clean and were wearing light summery clothes.

It was only out of politeness that Wayne had asked Harpur. At Detective Chief Superintendent, Harpur lacked the glow of staff rank, and could not tog himself out with the same distinction as Iles. In fact, the ACC had seemed not wholly sure Harpur should accompany him. 'This will be a school with gold-lettered award boards on the wall, naming pupils who've gone on not just to Oxbridge or management courses with the Little Chef restaurant chain, but Harvard, Vatican seminaries, time share selling in Alicante. There'll be ambience. I know it inside out, from my own background, Harpur. But you, Col – can you fit into such a place with that fucking haircut and your alleged garments?'

'This kind of occasion makes me think back to end of term at my own school, sir,' Harpur reminisced gently.

'And what did they give leaving prizes to eighteen-year-olds for there – knowing the two-times-table, speed at de-wristing tourist Rolexes?'

'Should we go armed?' Harpur replied.

'This is a wholesome, academic occasion at a prime girls' school, for God's sake, Col.'

'Should we go armed?' Harpur said. He remained obsessed by Louise's warning, but could not tell the Assistant Chief. The information, if that's what it was, had come from undercover, and she should not be undercover.

Iles said: 'I'd hate it for some delightful pupil, inadvertently brushing against me, to feel only the brutal outline of a holstered pistol, Harpur.'

'This sort of school, they're probably taught never to brush inadvertently against people like you, sir. It would be stressed in deportment classes, plus during the domestic science module for classifying moisture marks on trousers.'

Iles's voice had grown throaty and his breathing loud: 'I gather she's become a star now as scholar, swimmer, musician and so on, but I remember Fay-Alice when she was only a kid, though developing, certainly . . . developing, yes, certainly, *developing*, but really only just a kid . . . although . . . well, yes, *developing*, and we went to the Ridout house to advise them that she should –'

'There are people who'd like to do Wayne. Perhaps he's been grassing about the firms and their business plans in the new scene.'

'Which new scene is that, Harpur?'

'And he's helped put all sorts in jail for you.'

'For me?' Iles had replied. Again that gifted ignorance.

'He's helped put all sorts in jail for you, especially drugs people. The firms have seemed unsettled lately, sir. Stirrings? Perhaps the word's around that Ridout will be on a plate at Taldamon.'

'A striking-looking child, even then,' Iles said, 'despite Wayne and his complexion. Yes, the wonderful long, slender back, as I recall. Do you recall that, Harpur – the long slender back? Do you think of backs ever? Or was it the era when you were so damn busy giving it to my wife you didn't have time to notice much else at all?' Iles had begun to scream in that heartfelt way of his.

Harpur said: 'If we're there we ought at least to –'

'I mean her back in addition to the way she was, well . . .'

'Developing.'

When they arrived at Taldamon on Friday, Harpur had seen that Fay-Alice still possessed this long back, and the development elsewhere seemed to have continued as it generally would for a girl between thirteen and eighteen. There was a little tea party on the pleasant school lawns before the prize-giving, out of consideration for parents who had travelled a long way and needed refreshment. It was June, a good, hot, blue-skied day. 'Here's a dear, dear acquaintance of mine, Fay-Alice,' Wayne had said. 'Assistant Chief Constable Desmond Iles. And Chief Superintendent Harpur.'

Iles gave her a true conquistador smile, yet a smile which also sought to hint at his sensitivity, honour, beguiling polish and famed restraint. Fay-Alice had returned this smile with one that was hostile, bored and extremely brief but which still managed to signal over her teacup, *Police? So how come you're friends of my father and who the fuck let you in here, anyway?*

'Fay-Alice's prizes are in French literature, history of art and classics,' Wayne had said.

'Won't mean a thing to Col,' Iles replied.

'I wondered if there'd been strangers around the school lately,' Harpur said, 'possibly asking questions about the programme today, looking at the layout.'

'Which strangers?' Fay-Alice replied.

'Strangers,' Harpur said. 'A man, or men, probably.'

'Why would they?' the girl asked.

'You know, French lit is something I can't get enough of,' the ACC had said.

'Mr Iles, personally, did a lot with education, right up to the very heaviest levels, Fay-Alice,' Wayne said. 'Oh, many a book. Don't be fooled just because he's police.'

'Yes, why are you concerned about strangers, Mr Harpur?' Nora Ridout asked.

'Are you two trying to put the frighteners on us, the way cops always do?' Fay-Alice said.

'I recall Alphonse de Lamartine and his poem "The Lake",' Iles replied.

'Alphonse is undoubtedly a French name,' Wayne cried joyfully. 'There you are, Fay-Alice – Mr Iles can go straight to it, no messing. As I said, books are meat and drink to him.'

Iles leaned towards her and recited:

' "Let us savour the rapidly passing delights
Of the most lovely of our days." '

'Meat and drink,' Wayne had said.

'Don't you find Lamartine's plea an inspiration, Fay-Alice?' Iles asked. 'Savour. A word I thrill to. The sensuousness of it, and the tragic hint of enjoying something wonderful, yet elusive?' Trembling slightly, he had reached out a hand, as if to touch Fay-Alice's long back or somewhere fairly near it. But, moving quickly towards the plate of sandwiches on a garden table, Harpur put himself between the ACC and her. He took Iles's pleaful, savour-seeking fingers on the lapel of his jacket. In any case, Fay-Alice had stepped back when she saw the ACC's hand approach and for a moment looked as if she were about to grab his arm and possibly snap it in some kind of anti-rape drill.

'Or the history of art,' Wayne said. 'That's another terrific realm. This could overlap with French literature because while the poets were writing their verses in France there would be neighbours, along the same street most probably, painting and making sculptures in their attics. The French are known for it – easels, smocks, everything. It's the light in those parts – great for art but also useful when people wanted to write a poem outside. In a way it all ties up. That's the thing about culture. A lot of strands.'

'And you'll be coming home to live with mother and father until Oxford now and in the nice long vacations, will you, Fay-Alice?' Iles had asked.

'Why?' she replied.

Iles said: 'It's just that –'

'I don't understand how you know my father,' she replied.

'Oh, Mr Iles and I – this is a real far-back association,' Wayne said.

'But how exactly?' she asked. 'He's never been to our house, has he? I've never heard you speak of him, dad.'

'This is like an arrangement, Fay-Alice,' Nora Ridout replied.

'What kind of arrangement?' Fay-Alice had asked.

'Yes, like an arrangement,' Nora Ridout replied. 'There are all sorts of arrangements, aren't there, Mr Iles?'

'A business arrangement?' Fay-Alice asked.

'You can see how such a go-ahead school makes them

put all the damn sharp queries, Mr Iles,' Wayne said. 'I love it. This is what they call intellectual curiosity, used by many of the country's topmost on their way to discoveries such as medical and DVDs. What they will not do, girls at this school, and especially girls who do really well, such as Fay-Alice – what they will not do is take something as right just because they're told it. Oh, no. Rigour's another word for this attitude, I believe. Not like *rigor mortis* but rigour in their thoughts and decisions.'

'So, does the school come into it somehow?' Fay-Alice had asked. 'Does it? Does it? How are these two linked with the school, dad, mum?' Although she hammered at the question, Harpur thought she feared an answer.

'Linked?' Iles said. 'Linked? Oh, just a pleasant excursion for Mr Harpur and myself, thanks to the thoughtfulness of your father, Fay-Alice.'

'A business or social arrangement?' Fay-Alice asked.

'No, no, not a business arrangement. How could it be a business arrangement?' Wayne replied, laughing.

'Social?' Fay-Alice asked.

'It's sort of social,' Wayne said.

'So, if it's friendship why do you call him Mr Iles, not Desmond, his first name?' Fay-Alice asked.

'See what I mean about the queries, Mr Iles? I heard the motto of this school is "Seek ever the truth", but in a classical tongue which provides many a motto around the country on account of tradition. You can't beat the classics for things like seeking and truth.'

The ACC said: 'And I understand swimming has become a pursuit of yours, Fay-Alice. Excellent for the body. You must get along to the municipal pool at home. I should go there more often myself. Certainly I shall. This, also, will be an experience – to see you active in the water, your arms and legs really working, your wake aglisten.' Beautifully symmetric circles of sweat had appeared on each of his temples, each the size of a two-penny piece, although the party was outside and under the shade of a eucalyptus. 'The butterfly stroke – strenuous upper torso exercise, but useful for toning everything, don't you agree, Fay-Alice? Toning *everything*. Oh, I look forward to that. Wayne, it will be a treat to have Fay-Alice around so much in future.'

'Aren't you a bit old for the butterfly?' she'd replied. 'I can't stand watching a heart attack in the fast lane, all those desperate bubbles and sudden incontinence.'

Iles chuckled, obviously in tribute to her aggression and jauntiness. 'Oh, look, Fay-Alice –'

'We don't need *flics* here, thank you,' she replied. 'So, why don't you just piss off back to your interrogation suite alone and play with yourself, Iles?' Harpur had decided that, even without pre-knowledge from its brochure, anyone could have recognized this as an outstandingly select school where articulateness was prized and deftly inculcated, and scepticism about the police and other security apparatus obligatory.

Later, in the fine wide assembly hall, he had appreciatively watched Fay-Alice on the platform stride out with her long back and so on to receive prizes from the Lord Lieutenant. He seemed to do quite an amount of congratulatory talking and hand-shaking with Fay-Alice before conferring her trophies. All at once, then, Harpur realized that Iles had gone from the seat alongside him. Harpur wondered for a moment whether the ACC intended attacking the Lord Lieutenant for infringing on Fay-Alice and half stood in case he had to move forward and try to throw Iles to the ground and suppress him.

They had been placed at the end of a row, Iles to Harpur's right alongside the gangway, Wayne and Nora on his left. To help keep the hall cool, all doors were open. Glancing away from the platform now, Harpur had seen Iles run out through the nearest door, as if chasing someone, black lace-ups flashing richly in the sunshine. He disappeared. On stage, the presentations continued. Harpur sat down again properly. The ACC's objective was not the Lord Lieutenant.

After about a minute, Harpur heard noises from the

back of the hall and, turning, saw a man wearing a yellow and magenta crash helmet and face-guard enter through another open door and dash between some empty rows of seats. At an elegant sprint Iles had appeared through the same door shortly afterwards. The man in the helmet stopped, spun and pulling an automatic pistol from his waistband pointed it at Iles, perhaps a Browning 140 DA. The ACC swung himself hard to one side and crouched as the gun fired. Then he leaned far forward and used a fierce sweep of his left fist to knock the automatic from the man's hand. With his clenched right, Iles struck him two short, rapid blows in the neck, just below the helmet. At once, he fell. Iles had been in the row behind, but now clambered over the chair backs to reach him. Harpur could not make out the man on the floor but saw Iles provide a brilliant kicking, though without thuggish shouts, so as not to disturb the prize-giving. Iles was often damn fussy about decorum.

But, because of the gunfire and activity at the rear of the hall, the ceremony had already faltered. Iles bent down and came up with the automatic and crash helmet. 'Please, do continue,' he called out to the Lord Lieutenant and other folk on the stage, waving the weapon in a slow, soothing arc, to demonstrate its harmlessness now. 'Things are all right here, oh, yes.' Iles was not big yet looked unusually tall and might be standing on the gunman's face. A beam of sunlight reached in through a window and gave the ACC's features a good yet unmanic gleam. There were times now and again when Iles did look unmanic.

Afterwards, when the local police and ambulance people had taken the intruder away, Harpur and Iles waited at the end of the hall while the guests, school staff and platform dignitaries dispersed. Wayne, Nora and Fay-Alice approached, Wayne carrying Fay-Alice's award volumes. 'Had that man come for me?' he'd asked. 'For me? Why?' He looked terrified.

'My God,' Nora said.

'Someone hired to do a wipe-out?' Wayne asked.

'I'd think so,' Iles said.

'All sorts would want to commission him, Wayne,' Harpur said. 'You're a target. Have you been talking firms' business to Mr Iles?'

'My God,' Nora said. 'Attack Wayne?'

'To silence him. And people might want to get at Mr Iles,' Harpur replied.

'But why?' Nora asked.

'Things are changing,' Harpur said.

'How?' Nora asked.

'Like that,' Harpur replied. 'Someone had you marked, Wayne.'

'He'd have gone for you in the mêlée as the crowd departed at the end of the do, I should think,' Iles said.

'But how did you spot him, Mr Iles?' Nora asked.

'I'm trained always to wonder about people at girls' school prize-givings with their face obscured by a crash helmet and obviously tooled up,' Iles had said. 'There was a whole lecture course on it at Staff College.'

'Why on earth did he come back into the hall?' Nora asked.

'He would still have had a shot at Wayne, as long as he could knock me out of the way,' Iles said. 'He had orders. He'd taken a fee, I expect. He'd be scared to fail.'

'Oh, you saved daddy, Mr Iles,' Fay-Alice had replied, riotously clapping her slim hands. 'An Assistant Chief Constable accepting such nitty-gritty, perilous work on our behalf, and when so brilliantly dressed, too. It was wonderful – so brave, so skilful, so selfless. I watched mesmerized from the platform, but *mesmerized* absolutely. A privilege, I mean it. Oh, thank you, Mr Iles. You so deserve our trust.' She inclined herself towards him, the long back stretching longer, and would have touched the ACC's arm. He skipped out of reach. 'We shall have so much to talk about at the swimming pool back home,' she said. 'I *do* look forward to it.'

'Let's get away now, Harpur,' Iles snarled.

'Yes, I must show you my butterfly, Mr Iles,' Fay-Alice said.

'Let's get away now, Harpur,' Iles had grunted.

A couple of days later they heard Wayne was run over. Iles would feel responsible for that, of course. And now, in Harpur's office, the ACC determined on a home visit to the Ridouts.

Chapter Three

The thing about Ralph Ember was he liked to think he had climbed a good way up from the untidy, head-on aspects of ordinary commercial life, such as slaughtering rivals in their own homes or pub car parks. He considered that kind of work should be transitional only, and if you were still caught in it as you came up to middle age, you were most probably not naturally gifted and should possibly think about a new career in, say, house decoration or taxi driving. Ember could be very sharp and ruthless examining his own life and the lives of people around. Often truth seemed quite vital to him.

And yet here it was again now, that old necessity, startling Ralph, and yes, in a sense making him edgy and ashamed, although vibrant – that old rotten necessity, that old rotten compulsion, to kill. He had a couple of pistols stored, of course: a short-barrelled Smith and Wesson 47 Bodyguard .38 revolver, and, as second string, a 9 mm Parabellum Bernadelli PO 18 automatic. He felt unsure about a gun from Italy. Ember was offended by racism, yet he doubted whether Italy truly knew much about making handguns, despite the Mafia there. Italy could definitely come up with good, ancient architecture, brilliant fountains, grand foodstuffs such as Parma ham, and, naturally, first quality opera and singing, but Ember thought that for handguns he would prefer something German, if it could not be British or American. He always felt a handgun with a Germanic name like Walther sounded an undebatable fucking stopper.

He'd had a Walther once, but you did not hang on to any weapon very long. Now, he wondered whether he should scrap the Bernadelli *and* the Bodyguard and get something totally new, totally reliable, totally untraceable. Or totally untraceable by Forensic. The trouble with getting something new was, obviously, you had to buy it. He did not need to care about the cost, but he did care that the dealer might talk one day if things went rough, or sooner than one day if they went *very* rough, and Ralph had the notion that things might go very rough very soon. Ember considered himself dab at foresight. He could read trends. That was how he came to own a club and a country house with grounds, Low Pastures.

In any case, who *wouldn't* see signs in the deaths of Percy Kellow and Mildly Sedated like that up at the anti-aircraft emplacement, and then the harsh way Wayne Ridout was encountered by road traffic? Consider how the Great War in 1914 began with the shooting of just one man in Bosnia, Archduke Franz Ferdinand. On this patch, for God's sake, there were already three assassinations, and nobody done for them.

It was a real while since Ralph bought armament and he could not be sure the supply scene had stayed the same. Stupid and smug to let absolutely basic knowledge slide like that: did the Pope ditch christening skills because he had a palace now? In the club a night or two ago, chatting to some customers, he had moved the conversation towards handguns, though only very generally, nothing even to hint he might be in the market. No responses. The topic died. He would need to ask around with a bit more focus.

Occasionally, it was useful to have members at the Monty who might help on such queries. Yes, occasionally. On the other hand, it often sickened and depressed Ember that you could expect to find out in his club who flogged the best firearms, or which alarm system operated in which security vans. As the Monty's proprietor, Ralph yearned for a day when it would rank with central London clubs like the Garrick or Pratt's or the Athenaeum, mentioned now and then in the Press. There was a distance to go before the Monty made this status, no question. He could see the gap between Shield Terrace and Pall Mall. This was another instance of his damned frequent reverence for truth. At Pratt's they had apparently blackballed Michael Heseltine, the Deputy Prime Minister at the time, because he wasn't up to snuff. God, blackball the British Deputy Prime Minister! At this stage, the Monty would probably not be as choosy as that if Heseltine applied for membership. Realistically, Ember considered he would probably *not* apply, even if invited.

Ralph went down to the bar now from his private flat and office above the Monty and decided to do a bit of circulating and get some really thorough talk about guns later on tonight, when the club filled up. He'd be more direct but still take things gingerly. Ask the wrong person the right questions and tomorrow Harpur would know Ralph was rearming. Or even fucking Desmond Iles would know. They thought they had a fucking *right* to know, the pair of bullying big-rank bastards. This was another unpleasant fact about the Monty membership: you couldn't screen out blab-mouths. Just the same, Ralph prized the club: its real brass and mahogany fittings, its glorious brooding potential. The club always comforted him, brought him optimism. In fact, there had been a time before Ralph bought it when the Monty *was* different: a social gathering spot for the town's professional people and true businessmen. It could be restored, eventually.

Ember poured himself a good Kressmann Armagnac and did a survey of who was in. Small stuff yet, except for E.W. Fenton, sitting alone, as he generally did. Fenton would sometimes down a drink or two and then disappear. Or he might linger for most of the night, never getting helpless, though, and not seeming to talk much to anyone. Ember had failed so far to get a full idea of what Fenton did: not a proper occupational profile. Perhaps he kept an eye for one of the big London or south coast commodity suppliers: provided the local touch. He had money from somewhere, and not just Social Security. His clothes were laughable, but not cheap. He drove a newish big Citroën. People who could stay obscure like Fenton infuriated Ember, unnerved him. Their secrecy amounted to defiance. Who the hell did E.W. think he was? Right. Even now, tonight, when the Monty bar had been really balming Ralph's angsts in its unfailing style, he felt troubled to see Fenton there. Ember was certain this jumpiness in himself was another sign of general destabilization on the patch. Although he did not drop into one of his panics, or anything really like one of his panics, he felt off balance suddenly. He detested the way Fenton used only initials, like a fucking air commodore.

Fenton saw Ralph was watching him and beckoned: an urgent, short-arm wave. This enraged Ember. What was he, some waiter? Fenton had a table near the fruit machines, a glass of red wine and the open bottle near him. Ember gave a bit of a gesture back. It said, *I let you in. Be happy with that, you shady jerk.* Ember returned to his papers. As an exchange of intimacies this would do, do for at least a year or two.

Apart from Fenton, only non-people and idlers would turn up in the Monty as early as this: creeps, mainly – dole two-timers, layabouts, would-be heavies. A few watchful girlfriends in impulse-bought shoes waited around. Ember stayed behind the bar for the present and thought about prospects while he fiddled with some accounts. At least the killing he planned would not be a matter of hate. Ralph detested intemperateness, both feared and despised it. Even keels he adored. He loathed and was confused by this sudden sense of anarchy everywhere. It would spread. All right, many might have expected a long-time grass like Wayne to be knocked over two or three times much sooner, but the point was it had not happened, and it had not happened because, until now, tranquillity prevailed, cherished on all sides. Why was it splintering, and splintering so fast? As Ember heard it, the deaths of Perce Kellow and

Mildly Sedated Henschall had been damned efficiently done. And then Wayne was systematically hunted again immediately after an escape up at some school. Ruthlessness and determination seemed off the leash. Now, there came these cruel hints about a possible move for dear dribbling Mark Lane, the Chief, and, under his successor, the likely neutering of Desmond Iles to what he had always nominally been, an Assistant Chief, no convenient policy supremo.

Obviously, Ralph detested Iles: his vast, flashy fucking arrogance, effortless brutality, foully distinguished clothes, and unchummy so-called wit. But Iles did know how to create and guard the peace, that peace Ember also craved. Didn't peace ensure a settled, improving life for him and his firm, and his family and the Monty? If you earned from commodity dealing £600,000 a year rising and, inevitably, non-taxable, you were entitled to dread turbulence, surely, and to get yourself decently armed to kill it off early. In a disgusting sense, he and Iles were as brothers, each governed by that 'blessed rage for order', which Ralph heard about in some literature lecture during his mature student university course. Naturally, parts of the teaching stuck with him, although Ralph had suspended his studies for the present because of other interesting pressures on his time. How could that lovely, essential order survive if some new, headstrong, tough Chief Constable arrived and started a crudely all-out application of the law, for God's sake? Naturally Ralph knew the phrase 'law and order', but surely it was naive, even insane, to regard them as identical, though perhaps vaguely linked. Why would two words be needed otherwise? Almost all politicians, from Thatcher to Blair, slipped up on this. Iles might be the biggest shit ever to imagine himself acceptable, but he understood and skilfully operated life's basics.

Ralph glanced up and realized Fenton had left his table and come to stand at the bar opposite him. He was carrying the glass and bottle. 'You ever consider visibility, Ralph?'

'Whose?'

'Yours.' He turned and pointed towards the door, then at Ember's heart region, moving a finger through the air. 'Straight as a firing range. No obstructions, no shelter, not this time of night, before the crowds arrive.'

'I love the club's feeling of space early on.'

'Too much visibility.'

'People can enjoy the proportions of the club.'

'I heard you've been asking around,' Fenton replied.

'Asking what?'

'Of course you have. Shrewd, Ralph.'

'Asking what?'

'Of course you have. You can see the changes, *feel* the changes.'

'Which?' Ember asked.

'Changes that have already come, and those on the way. Why I mentioned visibility. In a way it's great in you. Brave. Bold. You know there's rough problems here already or en route but you still stand there.'

'What rough problems?'

'I heard you've been asking around, and it's wise, Ralph – if I may say.'

'Asking what?'

'But, look, what I can't match up – you're asking around because you can feel it, the change, the exposure, yet you still stand there.'

'Why not?'

'What I meant by visibility.' Fenton put the bottle and glass on the bar but did not take a stool and sit down or drink. He was heavy-cheeked, thick-lipped. He had a frown on, to show how puzzled he felt.

'What exposure?' Ember asked.

'That's what I mean, visibility.'

'Visible who to?' Ember asked.

'Whereas, listen, Ralph, over at the table we'd be . . . less visible.'

'Why do you use just fucking initials, anyway?' Ember replied.

'When I say visible you see what I'm saying, do you?'

'Is what you're saying *visible*, you mean?'

'I'm keen on humour,' Fenton said.

'I've enjoyed our chat,' Ember replied.

'Visible. A straight line. Someone comes in, he could just stand there at the door and you're so visible he'd be able to put you away and be back out through the door and never come into the club proper at all. Thought about that, Ralph? It's defiance? It's a challenge? In some ways, yes, terrific, full of valour, but, I mean, you've been asking around, indicating you certainly know the developments, but you still stand there, a straight line, your head down in papers, unvigilant. So some hired lad gets told: You want the eminence behind the bar, standing at a little shelf about quarter right from your position at the door and looking like a young Charlton Heston. Give him three rounds at least, five if you can manage before he falls.'

'Oh, that Heston thing,' Ember replied. 'People are always on about it. I get fed up.'

'I still say we'd be better over at the table if we're going to talk about things,' Fenton said.

'What things?'

'We all think you're wise to want something new,' Fenton replied.

'Which we?'

'There are technical improvements to armament all the time. Anyway, it's always bad to carry something that's got a history. First lesson in infants' school.'

'I have to get around the club a bit now,' Ember said.

'I'll wait at the table. For half an hour.' The voice crackled, like an ultimatum.

'A club like this doesn't run itself,' Ember replied. 'These are people who know life.'

'I'm not going to talk outside about your visibility, Ralph. That's not E.W. Fenton at all. I hope you recognize this. But it *is* a factor.'

'What?'

'The visibility.' Fenton took his glass and bottle. With the base of the bottle he pointed at his table. 'To talk about what you've been asking around about. Obviously. I've got suggestions.'

'In a club like this things start to build up from about eleven. I get busy.'

'I can't stay more than half an hour,' Fenton replied.

'Oh, dear. You turn into a pumpkin?'

'What?'

'So why the fucking initials?' Ember replied.

'Half an hour.'

'Sorry,' Ember replied. He took a bottle of Barolo from the rack, pulled the cork and pushed it across the bar to Fenton. 'For you in your loneliness.'

A party was beginning to form near the pool tables, to salute the arsoning of an alleged paedophile's house and car on the Ernest Bevin council estate, though without apparent loss of life. Often the Monty became the venue for community jubilees: wedding receptions, birthday get-togethers, champagne and canapes evenings to mark Parole Board successes, or trial acquittals, post-funeral drink-ups, shindigs for a coming of age, vengeance triumphs, accumulator racing wins. In some ways Ember was gratified to see the Monty favoured like this. But he would try to discourage quite a range of these occasions when he really started taking the club up socially. Probably, you would never get a paedophile torching celebration at the Athenaeum, or even the Garrick. Christ, Melvyn Bragg belonged to the Garrick. In a while Ralph might send over half a case of some middling stuff to the festive group. And a while after that he might even have a drink with them. This was hosting, whatever you thought of the people. If they wanted to do paedophiles, he might ask them if they'd thought of throwing a bit of flame through Iles's house. Ralph had the address.

Fenton went back to his table with the two bottles and his glass. Never before tonight had he talked to Ember for so long. It might be another evidence of disruption. Of course it was, and these symptoms would spread and increase. The health of the whole domain was sinking. In a changed regime it was certain Iles would be stripped of healing powers, so brilliantly exercised by the ACC under Lane, and regardless of him. They would choose as replacement someone hard enough and bloody-minded enough to annul Iles. That's why the Chief was to be promoted and removed. People in the Home Office wanted those absurd, folksy absolutes reasserted – good, evil – and the great gulf between them re-dug, re-dug deeper. There was even a whisper they'd put in a woman, just to humiliate Iles properly. At least one force was already run by a woman Chief. They could be really fussy about things.

Ember went out from behind the bar and did a slow tour of the club, having a word with people here and there, but only a word. Not many were worth more. He strolled to the door and looked back to where he had been standing. Yes, he would be a simple target from here. So, why had Fenton checked it? Most likely the sod wanted to get that kind of question asked by Ember. It made Fenton seem like an enigma, the fucking enigma. Ember moved away from the door. The view did trouble him. It upset Ralph to think of gunfire in the Monty, just as the idea of gunfire in a church or one of the Queen's residences would upset him.

He got his thoughts going on strategy again. Lane would probably be seen by the Home Office as almost as weak as he really was. They must know how Iles had come to domineer, but they'd be scared to attack the ACC direct. Probably he could pull all sorts of influence, and if he felt fucked about he *would* pull all sorts of influence – political, religious, professional. But Lane . . . Lane at his age and with his recent breakdown and possible recurrence, gave a nattier way of handling things. Someone powerful and passably benign would whisper to him and his wife that a good, sedate extension of his career was available in a realm where the ACC's £350 lace-ups would never tread.

The killing Ralph had in mind . . . well, was exactly that:

a creation of the *mind*, his thinking mind, an intent founded on good, intelligent process, not some foolish, cheap blood surge. As he saw it, if you were going to destroy someone you had been truly close to over years, there ought to be constructive meditation, producing what was known as a rationale. Another echo of his college course: the word had come up quite often there. Ralph totally approved of the notion of a rationale governing life and, in this case, death. During university classes, he had noticed that when he heard the term 'rationale', it did not remain just an abstract concept: in Ralph's head he would see a physical structure, at times like an actual building, at times only like the blueprint design of a building, and sometimes like a solid, unornate picture frame, bringing controlled and suitable shape to life, and, again, in this case, death. Ralph knew he could never contemplate annihilating somebody who had shared so many difficulties and triumphs with him if there were not a trim, intellectual basis first. As Ralph W. Ember, he often wrote letters for publication in the Press on environmental and civic matters, and he believed everyone had a duty to ensure society did not gallop, ferocious or giggling, to self-destruction. It would be irresponsible to ignore the continuing danger of this. Civilization was precious and fragile. Ralph knew it had to be defended and that he must be numbered as one of the few last people on earth ready to defend it.

Wasn't this why he had begun to think about a new pistol? It need not necessarily be of huge calibre, designed to fragment someone with only one round. But he did want something nicely lethal. The obligation to preserve order and harmony would rest even more weightily on him if Desmond Iles were depowered by an incomer. This prospect made Ember nervous but, surely, also affirmed his eminence and unique strength. He knew that people referred to him when he wasn't around as Panicking Ralph, or even Panicking Ralphy, and he also knew they were malevolently wrong. Yes, there had been one or two crack-up moments when things on a job had gone bad, but he felt sure almost anyone might have behaved the same, and, in any case, those bits of catastrophe lay far in the past.

For a second he considered getting straight back to the Kressmann Armagnac. It would help ease those awkward memories even further into the far away. Although Ember did believe fiercely in truth, you could definitely get too fucking much of it now and then and especially now. As he saw things, a man had a duty to be at his decisive best in the immediate present, in the current instant: to be strong and comfortable, and to forget those rotten bits of the past which would always try to bring you low and trample on your pride. Ember wanted to be a TODAY figure, and the Armagnac could help towards this.

But, no, no, no, sod it, he would not let himself sneak off to this bottled escape ploy tonight. There were matters to be faced and, by heaven, he, Ralph W. Ember, knew how to face them, how to grasp and hold that TODAYNESS. Often Ember could be like this for quite a period: unflinching. E.W. Fenton's cheap mysteriousness and know-all tricks must not break up his poise. For God's sake, giving in to tremors every time was hardly the way Ralph acquired the Monty and Low Pastures and the plump cash reserves nicely hidden about the roof space of both. He liked the idea of funds nested by the insulating fibreglass up there. That money was for insulating him and the family, too, in case things turned tough, which they could do so soon.

But, whatever happened, this was *his* terrain, the Monty, and he would behave in it like a duke, eventually nursing it up to a gorgeous glory role that nobody here at present, except himself, could visualize, not even E.W. Fenton, with his bloody gloating initials. Of course, Ember did wonder sometimes if it was farcical to imagine the Monty would ever catch up on the Athenaeum, but he did not let this doubt floor him for long. He felt ashamed of nearly crumbling just now because of that imagined view of himself as sacrificial victim from near the door. Entirely make-believe, entirely alarmist. Sensitivity was all right but you could get too much, the same as with truth. He must correct his recent feverish behaviour. Selfhood demanded it. To be Ember meant obligations.

And so he went unhurriedly, unswervingly, back to the spot to look once again in a wholly cool and practical way at the execution site so fondly described by Fenton. Yes, clearly the bugger had *enjoyed* describing it, because he thought this would rush Ember into one of his pathetic, uncontrollable frights, make him a pushover for whatever Fenton was trying to push. All right, that had almost occurred, but thank God not quite. Now, Ember meant to show he was clever enough to accept decent insights and advice from anybody, even someone like E.-fucking-W.-Fenton, but also show he would decide in his own way and time how he meant to use such insights and advice, if at all. Standing near the door he turned and looked indomitably towards the bar once more, his feet feeling exceptionally firm on the floor, his body bulky but not gross. Robust. Above all, formidable. He felt he must look like a man who had risen to his state by recognizing grave problems without evasion, and then resolving them. Ralph had always quietly admired the stiff upper lip, that British characteristic sometimes stupidly mocked these days. Now and then he would see himself as in a line from one or other of the great, uncomplaining adventurers – Clive of India, Rhodes, Shackleton. Although he might still buy a new gun, Ember did not need a pistol, new or old, to feel this link. It lived *in* him. He felt grateful. It thrilled him to belong to a tradition. Continuity was precious.

But, suddenly then, as he exulted, Ember realized one of his panics had begun. Oh, Christ, Fenton did have it *so* damn right about marksman possibilities from the door. Ember saw again that behind the bar he would be a parcelled gift, a sniper's doddle. He found he could not quell a double sob at the idea, the one rushing after the other, as if to beat any attempt at self-control. He gazed across the big room and had a terrible, graphic, created view of himself there, near his little shelf. The picture was clearer and much more chilling than previously. In this new glimpse of how it might be, he wore one of his fine, navy pin-striped suits and a white silk shirt, his head slightly forward over the accounts, just asking for fucking killer bullets. He seemed to show no awareness of how the city's whole commercial scene had turned pre-emptive murderous, how the era of turf slayings was ready for relaunch, with him so very high on any list. Highest. He felt a sudden, huge, crippling pity for Ralph Ember, as if momentarily he'd become somebody else: this horrifying, epically sad vision of himself in that famed, head-on-the-block spot. The suit was noble and deeply expensive, so how could he merit this kind of obliterating salvo? His intentions for the Monty rated as admirably ambitious and constructive, so who would have the sadism to cut him off before he turned them into brilliant fact? Ember never understood out-and-out cruelty, the shutting down of humanity. He believed a case often existed, even in commerce, for acting with humanity, humaneness.

He put out a hand to prop himself against the wall. He felt worse than when he first came to look from the door not long ago. Fenton's forecast seemed so much more real, its hellish suggestions so much wider: the point was, wasn't it, wasn't it, that if it didn't happen here now, soon, it would happen somewhere else soon? In any war, Ember was too considerable to be left alive. Once you became a figurehead you became also a target, and Ralph knew Ralph Ember could not be more a figurehead than now. Six hundred thousand a year untaxed made him a figurehead, as well as the Monty and his house, Low Pastures. Yes, the particular location of the assassination spot was irrelevant. Hate, envy, doom would relentlessly stalk him, remove him, for the sake of the pickings he would leave behind. Oh, God, should he have avoided eminence? But could he have? Hadn't eminence come to him as to its natural abode?

As Ralph had feared, the sweat of a prime panic was

starting. He could feel it in all the usual places, across his shoulders, in the small of his back, trickling down his thighs, soaking his scalp and making a poultice of his hair. And there came another sensation which always turned up as part of a full panic: Ember's foul suspicion that the old scar along his jaw line had opened up and was weeping some foul juice on to his neck and collar and jacket, like blame from betrayed accomplices. His free hand went up to it instantly and found, as it always found, that the scar remained as utterly sealed and dry as ever.

But, hell, how could he have broken like this? Nothing had actually taken place. He was nightmaring like a kid. Club members continued in their harmless, subdued way, even the arson team, so far. Only a fantasy, a scenario, a projection had brought on this disintegration. So, didn't he possess any centre, any core? It seemed pathetic and ludicrous to him now that minutes ago he had thought of himself as a confident duke. Clive of fucking India. He muttered, 'You sodding wreck, Ralphy.'

In his terror, he craved some kind of support, and some kind of support more than the wall. Where would it come from? Who would help him, bring him back to the famed steadiness and Toledo steel of Ralph W. Ember? The answer that presented itself dazed him, astonished him. He found himself needing E.W. Fenton: Fenton's knowingness, his bullishness, his solid, meaty face, his disgusting cockiness and sliminess, his shadowiness – that more than anything. Ember's ignorance of what Fenton really amounted to made him seem strong. His powers and connections stayed undefined and therefore infinite, like God's in the Old Testament or Colonel Gaddafi's. The casual insolence of telling Ember that he had only half an hour if he wanted a further audience turned Fenton mighty. How could he speak like that to Ember in his own club! This Fenton was solid, heavy with promise, as devious as Ember needed.

Ralph moved slightly, to try his legs. Would they carry him to Fenton's table without a give-away stagger or even a collapse? Sometimes during a panic they became temporarily feeble. Ember believed that his resemblance to Charlton Heston imposed exceptional image demands. Think of Chuck as El Cid, strapped on his well-known horse to hearten the troops at the end when clinically dead. How would it look if Ember, the Heston look-alike, could not even keep upright on his feet for a couple of dozen yards because of panic shakes? He tried a few small, very careful steps and found things pretty well all right. He had full feeling the whole way down to his toes. In a while, pride at this condition began to boom in him. He did not go direct to Fenton, though. Instead, he made his way to the bar for the Armagnac bottle and two glasses. But when he turned he saw that Fenton had stood up and was about to leave. The half-hour had passed? He could be so exact, so exacting? Ember yelled: 'E.W. E.W.' Frequently he had promised himself he would never address Fenton like this, but now Ralph longed to sound friendly, even like a colleague, perhaps like a supplicant. Fenton paused. 'E.W., please,' Ember called. He held up the bottle. 'Or I'll bring another Barolo.'

'Hurry,' Fenton replied. He frowned, pretty impatiently. 'I've other people to see.'

'Yes, of course, of course,' Ember said. It pleased him that Fenton was still so commanding. Ember *wanted* commands. He needed someone to take charge. Deliberately avoiding any cheap, egotistical flourish with the corkscrew, he opened a fresh Barolo, then carried it and the Kressmann Armagnac to Fenton's table. Fenton sat down again. Ember took a chair opposite him and filled Fenton's glass with the wine. He had a small, very delicate, even fragile-looking nose for such a face. This was the kind of nose mothers would like on a son. It seemed to give Fenton boyishness, a link to babyhood, even. A mother would think a lad with a nose like this had a splendid chance of staying out of jail. Ember poured an Armagnac for himself. 'Sorry, but it was just I wanted to ask how you, personally, see things, E.W.,' he said. 'This could be a help.'

'*I* see things as *you* see things.'

'Yes, of course.'

'You're sweating, Ralphy.'

'The air conditioning's off.'

'Everyone sees things the same,' Fenton said. 'Iles will be squashed, the street agreement will be squashed with him, then this territory's up for conquest once again and fighting starts to decide who's jungle king and who's eaten. Did you see in the Press that police in Nottingham carry guns as routine, because of drug trade battles? As *routine*. This is *British* police in a *British* city. We next? Can you face that, Ralphy?'

'I'm someone who –'

'Can you face it?' Fenton asked.

It was not one of those questions assuming the answer No, was it? The tone seemed almost kindly. Ember felt touched. 'Look, I'd like you to work with me, E.W.,' he replied. 'There's a place for you. The way you're observant, ahead of developments. You think of my safety. We could easily do something about your clothes. I'll give you an allowance and ask my tailor to get things as near to right as they can be for someone like you. It will make a difference. Concentrate on clothes. Unguents might help with your skin, but clothes are crucial.'

'What kind of thing were you looking for?'

'But working *only* for me,' Ember said. 'This will be salaried, plus bonuses. Proper paid holidays and sickness.'

'I think you want at least a semi-automatic,' Fenton replied.

Ember felt the panic begin to turn tail. It would be part Armagnac, part passage of time, part the belief he could shift some of his bigger anxieties on to Fenton, part the belief that Fenton would take them. The thick skin on his face could be a plus, mopping up trouble and never letting it out again. If Fenton had a scar he would not need to worry it might open up because for a scar to open up in skin like that would take a power drill. Perhaps he had actually come here tonight with the aim of scaring Ember and landing an adviser's job. Of course he had. Fine. E.W. recognized where the true status lay among dealers. He wanted to join the one who would be still around when the sorting out was over. 'I don't necessarily wait for people to come for me, you know,' Ralph said.

'Who were you meaning to hit? Manse Shale? Dubal?'

'I think there's sometimes a moral case for acting first,' Ember replied. 'A man is required to survive. Yes, *required*. There are duties to himself and others. We could have done Hitler at Munich.'

'Shale or Dubal?'

'Oh, I know they're both protected.'

'I've looked at a profile of you,' Fenton replied.

'What profile?'

'Not the Heston doppelganger bit. Dossier notes.'

'Which fucking dossier?' Ember asked.

'You can do something with a handgun, that's clear.'

'Which fucking dossier? You keep dossiers? You got your eyes on a police dossier? I've never been convicted, though. Of course I can do something with a fucking handgun.' This was better. He could feel a true fragment of anger barging its way through the sweat. Thank goodness for *fuck* and *fucking*. These words put a rhythm into him again and dignity. 'I'm alive, aren't I, for fuck's sake, with all my limbs, and I'm solvent?'

'But a long time ago, the handgun.'

'A skill like that never goes. It would be mad to let a skill like that go,' Ember replied.

The arsonists were at the speeches and toasts stage. There was some cheering and whooping and songs – 'There'll Always Be An England', that sort.

'Can you get me something?' Ember said.

'What?'

'I wouldn't mind if *you* decide.' So, he could fall low like that again, after the brilliant rage and structured cursing.

Christ, I can't even pick a gun. It's like handing myself over to him, the whole, helpless consignment. Squire me, E.W. Guide me, oh, thou great E.W. Favour me. Am I going gay? 'What are you using yourself these days, E.W?'

'Offensive, *de*fensive,' Fenton replied.

'Certainly.'

'When you say work with you, Ralphy, what are –'

'Your pay will be tidy. After all, we're talking about getting hold of the future, cornering the future. This will be the bliss of dominance. Do you realize the scale? It's worth spending on. Only, if you're in and out of my properties in the way of work keep your dick clear of my wife and daughters. One daughter's, well . . . volatile. She's away in France at a convent-type school to damp her down, but she comes back eager for closeness and the secular. Rifts we don't want.'

'Some kind of steel screen bolted to one of the pillars between the bar and the door,' Fenton replied. 'That's just basic. A start. It tells them we know the picture – I mean, if you haven't moved first and blasted Shale or Dubal.'

'I don't get called Ralphy,' Ember said. 'Look, I'm willing to call you E.W. despite everything, so don't fucking call me Ralphy.' He could always get anger going on this. He considered 'Ralphy' sounded like somebody's half-witted cousin who had to be made allowances for. Very occasionally, when he felt flat, Ember might think of himself as Ralphy, but this was private.

'Cash,' Fenton replied.

'Of course cash.'

'I don't mean just the salary and bonus. For me to get something for you.'

'Of course,' Ember said. 'Notes, no cheques. Before you leave tonight.' He stood up. One of the men from the firebomb group was dancing on a table, still wearing his shoes. Ember did not allow this. It was an image matter again. Could anyone visualize something similar in the Athenaeum, for heaven's sake? He did not want tales spread about. The shoes were poor. He walked over to the party, his legs perfect, and told him to get down. It looked for a moment as if he would refuse. A couple of the fired-up, liquored-up women shouted for him to keep dancing there. 'Seemliness is one of my basic things,' Ember snarled. The man gazed at Ralph, became still, then jumped down. One side of his head looked toasted. He must have gone too close. This again was probably something you would not see in any of the better London clubs – not just singeing but an authentic arson-based scorch. Ember said: 'The house buys the next round, boys and girls.'

Chapter Four

Harpur was always on edge at a funeral with Iles, especially when the ACC appeared in uniform. Insignia energized him fiercely. He seemed to feel he had a duty to participate in some active way, whether or not asked. Duty never left the Assistant Chief alone.

Although Harpur had suggested earlier that it might be an error to attend Wayne Ridout's funeral, they were here today to see him off. They sat together about two thirds of the way back in church: Harpur preferred it when the ACC was not in quick reach of the pulpit or altar. A theatrical, possibly ballet, element in Iles would often take him over during the service and cause what others might regard as very difficult behaviour. Harpur could see Nora Ridout and Fay-Alice up at the front, both in grey, apparently, not black, and both wearing hats.

Possibly Iles resented the attention received by the deceased at funerals. Was the Assistant Chief conscious of this envy? He did not go in much for self-knowledge and Harpur regarded that as shrewd, in view of the self. Harpur wished the ACC would not crave the sombre distinctions of death. There was already too much death around and more might be on the way, including the ACC's if Louise Machin read the pointers right. Harpur thought she saw a lot, and saw it well: rumour put this manor on the rim of chaos.

Ferdy Dubal and his mother were across the aisle from Harpur and Iles, and Dubal leaned forward for a moment to clear his mother and gave them a minor wave and mourner's small, brave but suffering smile. It seemed an excellent showing for someone who'd probably ordered the killing of Wayne at a second attempt, and might even have done it himself, once the hired boy failed, all fucking helmet and hesitation.

Once or twice or oftener Harpur had been forced into attempting physical restraint of Iles during funerals, and Harpur thought it would be poor if this grew usual. The Assistant Chief could not bear physical restraint, any more than, say, Dame Margot Fonteyn could have on stage, and a full fight between senior police around a loved one upset some folk and interested the media. Iles's formal uniform was a delicate blue and wrong for brawling at religious functions.

In the church forecourt, when Harpur and Iles arrived, Harpur had seen Mr and Mrs Panicking Ralph Ember, with Mansel Shale and one of his women, possibly Lowri, entering the church ahead of them. Contempt for Wayne would be widespread, as for all known grasses, and many folk wanted to say a personal goodbye, and check he was really finished. Harpur hoped Nora and Fay-Alice did not realize why some of these people turned up. When he and Iles had called at their house to commiserate a couple of days earlier, the ACC spoke of Wayne as 'much cherished by his community'. Nora had looked as if he were talking the horse shit he was but wished she could believe it, and felt grateful. Fay-Alice seemed grateful, too, and Harpur saw the ACC felt relieved she had not reverted to hate.

As far as Harpur knew, the ACC did not detest all vicars outright simply for being vicars, but he would grow restless and possibly disruptive if one of them tried to hog things in a church funeral. The Assistant Chief's uniform had a highish, stiff collar, enclosing most of his Adam's apple, and he considered he could make himself noticeable during the service without dragging the occasion into comedy. That he would never deliberately do. Iles had more than one streak of genuine sensitivity. Say, three. Not long ago, though, he had said: 'Some funerals are fucking heavy, Col.' When Harpur replied this might be in their nature, Iles did not dismiss it, but Harpur saw he still believed things could occasionally be brisked up and given an Iles touch. The Assistant Chief regarded funerals as a magnificent opening for some impressive moving about by him through the nave and aisles, plus a possible address to the congregation on policing or more general issues in the state or world. As he'd also once told Harpur, he did not turn up in his best duds just to hear 'some poncy Rev. simper about the corpse's well-known and enduring respect for his/her family and all members of the animal kingdom'.

It was Mark Lane who insisted Harpur and Iles should attend the funeral. He was ready to risk sending Iles despite previous troubles, because the Chief now had a bigger purpose. His reasoning was not bad. He said Press reports of the dreadful incident at Taldamon school showed that Iles and Harpur knew Ridout somehow. In the same way as Iles feared undercover work, Lane despised police use of informants, and the Chief would not want the relationship between Wayne and the ACC given a hint of secrecy by avoidance of the funeral. In any case, Lane said secrecy was no longer available, whether or not required previously. Now, it would look churlish if there were no police presence at St Luke's, when someone known to Iles and Harpur had been so monstrously killed.

'We owe that presence to our friends, Desmond,' Lane had said. 'We must be seen to respect our friends. This is the way to gather *new* friends. This is the way to preserve and, yes, to further, policing by consent. And what other effective policing is there? We are the arm of society, aren't we? You will be, as it were, the embodiment of that arm.' Lane's strange fluency with this vermillion corn made Harpur think the Chief must really be due to depart, and his terror of Iles therefore no longer at a wise maximum.

'I believe there's always a case for stating the great simplicities, sir, regardless,' Iles said.

If Lane were moved from his post he'd passionately want to pass on to the next Chief an outfit wholly esteemed by the people. He genuinely valued the people, thought their views counted in some ways.

Harpur said: 'Just a hired and hard London artisan, the gunman at Taldamon, sir.' They had been talking in Lane's office. 'We get nothing from him about his purpose or who sent him. The charge can only be attempted murder of Mr Iles.'

'But when people see you unimpaired at the funeral, Desmond – read in the Press about you at the funeral – they will realize how abjectly that attempt failed,' the Chief cried triumphantly. 'It will proclaim your continuance unharmed, and, through your personal continuance, the continuance of what you and all of us represent, the integrity of the law.'

'Frequently, sir, my mother would say to me, "Desmond, be an emblem!" ' Iles replied.

'Oh, certainly I've heard the complaints of excessive force during his arrest – cheekbones, ribs,' Lane said. 'Would I question the judgement of an Assistant Chief in such an incident?'

'Not *all* policing is by consent, sir,' Iles replied, 'and once you've got an armed piece of contracted, skid-lid shit on the ground and you're wearing a bonny pair of shoes, it's only natural to give him a –'

'Mr Iles is too self-effacing to tell you himself, sir, but the Head at Taldamon will create a special award called the Desmond Iles Assembly Hall Trophy permanently to commemorate that episode. It will be given to a pupil showing exceptional enterprise and resourcefulness and they hope he will present it annually.'

'This is splendid, Desmond,' Lane had cried. 'Wonderful for our image. Normally, as you know, I don't give much weight to modish, woolly concepts like "image". But public perception *is* important. It's fine the school acknowledges your fierce determination to look after its girls.'

'This is already widely recognized, sir, but yes,' Harpur said.

In the car on the way to St Luke's Iles had said: 'I do love that benighted jerk, Harpur.'

'We'll all miss him.'

'We would, we would,' Iles replied. 'But he'll never go. The Chief is anchored here, thank God.'

'Others might insist. That's the rumour.'

'He's ours, ours for ever, Col. We are blessed. Mark Lane speaks his mind regardless of what kind of mind it is.'

'What kind of mind *is* it, sir?'

'I've known others the same,' Iles replied.

'What happened to them, sir?'

'The school trophy in my name, Harpur – what the fuck was that about?'

'It seemed a lovely thought, and moved things away from the kicking, and just in time.'

'But whose lovely thought?'

'Oh, mine, sir.'

'And only yours?'

'But one the Head *should* have had, and might eventually. An *ideal* thought.'

'But only yours now?'

'Oh, of course, sir.'

Iles dwelt on this. 'So, there's absolutely *no* Desmond Iles Trophy?'

'There's the *idea* of a prize – the concept.'

'Where?'

'What, sir?'

'Where is the concept, you slippery fucker?'

'I told you, in my head, sir.'

'The other Head hasn't spoken to you about it?'

'Oh, no, sir. Entirely my notion and no more than a notion.'

'Well, thanks, Col.'

'It's the kind of testimonial which, if it existed, could be crucial for your standing with any incoming Chief, sir.'

'What incoming Chief is that?' the ACC replied.

They were early at St Luke's. Harpur looked around. He could feel quite comfortable in churches, apart from the anxiety about Iles. Although at Sunday School in the Gospel Hall Harpur was sent to as a kid he learned to suspect holy flummery, he now considered this blinkered. He could be intrigued by the mad overtinting and slabby, big-toothed portraits of people and saints on stained glass.

The Assistant Chief bent close and muttered from behind his prayer book: 'I'll ask him to call me. A courtesy.'

'Who?'

'The padre. Invite me.'

'To what?'

'This is what the Chief wants,' Iles replied.

'What?'

'Some assertiveness. Turn proactive.'

'What's that?'

'Jargon.'

'In what way proactive?' Harpur asked.

'A statement.'

'Who to?'

'Everyone,' Iles said. 'An address.'

'About what?'

'And if you grapple with me this time in that sodding carpet salesman's suit I'll throttle you, Harpur,' the ACC replied. 'Remember, this is a fucking church, for God's sake. Remember, too, it's a tribute to a dear dead husband and father.'

'Well, yes, sir.'

'If there's one thing I wouldn't want to do it's to disappoint the Chief.'

'In what way?'

'Failing him.'

'In what way?'

'He wants me to make an impression here, Col. That was evident in our briefing.'

'I took him to mean just by attending, sir. Our presence.'

'I was speaking more about myself as a wholly separate,

meaningful entity, not linked with some miserable, run-of-the-mill . . . well, not linked with *you*, Harpur.'

'I think the Chief feels that merely by being here and perhaps chatting afterwards with other mourners we'll be reaching out in acceptable fashion to the populace and broadcasters and Press.'

'Oh, he'd want more than that of me, as a separate entity, Harpur. Lane is looking for the Iles factor. And this is a man I cannot let down – cannot, as you know. An icon.'

'He spoke as if he wanted us to act with dignity, sir, to enhance the reputation of the police.'

'This *will* be with fucking dignity, you blind prick,' Iles replied. 'Such enhancement is my only aim. What else do I live for?'

A bit desperately, Harpur changed line. 'Possibly it's too late to ask the vicar to call you. Matters are pretty much under way. He'll have his programme worked out.'

'I certainly don't want to barge into things without a specific plea from him,' Iles replied. 'It would be arrogant, crude.'

'Right, sir. Undignified.'

'OK, I may have done something like that in the past, but Ridout has that lovely, aquatic, filthy-mouthed daughter, and I don't want to provoke abuse here, as you know. There were troublesome moments with her, yes, but these have been resolved. Now, we're part of a serious occasion. Can't you realize this?'

'The vicar will arrive with Wayne very, very soon, sir, and enter the church speaking those established words about the resurrection.'

Iles sat back in the pew for a while, then said: 'I think I'm in favour of it – the resurrection. Someone like Wayne needs that. He could do with another run at things.'

'But you shouldn't interrupt the parson once he's into that. It would be off-colour.'

'I hate anything off-colour, Harpur.'

'I know, sir. If there's one thing you're famed for it's that.'

'You're giving *me* instruction in what's off-colour?' The Assistant Chief and Harpur had been whispering, but now Iles's voice began to take on a familiar screaming malice and agony. Harpur could see from some twitching that a few people in the seats ahead wanted to glance back to see where the ranting din came from, but were scared. The ACC asked: 'Would you consider, for instance, Col, that shagging the wife of a prized colleague on flop house beds from all angles fell into the off-colour category, not to mention –'

'I think I heard the hearse, sir.'

Iles turned and looked back towards the doors of the church. 'I'll catch Mr Surplice before they get a clip on up the aisle.' He gave the people behind a very unscared stare. 'That pork-faced sprite E.W. Fenton's here, Col. How come? What the hell's moving?'

'The vicar might not have a space in the service for an outsider speech, sir,' Harpur replied. 'Or perhaps it's already arranged with someone else.'

'What fucking someone else?'

Harpur liked the tombs around the sides of the nave, with stone knights laid out above, wearing armour and visor, their qualities and details in Latin on beige plaques. At that time there were plenty of nobles who deserved memorials, most likely. You had to agree with the Chief a decline had taken place. Harpur thought Iles might look impressive in stone: his neat, snob features snug under a visor. Wayne would never get similar tomb recognition, no matter how brilliant a grass for the Assistant Chief he'd been. Did Latin *have* a word for grass, in that sense? These days, even the ACC himself would probably not rate much after death. And he might not rate much in *life* from now on, suppose he did stay alive and there was a new Chief – perhaps a woman, so the newest murmurs went. Harpur understood why Iles pretended ignorance of possible change. It dismayed Harpur to think of him crushed and humbled, though God knew such a malevolent, pirouetting, egomaniac vandal half deserved it, or a quarter.

Diminish Iles and you could undermine life's whole fragile scheme, as in the elimination of a species or act of genocide.

The ACC pushed out past Harpur and turned to walk down the aisle towards the coffin party. 'Fenton,' he called, en route, 'you're here as, Let the dead bury their dead, are you? You're the new tomorrow, I suppose.' In a little while Iles returned and took his place by Harpur again. Immediately afterwards the clergyman led the coffin on its glossy metal trolley up to the altar, intoning with big volume in his big robes the big, evasive, hopeful words. 'He was hesitant about offering me a slot,' Iles whispered.

'I feared that. The Church of England funeral service is strictly laid down.'

'He came round to it.'

'That right?'

'I hope I wouldn't personally use threats at a church door,' Iles said.

'I, for one, can believe you wouldn't, sir. And there'd probably be others.'

'I referred to you, Col.'

'In what respect?'

'Looking into the tales.'

'What tales?'

'About him and the choirboys.'

'What tales, sir?'

'In the matter of slots. I stressed what we heard might be mere rumour or false memory syndrome at this stage. However, then he seemed to decide suddenly that if I knew Wayne and his family well there might be a case for a small eulogy.'

'How small?' Harpur replied.

When the ACC responded to the vicar's request near the end of the service and went up into the pulpit, he stood silent for half a minute gazing out over the coffin and Nora and Fay-Alice and the congregation. Harpur considered he looked damn sane. Except for the uniform, you could have met somebody unexceptional like this anywhere: repairing

TV sets, running Bingo in a one-time cinema, presiding over a tripe art stall. Iles said: 'I am not Traffic.'

He would do this sometimes when making a public speech: depreciate himself so as to have a more spectacular rise in the rest of his address.

The Assistant Chief said: 'Although, as you see, I'm a police officer, my special area is not Traffic, yet I would like to speak to you today about road accidents. I'm here to tell you a little about Wayne, and I know that, if he were still able to advise me, he would suggest I use this opportunity to warn all of you about the increasing perils of crossing the road, as Wayne's own sad death demonstrates. He would wish me to as it were *use* that death in positive fashion so that others might be alerted and not suffer similarly.

'Very well then: clearly, there is the basic instruction we all, I'm sure, offer our children: look both ways before attempting to cross, and then look back once more to whichever side is the one for approaching vehicles. But, as Wayne's death shows, and as he would wish me to point out to you now, this is possibly no longer adequate. For what if – despite those elementary precautions – one is still struck by a vehicle, which leaves one lying helpless in the road? In this exposed position, one might desperately want to look both ways and then once more to the approach side, in case an encounter with a vehicle, or even encounters, threatens a further knock, or knocks, possibly fatal, and in Wayne's case tragically so, as we know.

'Because of injuries sustained in the first impact, it might be impossible for the victim to raise his/her head to look both ways and so on. And even if the victim can, he/she might not be able to do anything about avoiding a vehicle spotted during this survey because of injuries to, say, the legs or nervous system sustained during the first hit. There might be three accidents as one.'

Iles paused and smiled wryly at the tricky nature of the problem he'd set. 'I see several of you nodding sympathetically at the predicament one has described,' the ACC continued. 'I am sure, for instance, that Mr Ferdinand Dubal can envisage the doubled or even tripled pains of such an accident. Yes, yes, I see I have his assent. Now, if I *were* Traffic, I might be able to offer you some guidance on how to deal with such a multiple hazard. But my speciality is other. My speciality is, along with several other categories, murder. Hardly relevant, is it? I fear that all I can do now is ask people to be particularly careful when, as it were, out and about. This could be a time of increasing danger in our city. There is a sudden unease. At random I look around again and see Mr Ralph Ember, Mr Mansel Shale and even Mr E.W. Fenton. I think many would agree with me that our community would certainly be reduced in numbers if one or even all of them were, for instance, struck by vehicles, despite precaution, or fatally damaged in some other fashion.'

Iles gave a light, apologetic blow to the pulpit ledge: 'But I am here primarily to give a portrait, as I knew him, of dear Wayne, and perhaps what I've opened with is something of a diversion. I must correct this now. Ours was an enduring friendship, Wayne's and mine. It was founded in a shared fascination, almost an obsession, I must admit – a fascination, obsession, with *people*, with what might be termed humankind. I hope it's not boastful to say that we were both great observers of the folk around us. And we would exchange our impressions, compare them, contrast them, amend them, in the light of the other's views. Oh, this was very much a give-and-take relationship. Although we would certainly differ sometimes in our opinions of this or that person, the differences were rarely huge, rarely irreconcilable. It would be wrong for me to single out the folk we liked to talk about, but, since some are here today, perhaps I could be allowed to mention again Ferdy Dubal, Ralph Ember, Manse Shale, Fenton, E.W. I hope my naming of these four will not cause others unmentioned to feel, as it were, left out, slighted. It's just that these are unarguably prominent lads and are bound to sit big in my memory. Now Wayne has gone

I don't know where I shall find my little harmless chats on the quirks and qualities of our co-citizens. My life will be much the poorer for this, but at least I've still got it.'

So this, then, was the pulpited Iles, and the real Iles as well, most probably. Harpur reckoned that, as ever, the ACC saw pretty much everything and would deal with pretty much everything, but in his own eternally roundabout style, unless someone dealt with *him* first. When he was acting a vicar, he spoke parables. It would please him to behave in keeping. And the thing about parables was they told a tale but meant something else, something bigger. Iles was a performer, and performances observed rules. Dubal had received a message of destruction and would understand he had received a message of destruction, but could ignore it or shelve it or laugh it off for the present because it had come sounding like sweet friendship, churchy balm. Of course, he probably knew that Wayne had been the ACC's most revered grass and that Iles would be enraged and unforgivingly grieved by his slaughter. Dubal might imagine he could cope with these reactions. He probably did not know, though, that the ACC was in and out of love with the long back and so on of Wayne's daughter. This might increase Iles's urge to look for revenge. It would be part to satisfy himself, part to please and woo her, though not, of course, to produce in Fay-Alice the kind of slimy gratitude he detested. The two objectives gave an extra bitterness to the situation, and to the ACC.

Iles descended with quite a slice of elegance from the pulpit and, stepping around Wayne to Nora and her daughter, drew them up from their pew and embraced both, not hanging on to Fay-Alice very much longer at all than her mother and keeping his hands entirely in view and twitchless on her shoulder blades. The vicar went back into the pulpit and called for the final hymn, 'Out of the shadow land, into the sunshine'.

Iles returned to the pew and stood singing with Harpur.

Between verses he said: 'It will take him a time to cope with the light.'

'Who?'

'Wayne – out of the shadow land. Well, we all get so used to it.'

'Who?'

'Me. You,' Iles replied. 'Wayne, when with us. Your grass, grasses. Your undercover bint. The whole grey area crew.'

'I –'

'Listen, Col, couldn't you have a word with that Head about the trophy, and maybe the Lord Lieutenant who was there, too? It would seem pushy if I did it myself, and I wouldn't want to steal your . . . your concept, anyway. I really would like to feel a part of that jolly school.'

'Which?'

'What? Which what?'

'Which part of the jolly school would you like to feel?'

Chapter Five

In some ways, Ralph Ember felt pleased his club was chosen as venue for the drinks party after Ridout's funeral: great to see the Monty under his proprietorship had become so much a loved part of the community that folk wanted to mix there following the service and crem trip. Mix. He liked this. Truly, the Monty amounted to a miniature world. All sorts were here: the police, that twat Ferdy Dubal , the vicar in his robes still. The Monty could accommodate the lot, right across the range. When a day needed to be marked the Monty was the place for marking it. During Ember's university time there had been some chat about microcosms. A microcosm was just that: a small but complete example of human variety, class and complexity. You wouldn't get anywhere more microcosmic than the Monty.

Obviously, some outright fucking rubbish turned up among the huge crew who packed the club, the kind of rubbish he would have to kick out for keeps eventually when lifting the Monty into the Athenaeum category, to attract company directors, TV quiz masters, Nobel prize winners, NHS managers. But quite likely rubbish could sneak in even to the Athenaeum for a post obsequies piss-up, although the Athenaeum probably did not have membership deaths where someone had been attacked by a car three times for luck and certainty. The Monty might be one-up on the Athenaeum in the microcosm aspect.

The bar was no-pay. This happened very rarely in Monty celebration functions. Ralph thought the last time might have been on Quince Pargetter's release after nine years. Quince had managed to keep most of his trade gains intact and secret and insisted on paying the full Monty drinks bill. It was grand of him and stupid, a hint of hidden funds. Eighteen months later Quince was dead, most likely killed by former accomplices who believed themselves entitled to a capital cut of the gains, but who failed to talk him around. Quince could be impulsive, Quince could be stubborn. But this was a while ago now.

For tonight, Nora Ridout had given Ember £250 to cover things. Two hundred and fifty in used notes. She would have absorbed business protocol from Wayne. Two hundred and fifty would be nothing like adequate to go the whole long night when so many people wanted champagne and brandy cocktails, or doubles and triples of malt whisky or vodka, but Ember would certainly not ask her for any shortfall. This was a deep occasion, although Wayne had been such a whispering shit, and Ember felt he must host without any small-souled regard for cost. He was Ralph W. Ember. He had a prime status to guard. He had a muted, debonair leadership style to stick with. Say another £250 from him. OK. One harsh way of regarding it was, you did not get a grass of Wayne's dimensions burned all that often. The Monty must be in tune with occasion.

In the church, Ralph had been overwhelmingly moved, almost to a point when he cried out. It was a while since he had felt anything so powerfully, and he exulted in the fact that his sensibilities remained acute. This fine tumult of emotion in Ember came from the sight of what he took to be Wayne's daughter, a tall, neat-chinned, noble-arsed beauty in grey. Ralph could not let his excitement get obvious because he was with his wife, Margaret, as well as Manse Shale and one of the women who moved in with Manse at his property for a while now and then, when Manse felt like company and so on. Ember always noted women's chins. They could be the making or breaking of a face in his opinion. Although eyes were often regarded as the most significant items of a woman's features, eyes needed a good chin base. The haunches also obviously held importance, but it always seemed to him a bit crude and demeaning to a woman to dwell on these excessively, and this would be particularly true at a funeral, even of someone like Wayne.

Part of the hot disturbance to Ember's blood came from shock that a creature like Wayne could produce such a beauty. Ember would certainly not want to give any impression of commercial hardness or meanness to a girl with qualities like that by asking her mother to put more in the drinks pot. It could really mess up future possibilities. He had heard this girl was educated. Ralph always found it intensely heartening to imagine himself in bed with a lovely, academic girl, clambering very considerately on to her and taking an affectionate, meaningful, two-handed grip on her buttocks. He could see the girl across the room now. So far, she seemed to be staying near Nora in the Monty, but perhaps the mother would go home to mourn alone once she had spent a token time here.

Ferdy Dubal said: 'I've lost people as well, you know.'

'A dark time,' Ember replied. He'd just come up from the club cellar after checking supplies for this mob. Dubal seemed to have been waiting for him at the head of the stairs. They stood near the bar on the edge of the crowd.

'Did they go to *their* funerals?' Dubal said. Not a question. An accusation.

'Iles and Harpur?'

'Did they get to Perce Kellow's and Mildly Sedated's? Did they fuck,' Dubal replied.

'You're upset about that? Well, you would be, Ferd – very much *your* people.' There was a crummy sort of physical brilliance to Dubal, Ralph would never deny this. Even now when Ferd had turned to snarling, Ember could feel the glow. If Dubal was not who he was, Ember might have thought a friendship possible here. The glow stayed very inner, although at times you could see it in Dubal's large brown eyes and more or less uncreepy smile. But it was the glittering energy and sureness in Ferd you were most aware of, not so much his appearance. You had the impressive idea he had mapped the whole scene ahead already and that anything on the map he didn't approve he would blast out of the way. Of course, the trouble was *you* might be what he didn't approve, *you* might look like an obstruction, the arrogant sod. 'The gun emplacement deaths – this is an investigation that doesn't speed, I hear,' Ember said with good concern.

'Come on, Ralph, of course it doesn't. Would *you* make an investigation hop along if it might nail yourself? Two lovely boys, yet taken out like that. Did you ever hear Mildly sing those 1930s numbers, "Little Old Lady Passing By", "Red Sails In The Sunset"? A rounded personality.'

Dubal's clothes were expensive and right for him, clearly not always the same thing. They did not make you think of a country gentleman pose, or of daft effort juggling the money from six credit cards to meet the bill. Although Ralph would not say Dubal's grand suits definitely looked paid for, they were of such quietly glorious style you knew no tailor so talented could also be a money-chasing prick. Ralph had never seen Ferd in trousers with turn-ups at the leg bottoms and this showed true consistency. Anyone with the most basic intelligence was sure to realize Dubal could, if necessary, personally handle a drive-down death of Wayne done three ways, especially when a simpler, earlier effort had come unstuck. You could see why Dubal would want the assassination at that school prize-giving. *And now here's* your *laurels, Wayne the Mouth*. Ember himself still had an execution in mind, of course, but it would be carried out as a foul necessity, not from raw malice.

Ember said: 'Perce and Mildly were done up the hill, weren't they?'

'Who could help them – a remote area like that? Please don't tell me not to feel guilty, Ralph. Nobody was ever killed in that emplacement in the actual war – a full blitzkrieg fucking war and nobody killed there – but now my two lads in one fucking night. Irony? I do feel that's what it would be called.'

Ember could look past him and watch Wayne's daughter off and on, despite the gang of people in between. He tried to draw her gaze. Ralph considered she was the kind of girl who would need someone like him, and he would not hold back. He could have done without Dubal at this time and most others. 'What were they up at the gun site for in the night, Ferd? To commemorate the air raids of the 1940s? An anniversary?'

'These were two who followed their own whims, very much so,' Dubal replied. 'You had to allow them whims, or where's originality? I don't want clones. Yet very team conscious, also.'

'Only, if you knew what they were up there for it might give a pointer,' Ember said.

'They're not the kind of people a firm could insure.'

'It's so regrettable, but many's the tragedy we have to face in our work.'

'Wise, that big shield put up there,' Dubal replied.

'Where?'

'Fixed to the pillar.' Dubal pointed.

'Oh, that,' Ember said.

'All right, it spoils the lovely welcoming, very *personal* view of you behind the bar that members used to get as soon as they entered the Monty, but, may I say, I've always thought you were wide open from the door, Ralphy? I knew a barman knocked over just like that in Hoxton. It was bold of you, brave. But you're right to change – things grow much more dodgy now. Lane on his way? You *are* the Monty, Ralph. It would be nowhere if you went. I've heard this club mentioned all over. Hull. Stoke. Metal?'

'What?' Ember asked.

'The shield. Of course metal. What use otherwise? But nice the way you've decored it – decorated it – disguised it. The stick-on pictures.'

'A collage,' Ember replied. 'Prints.'

'What of, Ralph? Hard to make it out from here. Bare chests, but respectable.'

'Blake.'

'Oh, yes?' Dubal replied.

'The poet William Blake. He did "Jerusalem", that sort of thing. These are drawings he did for a quite famous work known as *The Marriage of Heaven and Hell.*'

'That right? *Heaven and Hell*? Colours and all. Vivid.'

'Blake was known for vividness,' Ember replied. If you were talking to an ignorant fucker you had to do what you could for him.

'We come from a funeral and then we're into a marriage. It's like the whole human tale, isn't it, Ralph? Taste. You're famous for that.'

'Collages always excite a lot of interest. The variety,' Ember said. 'I've got a responsibility to the club. I didn't want something just crude and blocky stuck there.'

'Right. But, on the other hand this is my point, really – it *is* blocky, isn't it? Blocky is exactly what it has to be behind the what-you-call.'

'Collage.'

'It has to block the bang-bangs.'

'I wanted to get away from something merely useful,' Ember replied. 'I hoped it would enhance.'

'Yes, yes, it does. And yet, of course – what's basic in all this – is it *is* useful, also. Really professional, the way it's bolted on. And can I inquire how many millimetres thick? Probably this would stop a Big Bertha shell.'

'The heating engineers,' Ember said. 'To do with air currents. The metal sheet diverts them, or something. We were wasting a lot of warmth, apparently. I must say I can notice the difference. So simple.'

'Whose idea?' Dubal replied. 'Is this E.W. Fenton? I hear he's been looking in on you. Fenton's got an eye. Was he the one to suggest not just the shield but the collage? He could easily have heard of that poet and *Heaven and Hell, The Marriage*. Probably he reads quite a bit when he's off on his own somewhere, nobody able to find him. He'd be crouched privately with a book – *Heaven and Hell*, *Jerusalem*, a real reading fan . . .'

'Heating engineers,' Ember said. 'Like the Gulf Stream.'

'Fenton? He can be a boon. He can be ruination.'

'Why the hell does he use initials?'

'Glock,' Dubal replied.

'Yes, I heard.'

'Glock pistol and perfect heart shooting. So, no wonder they can't go to the funerals.'

'Iles and Harpur?' Luckily, through business flair, Ember knew how to separate various thoughts about this or that person. He could look at, and listen to, Dubal now with definite admiration yet at the same time imagine his sweetly structured, ventless dark jacket torn all ways by bullets and disgustingly blood-dirtied in that small chest circle behind the fine left lapel. Ember dreamed of more than one assassination, if required, and Dubal's might be required. E.W. Fenton had not come up with new weaponry yet, but that was all right. Ralph would prefer he produced something fine and decisive, and he would understand if this took a while. He still had his other two pistols, a Bernadelli and the S. and W.

'Can I ask you, Ralph, doesn't this look like a police salvo that got Percy and Sedated? The weapon type. So, even those two didn't have the gall. But Wayne's something different, isn't he?' It was a full sneer. 'Oh, yes. Wayne is damn Wayne. So special. They looked after his daughter, you know. That school. She swims. Well, think what the idea of that would do to Iles – chlorinated water at municipal pool temperature nuzzling all her areas.'

'Wayne had a daughter?' Ember said. 'What age and so on?'

'Iles will be circling that piece. Or even Harpur. They think they have a right.'

'Pretty?' Ember asked. 'Wayne's and pretty?' At first in St Luke's, Ralph had seen the daughter mainly from the back, when she passed slowly up the aisle with Nora on her arm to their places alongside the pulpit. But when they stood to leave he could look properly and appreciate everything: a girl young and fresh, yet probably not *so* young that she would never have seen the early Charlton Heston films on television, and so miss Ralph's resemblance to him then. Although Ember would hardly ever agree to discuss this resemblance seriously, he privately hoped people would not see him only as Ben Hur or El Cid but as Heston in that other terrific role, Moses, full of spiritual force. Some women could be very unspiritual, and this always disappointed him. He would feel betrayed. This girl did not seem to him like that, even though her father was Wayne. Iles, wearing that fucking uniform, had been around the girl, pawing, in the church, regardless. Well, naturally. Dubal was correct about that. But no bugger would think Iles looked like the young Charlton Heston, or the *young* anybody.

Iles had come on to the Monty, plus Harpur, naturally. They loved to terrorize, especially Iles. Was he lurking near the girl now? Ember glanced away from Dubal to where she had been but could not find either Iles or the girl or her mother. More people had pushed into the Monty making it hard to locate anyone a distance away. Fuck Dubal. Ember asked: 'Did they have someone up there with them?'

'Who?'

'Percy and Sedated.'

'Take women up there?' Dubal replied. 'Why? Out in the open, in the weather? They've got cars, flats.'

'No, not women, not for that. But if they wanted to get rid of someone.'

'Get rid? Excuse me, but do I follow you, Ralphy? *They* were the ones got rid of, if I could point that out.'

'There'd be no interruptions up there,' Ember said. 'Or they *thought* there wouldn't be. An execution ground.'

'Exactly that, an execution ground. For Percy and Sedated. Tell me if you know why they should deserve that, please, Ralph. I mean it.'

'Say a rescue?'

'Rescue?'

'Of someone they'd taken up there,' Ember replied. 'You hadn't ordered them to take someone up there, had you? Well, clearly you'd remember.'

'Rescue? No rescue for Percy and Sedated. This is my point about blaming myself.'

'You're a conscience person, Ferd. I'd heard that.'

Dubal did not have a very big firm and two talented troopers eliminated would really weaken him. But, even if things had been different, you sensed he would feel upset about the deaths of colleagues. There were definitely very staunch things in Dubal and these might go against him in the long run, or possibly the short run. This was the kind of elegant, intrusive charmer who could be tolerated at a decently low trading level when the system was working as it should, but who might believe he could fight his way to monopoly if street wars began again when Iles faded. The deaths of Perce and Sedated would possibly make him fear he must start the fighting soon, before he lost more people.

Dubal said: 'I have to make excuses, you know – try to explain to Perce's and Mildly's dear parents why no police came to either service, despite violent deaths. Except, of course, I can't tell them the out-and-out truth.'

'Being?'

'These were Glock killings, Ralph. These were marksman killings, Ralph. Perhaps you can help me. Do I tell the parents their sons were shot by law officers? What degree of civic breakdown does that suggest, Ralphy? Where are we, Ralphy – Yugoslavia late 1990s? Jerusalem – not the poet's but the *new* Jerusalem when you can't be sure whose side the police are on? Each of them – Mildly *and* Perce – has two parents, Ralph, and both pairs on their original marriage. That's the kind of salt-of-the-earth families Perce and Mildly come from. Perce from the best sort of Travelling People – their own culture and systems.'

'I've heard several ask what were they doing up there, Perce and Mildly,' Ember replied.

'They've put some nobody, no-rank, on to the deaths.'

'Who have, Harpur and Iles?'

'An unknown called Garland. Not Harpur himself, naturally. How could he?'

'Chief Inspector Francis Garland? He's not dim.'

'Unless he's been told to be dim,' Dubal said.

'Garland often works second string to Harpur.'

'What I mean. You'll ask about funeral costs for Perce and Mildly. Please, may I beg you not to mention them? I want no publicity. Who else was going to pay?'

'Generous, Ferd. Typical.'

'But a different procedure altogether for them with Wayne. Don't tell me *that* funeral wasn't backed by public funds.'

'Unfair,' Ember replied.

He disliked the way Dubal often had his mother with him, though probably not when he did Ridout: he'd worry she might get hurt as the car jolted three times on impact. Ralph thought Dubal brought his mother to show he had proper feelings and to hint she was a dependant and would be unsupported if, say, Dubal prematurely died somehow. Obviously, Ralph normally regarded mothers as totally all right and possibly even of significance, but he could not allow any mother to be used as a political tactic. If a mother had a pushy son who might try to annihilate established commercial people such as Ralph, or Manse Shale for that matter, she must realize he would most probably get annihilated himself, especially if he called Ember Ralphy and compared him to some fucking destroyed hack barman in Hoxton. Plus, was that satirical about the Monty getting a mention in metropolitan highpoints like Hull and Stoke? Thinking of Dubal's damn self-belief, Ralph was pleased that never throughout this conversation had he felt even the beginnings of a panic, despite hints and those references to the metal shield. Dubal he could fit into a scheme, *and* his bloody mother. Ralph was not going to panic about Fenton's delay in coming up with new armament, either. Ralph wondered, in fact, whether he was growing out of panics. He felt he might have reached a plateau of coolness and poise.

'The thing about tragedy is it can be layer on layer,' Ember remarked. He leaned over the bar for a bottle and gave Dubal more champagne.

'And then one for my mother, if I may, Ralph. She's playing the machines.' One of Dubal's grand smiles came. His eyes were all matiness, the fucking invader. Ember found another glass and poured. Dubal took it and edged away through the gang of folk. He was tall and lean, as hard as curtain cord. Plainly, he had told the tailor to keep his trouser legs very slim as a show-off ploy and the non-turn-ups did help by letting the trousers taper really close to black ankle boots. It was strange but the actual lack of turn-ups gave a sort of completeness to Dubal. Looking at this trousers style, you could guess that if a couple of his people got shot on a hill in the night he would be sincerely troubled. His head was longish, not round, and Ember could imagine a brain on the job inside working out non-stop how to shove Ralph under and hold him there until lifeless.

Ember slipped into the crowd, seriously looking for Wayne's daughter now, but, of course, not making it evident he was looking for anyone. He gave good smiles all round, even to deadbeats. His role required this and he would not fail. He knew some called him Milord Monty. He did not mind this. He thought it a challenge. Ralph moved on. Before they disappeared, the girl and her mother had been standing near the big, framed photograph of club members setting out on their excursion to Paris a few years ago. After what had happened in France, Ralph would never organize another trip under the Monty name, nor permit others to, but he allowed the photograph to remain on the wall.

When Ember drew nearer to it he saw that the girl and Mrs Ridout had sat down at a table with their drinks and people standing around obscured them. Iles was also at the table, not Harpur. Iles gave Ember a bit of a wave: that was all, a bit of. It was the kind of wave Ralph had aimed at Fenton the other night. Done by Iles, it said, Kindly keep fucking going, Ralphy, dear, no fucker wants you here, meaning he, Iles, didn't, because he had things nicely set up, especially if Nora left soon. Ember found it almost unbelievably disgusting. This was a girl in mourning for a parent, yet Iles, a senior police officer, would undoubtedly still think of her only in that bodily way of his. Unbelievably disgusting, though not unbelievable for Iles.

But Ember saw the girl look at him and, in his opinion, it was fairly fervent. Ralph could understand: she must feel delightfully overwhelmed by the young Chuck Heston resemblance. In the kind of good school she had attended they'd have the Movie Channel for Heston's early pictures. Ember was very used to this sort of dazed reaction from women and did not pose in any way now, or deliberately give a profile. He despised such vulgarity, even when he was competing with someone as full-out foul as Iles. Ralph behaved with total, civilized ordinariness, no masterly flick of the jaw like Heston anxious about buildings in *Earthquake*. The sexual pull he had had to be his own, for God's sake, not a remake of something Hollywood. There were times when he found the whole Heston thing tedious, though it undoubtedly could produce fucks, and not only with the oldish and/or twitchy.

He smiled an absolutely formal smile at the girl on account of the grief circumstances and found a chair for himself, then brought it to the table: not next to her but next to Nora who *was* next to her. Stuff Iles. Ralph refused to be directed by him. Ralph had to show this was the *new* Ember, able to deal resolutely with whatever came, free from the spurts of confusion and panic Iles used to cause him previously.

In any case, Ember was in his own damn castle here, wasn't he? Milord Monty. All right, a joke, but one of those amiable jokes which also hit the truth. Even without the Heston help, Ralph added up to a presence, a force. He wanted the girl to observe this, it, yes, enjoy it. For the daughter to feel close to someone so solid and imperturbable might help offset her loss. This would be crucial, as Ralph saw matters. He never ceased to recognize an obligation to aid some weaker folk.

With his voice absolutely level and non-cringe, Ember said, 'Of course, I know Nora, but I don't believe I've met –'

'Fay-Alice,' Iles replied. It was terse, it was virtually rude, the interminably lech-driven, pathetically jealous has-been.

'Ember,' Ralph said, smiling moderately. 'Ralph W. Or simply Ralph.'

That prancing Hun, Iles, thought his damn uniform and sneers could do everything. It was time to show him matters were different now, especially as he would soon be on the decline and tied down in his real rank as a piddling assistant, not flitting high like some sun god. True, Ember did not want that decline. It would put the grand, wholesome tradition of peaceful substance commerce into real jeopardy. But if it did happen, he, Ember, would intelligently and systematically adjust. He had begun to adjust to it: the commission for new weaponry, the William Blake baffle board. This was what business competence, business leadership, amounted to. Another part of that adjustment, surely, was to show Iles how much his powers had already begun to wither, just as Ralph had made Ferdy Dubal tame, undisturbing, a few minutes ago.

The girl said: 'This is your place, Mr Ember?'

'I'm happy to put it at the disposal of you and your mother for the occasion. Of course, I would like to say how much I regret the death of –'

'Look, Mr Ember,' Fay-Alice answered, 'you might be able to help me, if you don't mind: dad was Mr Iles's special grass, is that right? He won't say – as you'd expect. The whole informant mystique. Secrecy. I read an article on grasses in the *Observer* that helped me work out things a bit, since the school incident. I need to understand.'

Ember said: 'Everyone sympathizes, I know, with –'

She looked around the noisy, cheerful club. 'I don't believe *everyone* sympathizes,' she said.

'Oh, yes,' Ralph replied. 'Wayne Ridout was –'

'I think it's kind of you to say that,' Fay-Alice answered, 'and so does my mum, I'm sure, but –'

'Wayne was known to many,' Ralph replied. 'Many.'

'I dare say,' the girl replied. 'Listen, I'm not *blaming*. Mr Iles saved my dad's life. I'm hardly going to loathe him, am I?'

'Something just by the way,' Iles said.

It was offhand, so bloody valiant. Ember longed to hate him at full power, but the relationship with Iles had to be complex. Although he was a vain, bullying shite, he was also, like Ralph, a lover of intelligent peace on the streets. Ralph detested him, Ralph sided with him. Soon, this complexity might end, though, when Iles's influence died. Ember had to be ready. Any great trade personage took changed conditions and built a triumph from them. Or think of how the Germans got their economy going again so fast after the war, despite devastation. He recalled a lecture on this from his twentieth-century background course in the university foundation year. This transformation had always seemed to him a truly inspiring model.

Fay-Alice said: 'As a matter of fact quite a few of the sixth form girls thought Mr Iles absolutely shaggable.'

'I could see that,' Nora replied.

'What?' Fay-Alice said.

'What?' Nora replied. 'What do you mean?'

'*You* could see he was shaggable, or you could see the girls thought him shaggable?' Fay-Alice replied.

'Yes,' Nora said.

'Which?'

'Oh, yes,' Nora replied.

'Who are we talking about?' Ember asked. 'Not Iles?'

'Yes. Desmond,' Fay-Alice said. 'The hautiness and thug eyes could be a turn-on – if you've had a couple of drinks or a smoke. I mean, a one-night job, only, naturally. Age and the greyness don't matter then. They thought me *really* lucky.'

Iles looked as though he might get up and leave, offended. Ember had heard he detested shows of affection or gratitude. So, fine: go, you smug prat.

'But I'm curious about my dad,' Fay-Alice said. 'Mum doesn't say much.'

'No need now,' Nora said. 'Wayne's gone. Does it matter why?'

'Yes,' Fay-Alice replied. 'Yes. How I came to be at Taldamon – all of it – the friendship – the so-called friendship – with Iles and Harpur. I must know. Was it Desmond placed me at the school?'

'What difference now, love?' Nora asked.

'Half of the people in the church and here look delighted dad's dead,' Fay-Alice said.

Iles, shaggable? Ember wanted to scream at her that shaggable Iles, one-night-stand-shaggable Desmond, was about to fall to fucking nowhere in his fucking doorman's uniform. Would sixth formers at that chic school think he was shaggable when all the Iles strut and sauce were gone and he was on the crawling kow-tow to a new Chief? The hautiness would be properly ruptured then. How could this kind of low talk be going on among women just after the funeral of what would unquestionably be a dear one to them? Ember thought of yelling Iles was such a sex hot-shot that a hulk like Harpur could take his wife from him for God knew how long and Iles was so ruined by it the memory still caused him fits.

'That name – Fay-Alice – I mean, it's a sort of version of Alice Faye, the forties film star, is it?' Ember said. These calibre schools that believed in ideas and the arts made kids so damn frank and coarse and full of questions. Didn't Ralph have daughters of his own at similar places? Ember wanted Fay-Alice sidetracked on to something stupid but safe. 'Intriguing, your name, names.'

'I should think you're in touch with the – with the sort

of milieu my dad lived in, yes, Mr Ember?' Fay-Alice said.

'Milieu?' Ember replied.

'You know – the milieu,' she said.

'Milieu?' Ember replied.

'It's French, Ralph,' Iles said. He spoke like Ember might not have heard of France.

'That right?' Ember asked. He thought of answering, My daughter Venetia's a damn resident there, you patronizing prick, but decided just to do sarcasm.

'Means underworld,' Iles replied.

A school like Fay-Alice's – they'd be able to teach them all the roughest slang, foreign and homegrown. 'Thank you so very much,' Ember said.

'No reflection but it's how you seem,' Fay-Alice said. 'In touch. Familiar with a lot of the people here. God, look at some of them! What's that line in the Woody Allen film when he's scared by men in the street – "like the cast of *The Godfather*"?'

Iles said: 'I don't think Fay-Alice has ever been in this kind of club before.'

'Which kind?' Ember replied.

'Like the Monty,' Iles said.

'Which kind is that?' Ember asked, his tone true steel. 'The kind that knows the dead should receive respect? I would hope most decent clubs were of that kind, for heaven's sake. Or are you saying this club is part of the milieu?' He really gave it the fat, greasy Maurice Chevalier vowels. He asked a waiter to bring more drinks: champagne for the two women, port and lemon as ever for Iles, Armagnac as ever for himself. He'd show Iles that if the Monty was the underworld the underworld knew bloody impeccably how to cater for guests, wanted or not.

When the glasses arrived, Iles asked, 'Who's paying for all this?' He glanced towards the drinks and then at the busy bars.

That was just like the plotting bastard. Normally, when he and Harpur came to the Monty to snoop and terrorize, on one of their supposed 'club licence inspections', it did not seem to bother him who was paying for the drinks. The Monty would be paying, and he expected the Monty to. This afternoon, though, Iles wanted to do a grovelling, thank-you-very-much display to Nora, didn't he, to help hook her daughter? He would think he knew who was paying, Mrs Ridout, as widow. Although by now that two-fifty was well swallowed and pissed against the wall, Ember certainly would never say so, whatever it cost him. There was a concept called gentlemanliness, one Iles had never heard of. Ralph must not come on like a fucking bar bill in front of Fay-Alice. This girl was much more than chin and arse. For God's sake, did that even need saying? Ralph could not bear to cheapen women. They had a valid role in quite a few of life's scenes. This girl might be a nosy nuisance but she showed perception. 'It's Mrs Ridout's party, of course,' Ember replied.

'Well, so kind, Nora,' Iles said, leaning across the table, big and shiny with promise, like Christmas wrapping. 'Let's drink to a great, much-missed man.'

He stood. The women got up, too, then Ember. He did not think he had ever drunk to a damn grass before and didn't now. But he did stand and put the glass against his lip in case Fay-Alice was watching. This kind of girl deserved some special care, especially today, regardless of all her questions and father. He had to make sure Iles did not gallop ahead, first by calling the toast and then drinking off half the port and lemon with a great, empathic, testimonial gulp, the sly, decked-out turd.

They all sat down again. 'Plus Desmond's words from the pulpit today,' Fay-Alice said. 'What did you think of them, Mr Ember?'

'Ralph,' Ember said.

'What did you think of what he said, Ralph?' Fay-Alice asked.

'Mr Iles often performs at funerals, I gather. It's expected now – some performance by him.'

'You were mentioned, Ralph,' Fay-Alice replied. 'Threatening? Did some of it sound threatening to you? *He* says not. But what about you, Ralph? Did it sound . . . Well, a menacing note? A man called Dubal referred to? Something like that. This name kept coming up in what Desmond spoke of. I don't know, I wasn't concentrating all that much on what was said, being alongside dad like that, and the sadness –'

'This is predictable, Fay-Alice,' Ember replied. He could get it out, say it, her name, but, Christ, what an idiocy.

'Desmond tells me the people listed were just acquaintances who would miss dad, but it didn't sound like that. What did *you* think, Ralph?'

What Ember thought was that probably one of them did *not* miss Wayne, but hit him three times with a vehicle, and would have liked a minion to hit him with bullets up at the school earlier. But, out of tenderness, Ralph stayed quiet.

'Leave it now, Fay-Alice,' Nora said.

'Who *is* Dubal?' Fay-Alice asked. 'That warning about crossing the road – Desmond's reading from the road safety tract. Do *you* know this Dubal, Ralph?'

'He's around,' Ember said. 'New to the city. On the commercial side. Sharp dresser.'

'But *what* is he?' Fay-Alice asked. 'He's here?'

'He'd probably be here somewhere, wouldn't he, Ralph?' Iles said. 'With his mother.'

'This is a community occasion,' Ember replied. 'That's another aspect of the club, I'm proud to say.'

'And you also spoke about murder in your spiel, Desmond,' Fay-Alice said.

'I explained I was murder not Traffic.'

'What did it mean?' Fay-Alice asked. 'What were you telling them?'

'Describing departmental boundaries, that's all,' Iles replied.

'It was good of you to give an address,' Nora said.

'A privilege,' Iles said.

'To get into the pulpit, did you have to bully the vicar?' Fay-Alice asked.

'A delightful, understanding man,' Iles replied.

'Mr Iles thinks he can take over anywhere,' Ember said.

'I like to *contribute*,' Iles replied. 'Surely we each wish to do this in our different fashions.'

'All that will finish very soon, though,' Ember said.

'What?' Fay-Alice asked.

'Taking star positions. He won't *be* a star.' Ember said it as if he were pleased. Yet if Iles's star crashed so much could crash with him. That's what disaster meant – bad vibrations from a sick star. But now, at this party, Ralph had to squash Iles.

'What's that about, then?' Nora asked.

'Ralphy needs to get his bile out occasionally,' Iles said. 'Wouldn't anyone so full of yellow?'

'Desmond, it sounded to me as if you thought Dubal killed dad,' Fay-Alice replied.

Iles had a weighty, comfortable, phoney fucking chuckle. 'Such an imagination, Fay-Alice! You mustn't speak like that.'

'No,' Nora said. 'Dubal has lawyers.'

'And as if you were promising him something, something bad,' Fay-Alice said. 'Is that how it struck you, Ralph?'

Yes, of course, it was how it had struck Ember. How fucking else? Suddenly, he began to feel very nervous. *Yellow*. This word could always knock him back and set his mind scampering for refuge. That bloody shield fixed up there on the pillar: what use if someone who wanted to do Ralph damage was already inside the club?

Now, he thought again of the twentieth-century background lectures, but this time the Maginot Line. These fortifications should have protected France from the Germans in 1940. But the Panzas just skirted it and attacked from behind. The same here, at the Monty? Dubal and maybe others were on the wrong side of the shield. If Iles in his own filthy style meant to get Dubal for killing Wayne, it could be an unspeakable mistake to sit at their table, as if Ralph were a steady pal of the Assistant Chief. Ember would look like an ally.

And, naturally, Iles *would* most probably mean to get Dubal. Didn't he settle with people after the undercover detective Street's death? Didn't it look as though Iles wanted to find a way to Fay-Alice? Could he manage that better than via a bit of vengeance for her? The girl was right and he had said it from the pulpit without saying it – the Iles mode. But Dubal would have interpreted the words like that for himself. And he was here somewhere now, watching, noting, getting his battle plans in shape, identifying enemies. Ralph was a pampered competitor in the trade and therefore probably seen as an enemy and obstruction, anyway, even before snuggling up to Iles. Now Dubal might be more certain still. He would not understand that Ember had joined the table only because Fay-Alice was there, her chin classical. To Dubal Ember might look like Iles's new, close talky-talky pal now Wayne had gone. Oh, God. Ralph could feel the start of a sweat again.

'As if a war had begun,' Fay-Alice said.

'Oh, we really don't want that,' Iles replied with another chuckle, so offhand this time.

'In the church I sensed it. And I sense it now,' Fay-Alice said. 'Don't you sense it, Ralph?'

Ember wished Harpur was at the table. He was big and looked loutish, a face that had survived all sorts and did not expect things to get easier. Although nowhere near as dangerous and evil as Iles, of course, he appeared *more* dangerous and evil, his clothes rough-house. They said he resembled the one-time undefeated heavyweight boxing champion of the world, Rocky Marciano, but fair-haired. Harpur could scare people just by presence, even armed people. Ember glanced about. He did not see him. Conceivably he had picked up someone in the church or earlier in the evening here and needed to avoid Iles. If you'd met a woman and wanted to get a harmony going with her you could do without Iles starting one of those famous froths and bayings about his wife and you.

'Why not nail this Dubal then, Desmond?' Fay-Alice asked.

'Nail him?' Iles said.

'Yes, nail him, the way police do nail people they think have killed someone,' Fay-Alice replied. 'Isn't that what the police are *for*? This is my dad we're talking about. This is your friend, supposed friend. You owe?'

They had all sat down again. God, she was talking vengeance direct to Iles. Then, abruptly, she swivelled towards Ember. 'Ralph, I'm glad you're here as an independent voice. Don't you think Desmond ought to get after this Dubal? He drives over my dad three times. All right, he was a grass. Grasses are despised, I know. But not by me, not *this* grass.' She stood up, her eyes wet for a moment. 'Where *is* Dubal? What does he look like? With his mother, you said.'

Hell, she was making a show. Ralph dreaded to be in it, to have attention drawn to him and his apparent companions. Why couldn't Nora control her? As before, one of those terrible backtrackings in his mind began. How could he have been so daftly confident just now, thinking he'd stand up against not just Dubal but Iles? What had he called himself – 'solid' and 'imperturbable'? Demented, more like. He'd made Dubal 'undisturbing and tame', had he? Oh, God, had he? There was 'triumph' waiting for Ralph to find it in the changing situation, was there, like the German renaissance of 1945? Like fucking *what*? Ember stood again, while his legs might still be all right. He felt nearly sure they were. Sometimes during a panic they failed last, after his ability to see properly. 'I must do a tour of the club,' he said.

'I'd just like to look at this Dubal, that's all,' Fay-Alice replied.

She also stood, then stretched out her arm and took hold of Ember's right wrist. It was an invitation to move through the crowd with her as a questing pair. Ten minutes earlier, Ember would have been delighted by this contact, giving lovely points against Iles. Her fingers were so eloquent, so essentially personal to Ralph. They horrified him. 'I *have* been eye searching. I think he must have left early – out of consideration for his mother,' Ember said. He detached himself from Fay-Alice's cosy grip.

'You can't be sure,' she said.

'Yes,' Ember replied.

'Yes, he'll have left,' Iles said.

Of course this sod wouldn't want her going off, fingers intermeshed, on a search with Ember. He understood that but couldn't do anything to counter Iles now. Ralph had to concentrate on his condition. He needed his right hand to reach up and check the jaw-line scar was still all right, not oozy. Unthinkable he should go with her to confront Dubal. What she had felt in the church was spot-on – a war approached, or had already started. Clever of her to see it at her age: but why wasn't the daft bird also clever enough to see that everyone had to be ceaselessly careful now, especially someone like Ralph, with his responsibilities and looks that might get damaged?

He moved hurriedly away from the table. Fay-Alice sat down. Thank heaven for this at least. Iles could make his play once Ralph had gone. Well, let him. All that was secondary, or less, now. Ember did some circulating. Yes, his legs felt good. Solid at this stage. Imperturbable to date, even brilliant. He could put up with the sweat and lack of breath. The scar still seemed OK.

He felt now a mixture of rage and fear that that fucking shifty enigma, E.W. Fenton, had so far produced no new armament for him. Why the wait? Was Fenton bought? Did he *want* Ralph unprotected, or protected only by William Blake art work? Earlier in the afternoon Ralph had regarded Fenton's delay with tolerance. He could not now. All right, Ember had those two pistols, the Bernadelli and the S. and W. Bodyguard, but this was not the heart of things, was it? He needed something specific to the altered power manoeuvres. Ralph had to know and feel he was actively preparing himself against enormous fresh hazards. He needed to *do* something. He had to garrison himself. He had to prepare in case he, personally, needed to do an execution, executions: some totally new weapon would be wanted then. If he dozed on these requirements he might grow vulnerable. *Would* grow vulnerable.

Sometimes, there could be a positive side to his panics. They were not all watery legs and brain stampedes. For instance, his panics would not permit him to idle. They intelligently destroyed the gross pride and lunacy of calmness. He saw calmness as unforgivable, even if he had two guns already. All right, the jaw scar never leaked but the point was, surely, if it had, he would regard this as a warning from the body against the cocky, lethargic absurdities of composure. And the fact that he *thought* it might leak showed he knew fucking composure could be treacherous, anyway.

He was clear what he needed to do. He must get across town to the Hobart pub just off Cork Street. Now. This afternoon. He wanted to see Leyton and Amy Harbinger. They were still the greatest armourers he knew. They would not mess him about with postponed delivery like Fenton. Fine new armament would bring his pulse rate down and give him back eye focus.

Ralph went to find the club manager and tell him to take care of things for an hour or so while he was out. They were still chatting when Ember noticed some movement on the Monty's small entertainment stage, and Dubal and his mother, with Maud Kale and her accordion, took up positions there. A spotlight found them. The microphone hummed. Backed by the accordion, Dubal and Mrs Dubal, standing close together in the circle of brightness, began to croon those two numbers he had mentioned as favourite performance pieces of Mildly Sedated, 'Red Sails In The Sunset' and 'Little Old Lady Passing By'. Dubal was weeping but continued to sing. At the end of 'Little Old Lady' they went back to 'Red Sails', as if by agreement, and did it again. Dubal's mother was large-shouldered, large-voiced. She pumped a lot of juice into words like 'way out on the sea' in 'Red Sails'. This seemed to be the part that made Dubal weep the most. Perhaps Mildly had been memorable on such lines, too. Sedated was a lout, but, then, Dubal was also a lout with no mentionable property to live in yet, so possibly the loss, losses, did truly affect him.

When Dubal saw Ember he beckoned him to join them. Ralph certainly did not ignore this. After all, the songs marked a double death. Some recognition from Ralph was due. He sent a small, definite gesture back, indicating, Fuck off, Ferdy. It was similar to the wave Iles had given Ralph earlier, and perhaps to the one Ember had given Fenton a while ago. Competing wakes could be troublesome. Ember knew he must be discreet about which mourners he backed.

When he left, people were still arriving in the club car park. Not all of them had attended the funeral, but whenever there was what Ralph would think of as 'an occasion' at the Monty the news always got around and folk wanted to be there and take part so they could speak about it afterwards, the way football supporters claimed to have been present at epic matches. Since Princess Diana, grief was quite a crowd thing. And perhaps even mock grief.

Ember felt proud of the club's magnetism. The Monty was a social beacon. Probably not even the Athenaeum or Garrick had this kind of come-to-me calling power: like one of those mosque muezzin voices that summoned folk to prayer. As he crossed to his Saab, he thought he saw Harpur talking to a woman in the front seats of a small green Renault. With his slob garments, ramshackle features and bulk, Harpur should have been reasonably easy to identify in a car that size, but Ember could not be certain. Moving vehicles came between him and them now and then, and he felt it would be intrusive to go closer for a real look. But Harpur was Harpur and this would be his kind of sordid setting. Ralph did not recognize the woman. She seemed in her early twenties, broad-faced with short blonde hair spike-cut, not Harpur's steady student friend, Denise. Harpur was Harpur. If he could pull a woman, almost any woman, he would, because he had the sense to recognize the luck of it, given his features and hair.

Ember drove to the Hobart. It was early evening. He would be back at the Monty before the wake party had anywhere near finished or moved into the danger spell. Funerals, like weddings, acquittals, christenings, prison releases and confirmations, sometimes produced bad fights with woundings at the club, but usually not until late when old and new hates had had time to perk up through drink and so on. He hoped Fay-Alice would cause no disturbance when she saw Dubal and his mother on stage. The manager must cope with that if she did.

'Why, Ralph,' Amy Harbinger called as he entered the Hobart, 'grief gear. But you'd bring distinction to anything. And the scar – still so chilling yet racy. Who got him at last? Who spread dear Wayne's ribcage and smashed the songbird?'

'The police haven't really –'

'No, but who got him, Ralph?' She pushed a large Kressmann Armagnac across the bar for Ember. Although the Hobart was on the lower slopes between basic and scruffy, it had plenty of customers with off-and-on cash enough to afford a palate, and so the Kressmann remained always in stock, not just for Ember. He used to worry about it occasionally, scared Forensic would work out a way to spot Kressmann traces from a Hobart regular at the scene of some killing or robbery and short-list the most renowned Kressmann devotee in the area, him.

He said: 'That kind of funeral, Wayne's, I feel I have to go, Amy, because –'

'I'd never blame you, Ralph, and I know Leyton doesn't either. We discussed it. You're a neighbourhood icon. It's expected. You and the club have a kind of, yes, *sacred* role in –'

'I *do* think of myself with a role. No matter how people regard Wayne, this rates as a community event. And Ralph

Ember has a duty to our community.' Although sincere, he felt this could sound inflated so did not put in the W. of his name.

'Plus there's daughter flesh.'

'Yes, I knew they had a child,' Ember replied.

'I've heard many speak of you as central to all big events. That was the word, central.'

'Kind.'

'And to keep an eye,' Amy said.

'There *is* a learning process.'

'The eye *you'd* keep isn't possible for everyone.'

'Just routine observation.'

'I heard Iles was present.'

'Things like that, yes. If you listen you can sort out quite a bit.'

'*You* can. It's a talent.'

'Well, I know the scene already.'

'Iles's scene?'

'I can make my guesses.' Ember would never say he knew Iles's mind or scene. You could guess and guess and get it haywire. Did Iles himself know his own mind or scene? That would have been a mark of total sanity, though, wouldn't it?

'Urgent?' she replied.

'What?'

'You being here now. Although I expect you've got something going in the *après* line at the Monty, you still come out to the Hobart.' She poured herself a Dubonnet and put the glass very near his on the bar. She was fiftyish, not past it, not at all, and wearing decent scent in very unstupid quantities. He hated purplish knuckles on a woman of any age, and someone pulling beer all the time might get like that, but not Amy. She had pale knuckles. When Ember thought of heroines in old tales their knuckles were always pale. Ralph loved to see women making a go of things with powder and dye and tactful yet by no means dowdy garments. Brave. A fight, like trying to stop the weather. Time was no kindly agent. It could produce the money and position if you were workish and lucky, but it dragged at you, as well. Chuck Heston would not be doing a *Ben Hur* remake. For himself, Ember felt pretty sound now. Getting out of the Monty for a while was good, and the Armagnac helped. His panic sweat had definitely eased. It always soothed him to hear testimonials to his scar, especially from women.

'Urgent?' he replied. 'Oh, I wouldn't say urgent. I just thought I'd look in.'

'How do you see it?'

'What?'

'Wayne.'

'See it?'

'A one-off for vengeance, or what?' Amy replied. 'And then Perce and Mildly. Is there a pattern starting?'

'Pattern? How so?' He approved of brightness in women but this did not mean you should give them stuff too easily.

Amy picked up his glass, as if by mistake, although the shape was different. She raised it to her lips and then, as she smelt the Armagnac, made out she had realized the error, laughed and put the balloon down. Shadow intimacy. Ralph did not mind. They deserved their bits of happiness at this age. They were reminiscing. Think of all the younger ones coming behind who would push women like Amy out of sight. He would never do anything with her but he could understand she might need a scratching post. A man recognized his obligations. Wistful the way she spoke of Wayne's young daughter.

'Or the *breaking* of a pattern,' she replied.

'Which pattern?' There were boxing photographs and souvenirs displayed on the walls all around the Hobart bar, including a couple of pictures of Marciano, one head and shoulder posed, another in the ring with Joe Louis. Although Ember could see Marciano's resemblance to Harpur, the boxer's face seemed less knocked about. Probably Harpur thought of his appearance as rugged, the fucking lost clown.

'Sort of balance of power,' Amy said.

'I've heard of that.'

'With Iles maintaining everything nice and placid, and Wayne to let him know in plenty of time if matters were liable to get awkward anywhere. *What is the wild Wayne saying?* And then Iles or you could knock it down early. But now Wayne's gone and saying nothing. Iles is weakened, and maybe weaker still, soon. Then, Percy and Sedated shot – to stir things even more. Who did *them*, Ralph?'

'I think the police are keeping one of those famous open minds.'

'Yes, but I'm asking *you*, who did them, Ralph? What significance? I heard a Glock.'

'Yes, I heard a Glock, too.'

'Well.'

'No officer would use a police gun on that sort of thing. Like a confession.'

'Someone sharp, trying to confuse?'

'Lots of sharp folk about, Amy. Plenty of Glocks.'

'Leyt's got some lovely stuff,' she replied. 'All untraceable, guaranteed.'

'By?'

'Oh, yes, guaranteed.'

'Not Italy. Not East Europe. *Not* Glocks.'

'He'll take care of you. He said the other day he thought you'd be looking in – because the pattern's breaking up, like we mentioned. You'd be a top target.'

A rush of customers started and Amy had to go to help the barmaids. She put the Armagnac bottle on the counter for him. Not all the people who drank in the Hobart were heavies. Staff from offices nearby looked in on their way home. It gave them a little thrill to be standing alongside smart lags. A parrot, usually silent, occupied a tall cage. Ember found it pleasant enough here in its seedy way, but Amy could irritate the fuck out of him. *He* hadn't said any pattern was breaking up, didn't even mention a pattern, didn't admit a so-called pattern existed. These were not matters needing words. All that came from Amy and her bloody brain. Peace existed because matters did not get spelled out. He resented being informed what he had said when he hadn't, even if what she said he had said was true. Ralph W. Ember's ideas stayed private to him until he chose to open up, perhaps in the Press, perhaps through mere conversation.

Also, it enraged Ralph that she and Leyton would discuss him and decide they knew what he was likely to do. They *expected* him to come looking for weaponry, or so she said. Such damn cheek, although, again, obviously right. After all, here he was. Predictable movements could be dangerous, especially if the pattern broke up – what she termed the pattern. Ralph assumed they'd had others in looking for handguns. To the Hobart, he would be just one of a string, whatever special fancy sex ploys Amy might try with his drink and the scar reverence. His anger climbed. He would have had no room for panic even if one tried to start.

When she came back to his spot at the long bar, Leyton was with her. 'Who else has been in?' Ember asked.

'In what sense in, Ralph?' Leyton asked.

'Buying.'

'Buying drinks? Oh, all sorts,' Leyton said.

'Buying,' Ember replied.

'Oh, *buying*. I didn't think you could be asking that, you see, Ralph,' Leyton said. 'You'd know it's a matter of confidentiality.' He was about forty, with a heap of gold curls. They quivered now when he shook his head in reproach. He looked very young, like a precocious head prefect. He never seemed bothered about Amy being older. There *were* men of that sort, Ralph would never deny it. In fact, he considered them humane.

'It's *every*one, Ralph,' she said. 'Buying weapons.'

'Which everyones?' Ember replied. 'I need to know where the customers are coming from.'

'All the firms,' Amy said.

'And that's as much as we can tell you, Ralph. You'll understand.'

'Manse Shale?' Ember said. 'Manse's people? That crud who drives him, Denzil? Ferd Dubal?'

Amy said: 'We can't tell you – more than the business and our lives are worth, and that sort of thing – but you don't hear any contradictions.'

Leyton looked annoyed she had given Ember even this much, doing his company chairman act now. Leyton had a lot of fear. He probably reckoned on plenty of sweet life ahead, provided he remained careful. And talking of songbirds, Ember wondered how long Leyton and his curls would keep confidentiality if Harpur or someone similar did a little leaning. 'What kind of item, then, Ralph?' he asked. 'Semi-auto, decent size magazine, I expect.'

'Is that what you've been doing big trade in?' Ember replied.

'You've got so much to defend, Ralph,' Amy said. 'Lovely family – one girl still out of the country for quietening? That's good, in a way. Safe. And then your splendid house, Low Pastures, and the Monty: we hear a metal screen erected – really wise. Plus, of course, business turnover. Such a shock for us to be back at these kinds of firepower preparations. And yet I suppose it was obvious the Chief in all his splendid frailty could not last. Nor Desy Iles's stolen dominance.'

Probably she was thrilled by the changes, really. Good for sales. Ember did not say this, though.

'When do you want it?' Leyton asked.

'Now,' Ember said.

'There's a book called that,' Amy replied.

'What?' Ember said.

'*I Want It Now.*' She offered Ralph a very communicative smile. He thought she was wonderful, the way she stuck at it with no bloody encouragement at all. It did not embarrass him. He was used to this kind of thing from women. You had to be tender.

'I can understand your hurry, Ralph,' Leyton replied.

'It's started, hasn't it, although Lane's still there to date, and the arrangement continues.'

'Precautionary only,' Ember said.

'Who was it said, You're twice the man with a pistol ready?' Leyton asked.

'Wittgenstein,' Amy replied. 'How will you pay, Ralph?' That's the way she always behaved, straight. Ember liked this. 'You can do an instalment down, then over three months. Your credit's good.'

'Cash. All of it. Now.' He had Nora's £250 in his pocket, plus a couple of hundred more about him, as usual. He felt unsure whether it was Amy's crude fucking tease to suggest Ralph W. Ember of Low Pastures and the Monty needed time to pay. He would always try not to turn rough with any woman as game and cheerful as Amy. Age and a place like the Hobart could make them loud and raw and envious.

'You'd better come upstairs then, Ralph,' Leyton said, lifting the bar flap. Ember wondered about this, but went. God knew how many of the Hobart's customers realized what other business Amy and Leyton ran. Ralph did not want it buzzed that he was gunning up. This could certainly make you a target: pre-emptive. But everyone would assume he was gunning up, anyway. All knew Ralph W. Ember could read the outlook, nobody more brilliant at it.

Chapter Six

'They'll sus you, Louise,' Harpur said.

'I'll try it.'

'A stranger, a woman, alone in there. They'll know you're police.'

'What are you saying?'

'I'm saying they'll suspect you, that's all,' Harpur said.

'Meaning, Dubal worked out I was undercover police, so these people will, too? You think I'm no good at it – have to be rescued all the time?'

'You're *very* good at it. But in the Hobart they –'

'For instance, I could be a tart.'

'The Hobart bans tarts.'

'I could be an out-of-town tart who doesn't know,' Louise replied.

'All tarts know tarts are banned from the Hobart. It's in their litany. And Dubal might have put a description around.'

'Do I look like police?'

'Women don't go to the Hobart alone. To them you'll look like police trying not to look like police.'

'As with Dubal.'

'It could work for a while with Dubal,' Harpur said. 'Did.'

'It's all interrelated, isn't it?'

'What?'

'Dubal, the hill deaths, the Ridout death, Ralph Ember, the Hobart.'

'Interrelated how?'

'I don't know, but *you* do,' Louise replied.

'Is that right?'

'I want to stick with it. Dubal tried to have me killed. I don't let him slip away. If Ember leads to him I –'

'We're police officers. We don't do vendettas.'

'No?'

'Of course not,' Harpur said.

'Of course not. This is a standard piece of investigation, that's all.'

'In the Hobart, the landlord's sharp, his wife sharper. Especially if they've been alerted.'

'Is Dubal going to broadcast something like that?'

'Like what?' Harpur asked.

'That his firm's penetrated by a youngster cop, Louise Machin?'

'Was.'

'All right, was.'

'Maybe not. Maybe.'

'I'll give it a go.'

'I don't think so,' Harpur replied. 'We ought to pull away now before Ember comes out, in case he did see the car at the club.'

'We don't even know why he's here. Or *I* don't.'

'Move away now,' Harpur replied.

'So, you're familiar with the Hobart? That's how you could pick up his route?'

'If he sees us here, all your clever tailing's dead.'

'Familiar with it how?' she replied. 'Because it's tartless?'

'Exactly.'

'Why do you have to sit on information, sir?'

Yes, why did he? High rank habit? That 'sir' squeezed out last – a sneer? Warranted?

'I'm on your side, you know,' she said.

'And very proud to have you, Louise.'

'Yes?' She quickly opened the door of the Renault, slammed it behind her and walked across the road to the

Hobart. For a second, Harpur thought of getting out and following, either to stop Louise or at least to be with her in the pub. But that would truly muck things up, wouldn't it? They might – *might* – not pick out Louise, despite what he'd said. And it was conceivable – more or less conceivable – that Dubal had put around no warning. They'd almost all recognize Harpur, though. Some he'd met. Some he'd interrogated, faces close. Some he'd put away. Even strangers would see what he was. He did not look like police trying not to look like police, he looked like police. He knew it. Harpur did get out of the car, but this was a reflex: gallantry – save a girl. He stood by the open passenger door briefly, then decided he would be less obvious in the Renault, climbed back aboard and tried to sit very low and inconspicuous, as in the Monty car park. He would give Louise fifteen minutes. If she had not returned by then he must go in, and to hell with keeping her anonymous.

It had been Louise's notion to follow Ember from the club. Harpur considered it impractical and failed to see what might be gained, anyway: or at least told Louise he failed to see. But, as he now knew, she thought everything 'interrelated', and what was strong enough to take Ember away from the Monty on a big night must be overall important. Bright: Louise had learned since she came in from the countryside that urban organized crime was . . . was *organized*, and that the components depended on one another, affected one another, were locked into one another. She had also wanted to prove she could tail unseen, because tailing unseen was part of the new career plan she'd picked for herself. She seemed to have succeeded with tailing Ember: again, it showed her bright, when the target was someone so fly and experienced.

Very bright, really. She had lain right back, always with at least one vehicle between hers and the Saab, and sometimes two. She seemed as aware as Harpur was that Ember might have spotted the Renault and the two of them at the Monty, although he had not reacted. Ember would be smart enough for that. After a couple of miles, Louise did lose the Saab at a roundabout, but by then Harpur could guess where Ralph was probably going and directed her. Knowledge of local geography helped occasionally. They got behind him again before he reached the Hobart, and from then on she stuck. Louise had all the skills. He would have bet on this, anyway. He meant it when he praised her. She had done brilliantly to hang on in Dubal's outfit for so long. She had been sharp to sense they meant to hit someone. They had hit Wayne. The motives were plain. Proof did not come so easily.

This afternoon Louise had turned up outside St Luke's from sick leave, half hidden inside a big, hooded coat, and, after the funeral, managed to speak unobserved to Harpur for ten seconds in the crowd as people dispersed. She had asked for the Monty yard rendezvous later – when he could slip out of the wake. She wanted to discuss what happened to her next. Undercover was impossible: at least one firm had identified her. Louise's head injuries still affected her eyes and hearing but she said that when she felt up to it she'd do some surveillance on Dubal – tracking him from a distance, now infiltration was not on. She knew plenty about Dubal and his routines, didn't she? This tailing of Ember by car to the Hobart was intended to convince Harpur she could watch Dubal undetected, too. He had thought she simply dreaded the notion of being sent back to her out-station. Later, though, he saw her motives went beyond this. She did not forgive Dubal. Harpur sympathized. She would feel weak and hopelessly young and crushed if she didn't try to do something about Ferdy.

Crouched in the Renault now, he, also, wanted to know what happened to Louise next, today. It was a professional worry, nothing more than this, he felt almost sure. She had been out of sight for nearly ten minutes. *Do not erase.* The Hobart towered, sombre and majestic, on its corner. He didn't really think she'd get hurt in there. Public violence among witnesses would be too risky. But she'd be noticed.

She'd already been noticed once, by Dubal and his people. A spy trip into the Hobart could make her terribly exposed again. If the word was around about her, people might come to regard Louise Machin as a supremely stubborn menace who had better be removed, successfully this time: the way Wayne was, at the second try.

Then, Iles would start nosing into how it had all come about and wanting to dish out blame. Harpur would get it, somewhere between plenty and the lot. Desmond the Merciful could sometimes forget he was. He already had Louise's name and suspected she figured somehow in the hill shooting. If she were killed now, Iles would want to know who killed her, obviously, but he'd also home in on who had put her in a situation where she might *get* killed. Whatever people thought of Iles, he did ferociously care for his people, remained integrally part of his people, unless, of course, one of his people, such as Harpur, wantonly allowed another of his people, such as Louise, into what Iles would regard as obvious and unnecessary danger. The perils from Iles had begun to move at geometric rate.

Louise came out of the Hobart and walked without hurry to the car. Nobody followed. The pub windows were too grubby for Harpur to see whether anyone watched her. Her way of walking had no sex in it, or none that got to Harpur. She took the driver's seat again.

'So, let's disappear,' Harpur said.

'They talked guns.'

'Oh, yes?'

'He went behind the bar with the landlord.'

'Oh, yes?'

'Possibly upstairs.'

'Upstairs,' Harpur said.

'They're armourers?'

'If you got close enough to hear what they were talking about, they must have seen you.'

'Crowds of office people in there, some girls with clothes and hair like this. I merged.'

'Grand work.'

'But you knew it all already?'

'Confirmation's valuable.'

'That's fucking condescending.'

'Confirmation's valuable,' Harpur replied. 'What kind of weapon?'

'I don't think they specified.'

'Just the same, you did well.'

'That's fucking condescending,' she said.

'Ralphy panicking, or steely?'

'If you know they're armourers why don't –'

'City policing's complex, Louise.'

'That's fucking condescending.'

'Shall we move?'

'I want to watch Ember leave,' she said.

'What for?'

'I'd like to see where he's wearing it.'

'You won't. It will probably be a nice, flat, Browning 9 mm automatic nesting neatly in a dimple on his left shoulder.'

'How can you –'

'Amy and Leyton are doing a good line in those lately.'

'To look at him carrying his new gun will be a kind of crucial midway stage in our operation,' she replied.

'Which of our operations is that?'

'The surveillance. The tailing. Important to see him go. Maybe pick him up again, find how it's connected to Dubal.'

'Interrelated.'

'Well, it *is*, isn't it?'

'Drive around the corner into Cork Street and we'll park on a side road and walk back. Just get the car out of his view.'

She did as he told her. That's how she was: sometimes she would listen to him, sometimes she decided for herself. If you had a brain you used it and made your choices, even when she was supposed to do what he ordered. A tough girl. They found a decently deep shop doorway on the other side of the road a little way from the Hobart and waited. Louise said: 'If people are all arming for war you'll obviously need someone to stick with Dubal. You must have realized that when you put me undercover, despite Mr Iles.'

'Who said they were all arming?'

'You.'

'Did I?'

'The Hobart's doing a big trade in Brownings. Remember?'

'They've got a steady little business. Always good activity there.'

'I'll stick with Dubal for you.'

'Thanks, but too dodgy.'

'He won't see me,' she replied.

'He might.'

'I feel I'm sort of entitled.'

'What's that mean?'

'Have a right.'

'Why? Because he nearly had you killed? That doesn't give you a right. The opposite. It disqualifies. He'll be looking out for you. You know him, yes, but he knows *you*. And all sorts of others might.'

'Not undercover, obviously. Far-away watching. Like this.'

'Too tricky.'

'Just promise to think about it,' she said.

'I *have* thought. No go.'

'You're scared of Iles?'

'Scared for you.'

'That's the same thing,' she replied.

'Shall we close the topic now?'

'I don't agree.'

'No?'

Louise could use rough leverage on him, of course. She had some awkward information. Nobody except Harpur, Jack Lamb and herself knew how she had been recovered from the hillside gun site, nor who so sweetly stopped Mildly Sedated Henschall and Percy Kellow there. Nobody alive except Harpur, Jack Lamb and herself were even aware she had been on the hill at all. Well, Dubal also might know, if he'd ordered the execution there, but he would not be disclosing much. This general ignorance was good, had to be ferociously preserved. A detective owed that much to his grass, especially when the grass's nimbleness up an incline and beautiful shooting with a police-type gun in the dark had unquestionably saved a young woman detective's life, and done a lot for Harpur's welfare, too.

After that destruction of Mildly and Perce, Harpur and Jack Lamb had taken Louise down the hill, given her first aid in Jack's van and a good slurp of whisky from the bottle, then driven her to Casualty and left her. During all this, Lamb had never been named, but at 260 pounds and six feet five inches he might be easy to trace, if she talked, and Harpur knew how well she could talk when she felt like it. Despite her shocked state, Louise would have noticed everything there was to notice about the van, including a routinely traceable registration number.

For now, she would be too respectful and subtle to pressure Harpur directly, but she must know he recognized her power. In fact he thought he heard fragments of that power in her words and tone. This amounted to more than simple belief in her own intellect. It was not usual for a detective sergeant to tell her detective chief superintendent that she disagreed with him, nor to claim they had run an 'operation' in partnership. It was not usual for a detective sergeant to accuse a detective chief superintendent of condescension, *fucking* condescension. And then the mention late on of Iles. That was shrewd, wasn't it? Harpur felt sure again that he had picked a very clever girl, sod it.

Ember came out of the Hobart and they retreated a bit deeper into the doorway. 'He looks damn confident,' she said. 'Formidable. He reminds me of someone.'

'Ralph's bored by all that Heston doppelganger stuff.'

'There was a silly-ass comedian called Cardew the Cad. My parents have videos.'

'See a bulge? On his shoulder, I mean.'

'And they call him Panicking? Why?' she replied. 'He seems so . . . yes, so solid.'

'The holster harness keeps him in one piece.'

They watched Ember reach the Saab and drive away. She did not seem to want to follow him back after all, knew where he would be going.

'I'd never actually attack Dubal,' she said. 'You don't have to get anxious about that. What with? I'm not gun-trained. I'll just observe and make the case against him for you. Due process. That's if you *want* due process, a case made. Do I understand city policing? I'm off work for a while with my injuries. It will be a kind of hobby.'

'They bear grudges, people like Dubal.'

'So do I.'

Harpur said: 'Let me hear the rescue phone number again.'

'Will they respond? I'm not officially on duty.'

'They'll respond. You weren't officially on duty before.'

She recited the number. 'If they're called out it's going to be known to everyone, isn't it, Mr Iles included.'

'Listen, if it gets bad, ring them. I'll cope with Mr Iles.'

'Really?'

'And my address – you've got my address?'

'In the phone book.'

'You might not have time for the phone book.'

'Arthur Street.'

'Number?'

'One two six.'

'If I'm not there and my daughters are about they'll probably think you've turned up because I've made you pregnant. Make it clear at once you're just a colleague.'

'You get a lot of that?'

'What?'

'Women they think are pregnant visiting the house.'

'They're kids. They imagine drama everywhere.'

'Do women get made pregnant these days, if they don't want it?'

'Exactly.'

'How old are your daughters? Don't they understand that?'

'We used to have a lot of books there, gone now, thank God. My wife read Victorian novels to them – one called . . . is it, *Adam's Bed*?'

'*Adam Bede*. Yes, Hetty gets pregnant by the squire.'

'They think they have to look after all womankind,' Harpur said. 'It means nothing. Sometimes I think it's only their idea of humour.'

'And there's a girl there off and on, I heard. Adult.'

'I've a friend who comes in to watch the children.'

'Is *she* going to think I'm there looking for the father of my unborn child, as well?'

'As I say, explain at once,' Harpur replied. 'Denise is sensible. She knows about police work.'

'They don't think you'd make a colleague pregnant?'

'Explain it's an emergency.'

'I suppose a pregnancy could be an emergency.'

'Explain it's operational,' Harpur said.

'OK. So, is this a kind of permission for me to do it, to watch Ferdy?'

'No it fucking isn't. But can I stop you?'

'It's blind-eyeing?'

'Not that either. It's a kind of surrender,' Harpur replied.

'Surrender to what?'

'Surrender.'

'I've got influence I don't know about?' she asked.

'Oh, you *know*.'

'Do we return to the Parents Evenings for meetings?' Louise replied.

She drove Harpur back to a street one block from the Monty and he walked. The crowd in the club had grown and there was some dancing now. He could not see Iles or Nora Ridout and Fay-Alice. Dubal and his mother were at a table with Mansel Shale and some of his people, everything tranquil enough. Ember stood near his little accounting desk behind the bar, part shielded by the decorated steel plate. When Harpur went over Ralph put a half-pint glass on the counter and mixed a gin and cider for him. Harpur had been right and even from very near like this he could see no outline of a holster under Ember's jacket. Almost certainly he would be wearing whatever he'd bought at the Hobart. It must have been a crisis trip, as Louise suggested. Ember had wanted something for tonight, for now. And, since Dubal was still here, Ember would probably still want it, and want it handy. Ralph poured himself a hefty Kressmann Armagnac.

Harpur said: 'In many ways, this hospitality at the club has been a drawing together of people from opposed camps, a kind of reconciliation, and I think you're to be truly commended for it.'

'Thanks, Mr Harpur. This is how I always see the Monty – a healing influence. There's an obligation on me to provide a venue where rifts may be attended to, repaired. Out of the death of Wayne, then, some gains may flow. Always I look for the positives.'

'Oh, yes: let us hope this peacefulness in the club may be a joyful omen that the peace on our streets will continue, also,' Harpur replied.

'Certainly, certainly. And my own feeling is, this street peace is by now so wonderfully established and appreciated, it's bound to endure.'

'I do hope this is right, Ralph.'

'But surely it must, Mr Harpur. Aren't we all beneficiaries – the city itself and every one of its folk: business people, the authorities, such as yourself and superiors? All, all enjoy this calm and would never let it slip. It is envied throughout the country, I know.'

'And yet a certain frailty,' Harpur replied.

'It must not, cannot, be.'

'Rumours of change,' Harpur said.

'Is that so? Of what nature? Are you at liberty to say?'

'And, of course, the terrible deaths.'

'Tragic, admittedly, Mr Harpur,' Ember replied. 'Yet in my view these must not be allowed to shake the –'

'That fucker Dubal, for instance,' Harpur replied.

'Dubal?'

'Does he scare the shit out of you, Ralph, no easy thing?'

'Dubal? Is that the lad over there, with his mother?'

'Talk of people gunning up.'

'Gunning up? But why, why?' Ember cried. 'How can that be necessary?' He gazed around the club. 'Everything so harmonious, so unified.'

'You didn't do Perce and Mildly Sedated up the hill, did you, you sly sod?' Harpur replied.

'Piss off, Harpur. I heard it was you or yours. A Glock.'

'Someone wanting to weaken Dubal might go for his people.'

'Dubal? Is that the lad over there with his mother?'

'A lovely busy club like this – you're bound to hear things,' Harpur replied.

'What are you telling me?'

'Original mahogany fittings and beautifully cared for brass on the pumps and so on. They're certain to attract people. Well, only look at the turn-out now.'

'What are you telling me, Harpur – that I give you bits of insight or you'll fix me up for Perce and Mildly?'

'Dubal,' Harpur replied.

'What?'

'A problem?'

'You're frightened of him?' Ember asked.

'He doesn't understand the way things work. Or he does and he doesn't like it.'

'You're frightened he might hurt somebody of yours?'

'If I could be kept up to date on him, that's all,' Harpur replied.

'Hurt who?'

'This would be a general anxiety rather than particular.'

Ember said: 'The tale was around you had someone in his outfit. A girl? What happened there? Did you get a tip they had her marked? Who? A brilliant rescue? Two dead. And now you're worried about her again?'

'I have to look at the whole trade structure,' Harpur replied.

'And then Iles might be stalking Dubal as well, yes? Wayne was Iles's feed, wasn't he? He'll want to do Dubal, to comfort the daughter. So he can go on and comfort the daughter some more, in his own ram style.'

'It would be a help if you could keep a real eye on Dubal, Ralph.'

'Is that the lad over there with his mother?'

'Are you carrying something?'

'This is a fucking funeral aftermath, for God's sake, Harpur. Haven't you heard of fucking decorum?'

'And then what about the partnership treaty with Manse Shale?' Harpur replied. 'That holding up all right? There've been times when I wondered whether you'd feel forced to annihilate Shale, before he does you.'

'Are you banging this undercover girl? This why you're anxious?'

'If things get volatile – are Shale and you still totally comfortable with each other?'

'What's the other one going to say, the undergraduate – Denise? – the occasionally live-in one . . . what's *she* going to say if she finds out about the undercover girl, also very young?' Ember replied.

'I recall Shale lost someone, didn't he, someone well up in his crew – Ivis? Alfie Ivis? – I think so – well, well up – and this is another death we've never really got anywhere with. I don't know who Manse blames for that killing. Such things rankle. Did you see off Alfie? These are all factors. I mean, they *could* all be factors if the general picture grew . . . yes, *volatile*. I'd be really indebted to hear of any . . . any, well *shifts*, Ralph. Yes, shifts. Indebted.'

'A girl is bound to feel true gratitude if her life has been saved – suppose something like that happened – and she'd obviously wish to proffer thanks in that fashion they have,' Ember said. '*I* can understand that and so would many, but I don't know about the other one – Denise, is it?'

'Manse has these monopoly dreams – like most, I suppose.'

'What volatility?' Ember replied.

'Yes, volatility. You've got the word exactly, Ralph.'

Now and then when Mark Lane, the Chief, could not sleep because of anxiety and self-doubt he might call on Harpur at Arthur Street in the middle of the night. Lane was a wreck and a good man. There had been a breakdown not long ago. It was brought on by Iles, of course, but also by the Chief's dread that evil would swallow the universe, starting very specifically from his domain. Responsibility mercilessly badgered Lane – a religious thing, a hierarchy thing. Although, in his way, Iles loved the Chief it *was* in Iles's way, and this could sometimes appear like contempt and/or malevolence. Iles did not really answer to any known human formula.

Lane's worries would amass gradually and unbearably some nights. There was also another reason for arriving at Harpur's house so late: secrecy, above all from the ACC. Lane naturally did not want these calls for aid known about. Harpur always felt a duty to bring the Chief comfort. He had sallow, porous-looking skin that seemed made to suck up pity, and some of his clothes demanded compassion. It was terrible to watch a man crumple, especially someone like Lane. Harpur could remember him as a fine detective on the neighbouring patch, and occasionally worked with him then. Elevation had brought him low. Iles diagnosed it to Harpur as a well-known process: people were promoted just beyond their abilities and fell back disastrously, much further than the step they'd been on immediately before. Iles said St Peter would be an example, and, of course, J.F. Kennedy. Iles also found Lane 'fatally humane'. Harpur longed for him to retire or take a job elsewhere, before he became wholly derelict, his fine soul trampled.

Lane knocked the door tonight at just after 3 a.m. His wife was with him. Devoted, she would usually accompany the Chief on therapy visits. Harpur had been home from the Monty for about half an hour. When he got into bed Denise had woken in that lovely warm, welcoming style of hers, snaking an arm around him. Harpur was moving very carefully so as not to disturb her.

'You're so considerate, Col,' she said.

'Funerals do that to me.'

She shoved up with her shoulder under his right arm. 'But I'd prefer you considerable,' she replied.

'I'll do my best.'

'That's been good enough for many.'

'No, no.'

'Not good enough?'

'Not many.'

'We're grown-up people,' she said.

'Is that right?'

'One doesn't expect you to be super-chaste.'

'Which one doesn't expect me to be super-chaste?'

'This one,' Denise replied.

'What about this one?'

'What?'

'Should this one expect *you* to be super-chaste?' Harpur asked.

'I don't see how that can be. I'm in bed with you and have been before.'

'But *before* you'd been in bed with me before.'

'We're grown-up people, I think,' Denise replied.

'You're certainly a grown-up person, but also a young person.'

'That's so, Col.'

'So you must have been even younger before.'

'Before what?'

'Before you were in bed with me before.'

'Yes, younger, definitely.'

'At some stage then you must have been super-chaste.'

'True.'

'When?' he asked.

'Before.'

'How long before?'

'Before.'

'This is unhealthy, isn't it?' Harpur said.

'What?'

'Trying to possess your past. This dirty curiosity.'

'Yes, it *is* unhealthy. And dirty. But I think I like it.'

'Why?'

'It proves a caring side to you.'

'Do I have to prove that? Aren't all my sides caring, port, starboard and in-between? Didn't I creep into bed so as not to bother you?'

'But sometimes I want you to bother me.'

'Of course,' Harpur replied.

'What's that mean?'

'Appetite.'

'But there's nothing "of course" about appetite, Col, is there?' Denise replied. 'It's only for you.'

'Is that right?' Harpur asked.

'Well, what do *you* think?'

'Partly right. Variable.'

'There's an element of that. But, now, in this bed at this time, it's you only, isn't it?' Denise replied.

'But is that enough?'

'Let's see. Let's see again.'

'That's an idea.'

Soon afterwards, Harpur heard a mild tapping on the front door. It was apologetic, it was insistent, it was high-rank. Denise said: 'Is it His Eminence, Coitus Interrupt Us, again?'

'He's having a bad time. We could go on lying very quiet until he gives up,' Harpur said.

'We weren't lying very quiet, or even quiet.'

'We *could*.'

'Could we? What bad time?'

'I think like seeing himself as he is. This hits him now and then.'

She frowned and seemed about to weep. 'Oh, God, the poor love. Everyone should be spared that. Self-knowledge. Unspeakable. Who was it said, "Human kind cannot bear very much reality"?'

'Walt Disney? The Chief believes in all that – reality, truth, unflinchingness. Unflinchingness especially he prizes. He thinks people should face up.'

'You mustn't leave him out there in the porch, Col. Not if he's sick.'

'No.'

'I'll be here when you come back.'

'Awake?'

'I don't know if I can say that.'

'Ready to be awoken?'

'*Re*-awoken. But I've got a French verse seminar in the morning.'

'Luckily I'm clued up on French verse,' Harpur said.

'That right?'

'Iles mentioned some at a school prize-giving. Plus recitation, translated.'

'Oh, well, yes, wake me up, then. You can give me coaching. I'd be a fool to miss it.'

'That's what *I* thought.'

Harpur put on a dressing gown and went downstairs. He felt like Florence Nightingale. He opened the door and took the Chief and Mrs Lane into the sitting room, guided them to armchairs, and poured drinks. Harpur sat opposite on a sofa. 'Don't, don't, don't pretend that you have not heard the whispers, Colin,' Sally Lane said. It was playful, it was harsh and sad. 'You, you only can help. Why we are here at this hour.'

'Whispers?'

'There you go! Damn police deviousness, damn discretion. All right – the rumours that Chief might go. Promotion.'

'But this is brilliant news,' Harpur cried. 'So deserved! You would be greatly missed here, sir, obviously but –'

'Don't, don't, don't pretend that Chief runs this outfit, Colin,' Mrs Lane replied. It was no longer playful. It was still harsh and sad – and businesslike.

Harpur said: 'But of course he –'

'Chief and I have come to acknowledge he is an emptiness,' Mrs Lane said. 'An emptiness.' She spoke this flabby, woozy word as if they had spent weeks selecting it as uniquely spot-on. Her face was long and oval and beautiful in that style: solemn, aquiline, commanding. Iles referred to it sometimes as 'a rowing boat face'.

'Emptiness? That's so absurd it doesn't need an answer,' Harpur replied. Sick to say of any man he was an emptiness. Sick for any man to think it of himself. From his Sunday School days Harpur remembered a verse saying our bodies were the temple of the Holy Ghost, and this had to be more like it. He almost yelled at both of them that they must not embrace despair, the unforgivable sin. But this would be too brutal. God had breathed into Man to bring him life. How could he be empty?

'Wouldn't I once have fought that description of Chief with all my strength and rage?' Sally Lane said.

'Yes, an emptiness, Colin,' the Chief said.

'Chief has been a great, great man,' his wife said.

'Is,' Harpur replied.

'Iles runs this domain,' Sally Lane said, her dark eyes full of bleak certainty.

'Mr Iles would not claim that, although he's certainly a fine officer,' Harpur replied. True. Of course Iles realized he ran things, had worked and schemed and elbowed to run things, but he would never speak the fact. That would be to undermine the system and Iles revered and needed the system. *He* would be an emptiness without it. Mrs Lane shivered slightly, as though Iles's arrival were a hellish possibility even at this hour. It was not an *im*possibility.

'Yet a *useful* emptiness, you see, Colin,' Lane said. He sipped minutely at the whisky Harpur had poured for him.

'This is the point,' his wife said.

'It is an emptiness that would be lost if I moved on,' Lane said.

'Chief fears everything would be destroyed, you see,' Mrs Lane said slowly, like explaining an undifficult problem for a child. 'Iles would be reduced, neutralized.'

Harpur said: 'But, there was a –'

'But there was a time when I longed for that,' Sally Lane replied. 'This is what you meant to say? Correct. I loathed Iles for stealing Chief's . . . Chief's role and grandeur, the grandeur he was magnificently fitted for. I knew – knew with all my brain and body – that I must save Chief, must keep him Chief, buttress him. The only way – to fight Iles.'

'Always, Sally has been that buttress,' Lane said. 'She never ceased to see the danger from Desmond.'

'Yes, sir, a wonderful support, but we have *all* believed in you,' Harpur answered. 'From Mr Iles through all ranks. Yes, Mr Iles was and is a buttress, too. He brings undiluted loyalty.' And, in a sense – an Iles sense again – this was fair.

'You're kind, Colin,' Sally Lane said, 'and a right fucking liar.'

Had Harpur ever heard her curse before?

'We've drawn you from your bed, and I apologize,' she said. 'And then, also, your young friend might be here. She must find this kind of late visit upsetting.' Mrs Lane had worded it carefully so as not actually to suggest the bed they drew Harpur from contained this 'young friend'. The young friend might have heard the tapping on the door from a different bedroom. 'And *is* she here?' Once, when the Lanes called like this in the night a little while ago, Denise did not wake as Harpur left the bed, and she came down half an hour later, troubled by his absence. She was wearing his raincoat, which dragged on the ground. Somehow this had made her look especially dissolute. The Lanes had been startled.

'I like her to come in and sit with the children if I'm out at night,' Harpur replied now.

'Oh, quite,' she said.

'I must not desert this patch, Colin,' the Chief said.

Sally Lane grew more animated: 'Don't you understand that what Chief calls, perhaps justly, the "emptiness" of his role, the negativeness – you appreciate that this very negativeness has become a positive, a kind of triumph?'

So they really meant it. For them this null word was not despair. It had a weird, contorted value.

'Chief wields a splendid, though unobtrusive, influence,' Mrs Lane said. 'We see it now. That unobtrusiveness has always been in Chief's character. Perhaps it was this quality, posed against the mighty demands of leadership, which made his personality splinter and caused breakdown.'

'Sally can analyse these psychological matters, you see, Colin.'

Harpur thought her theory sounded feasible.

Lane said: 'If I go, and Desmond Iles is diminished, the peace pact will end and the carnage of battle resume: trade war, turf war, gang war. I'll look back on this domain and see only violence, feel only consummate failure.'

'Chief's health would not stand that degree of self-recrimination. Guilt would stifle him. People joke sometimes about Catholic guilt, but in Chief it is a real and terrifying power. And, yet, now and then, a constructive power.'

'Something has been created in my time here,' Lane said. 'Peace. I cannot allow its obliteration. This would be negligence, indeed, vandalism.'

'But you will say, Colin, that Chief was always opposed to an arranged peace with criminals – regarded it as conniving with villainy for the sake of a quiet life.'

'I was, I was,' Lane said.

'For a while Chief and I fought the notion of pacts and understandings.'

'We did, we did,' Lane said.

'We've changed,' Sally Lane said. 'We have *been* changed – by events. It can be foolish to oppose change. Certainly the creation of that peace was not directly of Chief's doing. But it has been accomplished *while he was in command*. He *allowed* it to be created. It has been created by Iles, but under, as it were, licence. A licence from Chief. Chief is the framework without which none of it could have taken place. Isn't this only a standard feature of leadership, the ability to delegate?'

'*Crucial* to leadership,' Harpur replied.

'These pacts exist,' Sally Lane said. 'The routes to peace are never plain and simple. I cite Northern Ireland. Now – as there – a kind of peace has been achieved, and we have come to feel it must not be lost through stupid casualness, or its opposite, extreme severity.'

'We thought of *you*, Colin.'

'One reason we're here,' his wife said. 'If peace ends and Iles relegated who must deal with the eternal horror of renewed street war? Obviously, Detective Chief Superintendent Colin Harpur – someone who has already tragically lost a wife and is single-parenting his daughters. Too much.'

'I cannot, cannot, leave you a foul legacy of that kind,' Lane said. 'You who have been so steady in my defence, Colin. I will not go.' His voice was resolute, his body tensed against all pressures. These last years he had learned how to mimic the strength he possessed when Harpur first knew him.

Harpur said: 'I do appreciate your –'

'But you will ask how can Chief's move be stopped? How, in fact, can this well-meant but dire promotion be averted? Well, we do not know the status of the rumours about his future yet.'

'How, Colin, could I join the Inspectorate of Constabulary – appraising other police forces while knowing that my own force – what I will always regard as my own force – knowing my own force was torn by drug trade confrontations – as if another Manchester or London or Liverpool – and that you had to try to stop them?'

'Perhaps the forecasts about Chief are *only* rumours, and therefore reversible,' Mrs Lane said. 'The proposal, if there is one, could be squashed. You can bring this about, Colin. And so we arrive tonight. You intercede. For instance. Iles undoubtedly has political friends. How otherwise could he have built such improper power? He knows Home Office people. And some of those he has formed his arrangement with – Ralph Ember, Mansel Shale and so on – these, too, have probably a network of contacts in Westminster and so on. Commonplace these days – the *purchase* of Members of Parliament. These people – Iles, Ember, Shale – must help us, must, Colin, and in doing so help themselves. They must apply influence to make the move away for Chief impossible. Perhaps Iles has already begun to use such influence. If so, good. He might realize that a replacement would cut him down. But it is also possible that Iles would regard disappearance of the Chief like a victory – as if Iles had outlasted him, got him kicked upstairs. That attitude would be folly.'

There had been a time when Harpur was appalled at how much police business Mrs Lane knew. He had grown used to it. Iles referred to her as the power behind the clone. If a woman's man was sick, she would try to save him, as she had said – even if it meant taking over.

'You, Colin, are the one person who could persuade Iles and, perhaps, through him, persuade those others – Ember, Shale et cetera – to ensure things are kept as now,' she declared.

'For the peace and order of this patch and the whole country and even, yes, beyond,' Lane said. Always, he sought a global perspective. The big-time habit of his rank.

Harpur said: 'I don't know whether –'

The sitting-room door was pushed open and his daughters came in, both wearing blue pyjamas. Jill said: 'Is dad looking after you properly, Mrs Lane, Mr Lane? Sandwiches?'

'We heard something,' Hazel said.

'I thought, emergency,' Jill said. 'We're used to things late, but this is really *very* late. Or there might be quiche.'

'We were just leaving,' Sally Lane replied.

'Dad doesn't think of things like sandwiches, quiche,' Jill said. 'What emergency? I mean, for people to be here *so* late it has to be an emergency. Is it to do with Desmond Iles? Hazel thought it might be Mr Iles here, which is why she wanted to come down, pyjamas regardless. She's *interested* in Mr Iles, you know.'

'Mouth,' Hazel replied.

'She's only fifteen but will soon be sixteen,' Jill said, 'though many girls regard this silly age limit as . . . as silly. I don't mind Mr Iles. Oh, he's flashy – a red scarf and so on. But a *bit* of flashiness is all right. It lightens things up. Hazel's got a boyfriend, obviously, but she likes maturity, also. Mr Iles is quite mature sometimes. I've seen it happen.'

'Drip, you're boring people,' Hazel said.

'What *kind* of emergency?' Jill asked.

'No emergency,' Harpur replied. 'You're not required, thanks. You can go back to bed now.'

'When we say emergency we're thinking it might be to do with if Mr Lane leaves the area,' Jill said.

'That's the buzz around school,' Hazel said.

'Back to guns in the streets,' Jill said. 'Some kids in school say everything on the streets now is sort of *arranged*, so business can go on all right and nobody gets hurt, business meaning drugs. But if Mr Lane went . . . well, where would we be? Where would Des Iles be? This makes Hazel nervy. She doesn't want someone ordinary and crushed, does she?'

'You don't know what Hazel wants, you blabbing infant,' Hazel replied.

'Chief isn't going anywhere,' Mrs Lane said.

'Is that really right?' Hazel asked.

'You see, she's jumpy,' Jill said. 'So what *is* the emergency? To do with the murders in the Press? Does dad know about these? Is that the conversation? Often he knows things. You might not think it, but he does. But if we're going to have a big discussion maybe I should get Denise as well. She can be quite intelligent off and on.'

'As a matter of fact, this meeting's closed,' Harpur replied.

And when Mrs Lane and the Chief had gone and the children were back in bed, Harpur sat for a while downstairs with his drink. He felt unnerved by the Lanes' cave-in to an Iles policy of peaceful coexistence. That's what it was, cave-in. Suddenly, Harpur realized why until now he had been able to tolerate Iles's acceptance of the drugs game in return for non-violence: Harpur had known Lane disapproved and had known, also, that Lane was in charge, nominally in charge. Always then the possibility existed that the Chief would intervene and dismantle the arrangement. It was not likely – probably only Harpur deluding himself – but at least he *had* been able to delude himself. Now, though, Lane and his wife would surrender to Iles's thinking. They had come to prize street peace, regardless of cost. The Chief wanted to stay and ensure the arrangement would last. This depressed and frightened Harpur. Was it an endorsement by Lane, and therefore by the Service, of that most smelly precept, the end justifies the means? Harpur did not want street war: the street war which would almost certainly come if Lane were replaced and Iles's comfy agreement with Ember and Shale ended. But neither did Harpur want Lane in charge if he and his wife had openly ditched their opposition to pacts with villains. Lawlessness was then normality.

When Harpur went to bed he had not resolved these anxieties. Denise woke up immediately and seemed to have forgotten she needed her sleep before tomorrow's seminar.

'It's like you need consoling, Col,' she said.

'Well, yes.'

'What have they done to you?'

'Suddenly, I see some things too well.'

'God, that's always dangerous.'

'But, at the same time, other things are so damn cloudy.'

'God, that's always dangerous, too.'

'I don't see you as someone who's here just to console me,' he replied.

'I know that, Col. But I can console you all the same, can't I?'

'Well, yes.'

Chapter Seven

'Come with me, Mr Harpur, come with me now,' Mrs Dubal said.

'As a matter of fact, we get a lot of people calling here late at night to see dad like this,' Jill said.

'Come with me, Mr Harpur,' Mrs Dubal said. 'I'll show you.'

Jill said: 'But if I really, really, think about it, nobody has called here late at night for dad like this since . . . since, oh, the summer. Yes, six months ago. More? And do you know who it was? It was the Chief Constable himself. Well, he *was* the Chief Constable, then. Mr Lane and his wife drove over all that way from their house at Baron's Hill. Important – had to be, I mean, they arrived at three o'clock in the morning. Honestly! Well, maybe even later! Woke us up. We had to come downstairs to find out what went on – all the talking. In this room, the same! So you can see, Mrs Dubal, we're used to it. No need to feel bad about coming very late now.

'That other time, in the summer, was just before Mr Lane got promoted and had to leave this patch altogether. Gone now, yes. He was so nice, but really dodgy and a bit bubbles-on-the-lips after his illness and kicked about by Mrs. Ever hear that not very nice saying, "pussy whipped"? He didn't want to take the promotion, you know, did he, dad? This was what we were talking about that night, oh, many arguments, all sides, yes. But the promotion could not be stopped, could it, dad? In what's known as "figurative expressions" in English in school it was what's called "wheels within wheels", meaning so complicated and shady.'

'Dad will definitely go with you now if it's urgent, Mrs Dubal,' Hazel said.

'Yes, in a way, urgent,' Mrs Dubal replied. 'And then in a way, I suppose, not urgent at all. Come with me, Mr Harpur, please.'

'Which way? Urgent, which way?' Hazel asked. 'Dad, do *you* know? Did Mrs Dubal tell you something before we arrived?'

Yes, Mrs Dubal did, but Harpur said only: 'This is probably another of those private police matters. Mrs Dubal might not wish to –'

'It looks to me like Iles,' Mrs Dubal replied. She spoke it pretty well deadpan, as though of course, of course, it was Iles.

'What? What does?' Hazel asked.

'Hazel gets like keyed up when people talk about Des Iles,' Jill said.

'*What* looks like Iles?' Hazel said.

'You see?' Jill asked. 'Poor Haze. All edgy.'

'That's my view,' Mrs Dubal replied. 'Ferdinand was always troubled about Iles.'

'What's it mean,' Hazel asked, '"looks to me like Iles"?'

'Shall we go, then, Mr Harpur?' Mrs Dubal replied.

'You know, I could have guessed it was urgent,' Jill said. 'So late again, though not as late as Mr and Mrs Lane. Obviously. And also it's in your face, Mrs Dubal. It *looks* urgent. Pale. And your eyes – like hurt.'

'Yes, hurt,' Mrs Dubal replied. Her voice grew weak. Briefly, she turned away from everyone.

'Do cry if that's what you want, Mrs Dubal. Sometimes it's good,' Jill said. 'This is well known these days. Better to express things.'

'I'll go with you, of course,' Harpur said. 'I'm grateful you came here. Logan's, you say?'

Hazel's boyfriend, Scott, said: 'Although a senior officer,

Mr Harpur will often go out at night on vital police matters, even very late. Duty. It *is* a police matter, is it, Mr Harpur?'

'What do you think it is, jerk?' Jill asked. 'Didn't I say it was urgent? If it's truly urgent it's police, isn't it? Oh, Scott, you can be all right now and then but no wonder Hazel's sniffing around for someone more grown-up.'

'Not so much snarl, Jill, love,' Harpur told her.

Scott said: 'My mother says that a lot of the time when police *seem* to be doing police things they're really –'

Jill said: 'Your mother's a –'

'So I'll get a coat,' Harpur said. 'Look, I'm afraid I'm going to have to leave the four of you here by yourselves briefly.'

Jill's boyfriend, Darren, said: 'That's all right, Mr Harpur, We'll be fine. No probs. We'll look after the place et cetera.'

Harpur had been talking to Mrs Dubal in the sitting room at Arthur Street when Hazel, Jill and the two lads came back at just after midnight from wherever they went on Saturday evenings. They were going to watch a late TV film and drink some of Harpur's cider and so on. Denise would not be here to keep an eye and sleep over because her parents were down for the weekend from Stafford.

'As a matter of fact, I've heard the name Dubal, Mrs Dubal,' Jill said.

'My son. A famed businessman.'

'Ah,' Jill replied. 'Yes, a businessman. I knew I'd heard of him. That's *Ferdinand* Dubal. Of course. You mentioned him. People on the street – they mention him, too. Yes, on the street. Is it some crisis to do with this businessman? Crisis, crisis – there's quite a lot these days, since Mr Lane went, and this new one. Mostly people who come here late are young, though not Mr and Mrs Lane, I suppose.'

'One thing Ferdinand always said,' Mrs Dubal replied, '. . . he always said: if things got so filthy that I needed the police – if things got as filthy as that, still don't go to them. Never. But now – well, I have to decide things for myself, haven't I? And I've seen you on TV sometimes talking about a crime, Mr Harpur, or your picture in the paper. I looked you up in the phone book.'

'What do you mean, have to decide things for yourself now?' Hazel asked.

'People are like that with dad,' Jill said. 'They see him and think anybody who looks so rough and with such a haircut can't be sly and crafty, like some police. Quite a few people believe in him and *I* –'

'I'll be back really quickly,' Harpur told them.

'And it's right,' Jill said, 'they *can* believe in him because he's definitely got some honesty. Many would admit that. Not just the way he looks on TV.'

'We'll be fine,' Scott replied. 'I should hope we know how to behave in someone else's home.'

'Right,' Harpur said.

'Oh, yes, indeed,' Scott said.

'Mrs Dubal, what did you mean, "Ferdinand always *said*"?' Hazel asked.

'Yes, he always said that about the police,' Mrs Dubal replied.

'But *said*?' Hazel asked. 'Doesn't he still say it? Why not? What's happened to him? And you were crying, weren't you?'

'Yes, he always said that about the police,' Mrs Dubal replied. She'd be in her sixties, hefty, wearing a long, Cossack-style, wrap-around, navy greatcoat, low-heeled black shoes, and a dark pudding basin style hat. Her face was large, kindly. Despite the outfit, you would have known she was a mother, although it might be a shock to discover she was the mother of someone like Ferd.

'So what's it to do with Desmond Iles?' Hazel asked. 'How do you mean, "filthy"?'

'Have we always got to talk about *him*?' Scott said.

'I told you,' Jill replied.

'What?' Scott said.

'Didn't I tell you?' Jill answered.

'Do you mean your son's . . . well, in some way . . . well, dead, Mrs Dubal?' Hazel asked.

Scott, lying out on the settee with his shoes off and feet in Hazel's lap, gasped and put a hand to his mouth, as if the words had come from him and he wanted to stop them, even now: 'Oh, she didn't say that, Haze. In this house sometimes it's like being taken to a different kind of world.'

'Is he in the past somehow, Mrs Dubal?' she asked.

'Scott's right – you're pushing too hard, Hazel,' Harpur said.

'You do know what it is, don't you, dad?' Hazel replied.

'Come, Mr Harpur,' Mrs Dubal said.

'Why, why do you think it's to do with Desmond Iles?' Hazel asked. 'People always say this sort of thing. It's because of all that trouble before – Raymond Street and what came later. Everyone's heard of it. If somebody mentions Desmond Iles everyone thinks violence straight away.'

Mrs Dubal drove ahead in the Volvo estate. Harpur followed. These days and nights he was using an old, small Peugeot 106 from the police pool. Harpur thought it helped make him unnoticeable, although he also knew he looked bulky behind the wheel. She led down to the new marina area near Valencia Esplanade in the docks. On the edge of the redevelopment, several big, abandoned Victorian warehouses and factory buildings still stood, waiting for demolition and replacement. One warehouse had been partially knocked down so it was possible to drive through where a wall had been removed to the former wide, ground-floor storage area. She took the Volvo in, very slowly. Harpur followed.

Immediately, he saw in the headlights of both cars the body of Ferdy Dubal on his side in an autism crouch among the debris and litter. Even before he left the Peugeot and went nearer Harpur thought it clear that Dubal had been run over more than once. At a guess, three times. His face and legs seemed to have taken the worst. Despite death and the adult clothes Dubal looked astonishingly young, like a shock ad to teach kids road safety, a visual aid to Iles's lecture at Ridout's funeral. Yes. Ferdy's suede jacket and beige slacks were obviously top of the range and the blood and muck around him could not absolutely cancel his traditional air of creepy brilliance. It had seemed to promise him a good, long crooked career or maximum security jail life.

Mrs Dubal climbed out of the Volvo and stood with Harpur near her son, both cars' lights still on Ferdy from behind them. Their shadows were huge and fell across the body, but they could see enough. 'You shouldn't have come here again,' Harpur said. 'I would have found him from your directions.'

She raised both arms in a small, impatient movement: 'The picture's in my head, isn't it? It will stay there. What's it matter that I see him once more?'

'I'll need to call other people at once.'

'Of course. Will Iles come?'

'I meant the Scenes of Crime team.'

'Yes. Will Iles come?'

'Mr Iles is an Assistant Chief Constable, Mrs Dubal. He doesn't attend every incident.'

'This is an *incident*?'

'A technical word. Every crime.'

'But sometimes?'

'If he was especially interested,' Harpur replied.

'Would he be?' she said.

'Mainly a desk man now.'

'People might like to check they haven't left anything about.'

'Which people?' Harpur replied.

'Or have a gloat; a quiet gloat.'

'Which people?'

'Someone, maybe more than one, will regard this as a triumph. Dead *and* mangled. The city's into that kind of situation now, isn't it?'

'The phone call?' Harpur replied. 'You said it simply named this building?'

'Plus Ferdinand.'

' "Ferdinand. Logan's Warehouse," ' he repeated. 'That's all? Exactly.'

'Three words. Number withheld, naturally.'

'Male. No accent.'

'I've said. No accent I could recognize.'

He felt as he had when badgering Louise about precautions, as if getting her to chant the obvious was a kind of protective spell. Louise. Yes, Louise. Might she know anything about this? Wasn't she supposed to be doing her freelance, distance watch on Dubal now? Her head injuries didn't improve as swiftly as expected and she had only lately felt able to start this self-given duty. The concussion had lingered, the lack of focus in her eyes and fuzzed hearing. Technically, she was still sick: official explanation, a mugging. But she'd told him a week or so ago she could manage this kind of work now. So, how distant was distant? Wouldn't she have tried to reach Harpur if she'd seen Dubal attacked? She had all Harpur's numbers for any crisis moment between scheduled meetings. This would rate as a crisis moment. She would recognize that, surely to God. Bright girl, even if the hillside beating had upset her brain temporarily. It was mad, but for a second he found himself staring into the blackness of the warehouse wondering whether she might be lurking behind a pillar.

'Did you know Logan's, Mrs Dubal?' he asked.

'I'd read about the redevelopment in the Press. It gets mentioned. I came down and found it and him. Not difficult. I stayed a while. Of course. Grieved in my fashion, had a think. I remembered what Ferdinand had said about the police, but wondered if he'd realized how . . . how filthy, as he called it, things *could* become. How fully, deeply filthy.' She nodded towards the body. 'I decided to see you. Do you want to search him?'

'We leave things as they're found until Scenes of Crime have done their work.'

'Yes, yes, absolutely, but do you want to examine him before they come? I don't mind.'

Harpur said: 'There are procedures.'

Again that irritated little wave. She was pushing the rule book out of sight. 'It might put you ahead. You can control things better if you know more sooner.'

'Murder investigations are very much a team matter.'

'Oh? But, yes, police believe in teams, don't they? The members look after one another. That's what teams are for.'

'Teams are for finding the truth, usually bit by bit, each one in the team contributing,' Harpur replied.

'As long as the truth's all right for everyone in the team and above.'

'The truth,' Harpur replied.

'Does Iles suppose Ferdinand was behind Wayne Ridout's death? I ask because Ferdinand felt sure Iles thought so. Wayne and Iles had a long-time connection, didn't they? Close. And then Iles has been doing something with Wayne's daughter, hasn't he? Still?'

Harpur went forward and squatted down alongside Ferdy. Low life with low life. God, what kind of job was it that had you every so often breathing brick dust, glass powder, stone fragments, wood decay, blood odour? *His* kind. But he knew he fancied a bit of self-pity now and then. These derelict places had become convenient, unfrequented sites for murders. Not long ago, Harpur had found the body of a famed drug dealer, Elcri ap Vaughan, in a similar off-Broadway spot. It used to devastate Mark Lane that an area certain of a chic and worthy future should also be the place for present, terrible, routine violence. The former Chief saw depressing symbolism, felt violence and taint could never be removed, regardless of dinky new building.

Ferdy Dubal's eyes were open. They added to the childlike impression: large, brown, possibly puzzled, though that might be Harpur adding a bit. Folk did find it puzzling that someone wanted to kill them, even folk like

Ferdy, and even though two of his lads had been removed like that on the hill. Most people felt entitled to life and regarded early extinction as for others. You could not blame them: a survival need. Harpur gingerly unbuttoned the suede jacket. Ferdy was wearing a very plain tan leather shoulder holster tucked in on the left against his custom-made beige shirt. The holster was buttoned down. Just below the holster, Harpur saw a jagged, blood-touched rip in the shirt. This tear had not been made by car impact: too precise and small. Harpur hesitated for a couple of seconds before deciding to open the holster. It was interference. It flouted rules. What was he going to learn, anyway? That Ferdy went around armed? Harpur would have reckoned this, especially now peace on the streets grew so shaky. Worse than shaky. Was a shot then car-mashed, high-fly villain peace on the streets? As Mrs Dubal said, this displayed the new situation.

Harpur went back to the 106 and found a pair of plastic gloves, then bent down again near Ferdy, undid the holster and pulled out a .38 Llama Piccolo revolver, small but capable. It was fully loaded. He sniffed at the barrel. He'd seen gun people do that. The Piccolo had not been recently used. This, plus the buttoned-down flap, said Ferdy had tried no defence. So did you know and trust who did it, Ferd? Did Ferd trust *anyone* apart from his mother? Harpur replaced the pistol and fixed the holster.

'He was making his way, like any young careerist, simply that,' Mrs Dubal said. 'The gun – just an aid, like a laptop or mobile.' Harpur glanced up but could not see her properly because of the headlight glare. She seemed all right, her voice steady now. Perhaps what she told Harpur a little while ago was correct and she had gone through the worst of the shock when she first saw Ferdy. It was her shoes Harpur could examine best at present. She said: 'He wouldn't usually be around by himself, open to this sort of grossness, but he'd lost both boys who used to do the minding, Perce and Mildly Sedated. Did you know anything about that?'

'We're looking at it, of course.'
'This is six months plus.'
'Some investigations are very tough.'
'But you're still looking?'
'Certainly,' Harpur said.
'Did you have anything to do with it?'
'I'm head of CID, so I'm in charge of all inquiries. But one of my officers is handling it day-to-day.'
'No, I meant, did you have anything to *do* with it?'
'In what sense, Mrs Dubal?' Hunkered down like this, he felt battered by the questions. 'We can all contribute to the investigation.'
'Yes?'
'Certainly.'
'Might there be such a thing as a law and order killing, killings?' Mrs Dubal asked.
'There *were*, of course. Capital punishment. Still so in Texas. Not for us.'
'Unofficial.'
'In what sense?' Harpur replied.
'A hillside sense.'
'How could that be?'
'Why were Mildly and Perce out there?' Mrs Dubal replied. 'At night.'
'Obviously, we want to establish that.'
'After six months?'
'There are several theories.'
'Were they killed to protect someone?'
'Who?' Harpur replied.
'Who was with them?'
'Was anyone with them?' Harpur asked.
'*Was* anyone with them?' Mrs Dubal replied. 'This is a damn solitary place at night, as I understand. If they had something to do, that might be a place for it.'
'Something to do?'
'You know.'
'It *is* remote. That comes into our thinking, obviously.'
'This is what I meant by a law and order killing.'

'What?' Harpur asked.

'Say to save someone. If it was discovered they had someone up there. A rescue. I wondered occasionally if Ferdinand knew.'

'Knew what?'

'Knew who was with them,' she said.

'You're assuming someone *was*.'

'If he was even involved somehow.'

'Why do you say that, Mrs Dubal?'

'From the way Ferdinand spoke of the deaths.'

'He mentioned someone?' Harpur asked. 'Mentioned someone as being with Perce and Mildly?'

'The *way* Ferdinand spoke of it. As if he understood why it happened. Almost accepted why it happened,' Mrs Dubal replied. 'Tit-for-tat?'

'Did he say this?'

'I'm his mother. I know Ferdinand. Or, I know him up to where he'd closed things off to me.'

'Where was that?'

'I think he considered it was best – best for me. Best not to know everything. He wanted my image of him kept reasonably clean. There was a lovely consideration in Ferdinand.'

'So, what do you think you didn't know, Mrs Dubal?'

'Oh, plenty.'

'But can you guess at some of it?'

'And will this investigation – the one for Ferdinand – will this one also be very *difficult*, just like for Mildly and Perce?' she replied.

'I don't necessarily see a connection with the other two.'

'No, but will it be very difficult – I mean, will it get nowhere, like with those two?'

'I didn't say that inquiry is getting nowhere, Mrs Dubal.'

'Will the inquiry into Ferdinand's death unfortunately get nowhere? Do two kinds of justice operate?'

'Which two?'

'Oh, the courts, obviously. But then something outside, maybe even above, like vaguer. A righting of things privately, say on a hillside, say in an old warehouse.'

'That's not justice, Mrs Dubal. Not as I understand it.'

'How do you understand it?'

'Proper process,' Harpur said.

'But if proper process didn't work?'

'It has to.'

'Do all your colleagues believe in proper process?'

'This is how policing has to function, Mrs Dubal.'

'Do all your colleagues believe this is how policing has to function?' she replied.

'I must call the Scenes of Crime people here now.'

'Are things different under the new Chief? I mean different as far as investigations are concerned.'

'Mrs Dubal, whichever Chief is here, murder inquiries are murder inquiries and are pursued with all our energies and resources.' Harpur found it hard to sound weighty and meticulous folded down with Ferd and her shoes and he stood up.

'Someone like Mr Iles wouldn't be able to influence things so much now, would he?' she replied. 'No, not someone *like* Mr Iles. There isn't anyone like Mr Iles, is there. I mean, Mr Iles.'

Harpur wanted to stay with the matter-of-fact: 'Mr Iles is still Assistant Chief Constable, Operations, and a murder inquiry is an operation. I answer to him.'

'Yes, but can he *influence* things?'

'He'll naturally be kept informed throughout.'

'Throughout?'

'However long it takes.'

'How long will it take?' she asked.

'There are difficulties here. Nobody about, as witnesses.'

'As on the hillside.'

'I don't believe Ferdinand was killed by a vehicle,' Harpur replied.

'The bullet wound in his chest,' she said. 'Shot elsewhere, then brought here for the car treatment as an extra.'

The last words silenced Harpur briefly. 'The car treatment as an extra.' God, it sounded almost offhand, jokey.

'That's what I mean,' she said.

'What?'

'Someone giving a message, balancing up.'

' "Balancing up"?' Harpur replied.

'You know. Like: this is what happened to Wayne Ridout, and now it's *your* turn. Someone who likes vengeance and likes it to . . . well, yes, balance up. I've heard of this sort of thing. Wasn't there a detective killed once, and then a kind of . . . a kind of balancing up on the men accused of doing it? Or what someone *considered* a balancing up, regardless of acquittals?'

'This is another file that remains very much open,' Harpur replied.

'I'm sure. Ferdinand's father wanted him to go in for landscape gardening, you know, laying patios, that kind of thing. In his view patios were sure to come into their own with the spread of barbecues and improved sun-barrier cream, and it's turning out very accurate. But his father went off to Kenilworth with that flat-chested museum guide dame, so could Ferdinand respect his advice? It's on oddities like this that life and death can turn. His father was a sucker for anywhere with literary connections.'

'I found Ferdinand in some ways a –'

'Oh, he had swagger. No business judgement, though. Not like his father. To take on Ember, Shale, Iles – I mean, is this making things hard for yourself, or is it? Ember with all that civic cred – letters on high topics in the Press, children at pay schools. So Ferdinand wore a Piccolo revolver. All right, it's a man stopper, no question. Which man did it stop, though? Which man *didn't* it? Adornment. The holster still buttoned down like that. He'd discuss them – Ember, Shale, Iles. He rated all three, but thought himself able, just the same. Such confidence was part of his appeal, as all sorts would testify. Even looking at him there now, I can't regret that aspect of Ferdinand. He had a soiled distinction.'

'Mrs Dubal, I'm afraid the jails and House of Lords are full of people with soiled distinction.'

'But that must have been really some confidence, mustn't it, if it can't be crushed out of him even here? Although you don't come across many white Ferdinands in this country, this was a name that seemed to capture his aura and yet to which he added his own aura, as if he knew he had to live up to it, the name of many kings.'

Harpur reported in. Mrs Dubal went home. Harpur said he would stay with Ferdinand until colleagues arrived. He started the Peugeot engine to keep the battery up. It was December and icy. Once Mrs Dubal had left he began a proper search of the body. Even with her permission, he would have regarded it as unseemly to do that while she remained. Though she appeared controlled, he still could not have presumed. A search was invasive: less invasive than an autopsy, yes, but invasive. If Harpur's clothes became messed up he would have an explanation for the Scenes of Crime crew: he might have gone close only to see whether first aid would do anything, despite how far Dubal looked beyond it. The gloves were blood-soiled now and he took them off. Anything he touched he would have to wipe with a handkerchief.

He brought out Ferdinand's wallet from the breast pocket of his suede jacket. It was full of twenties and tens and half a dozen credit cards, plus some of his own very nicely embossed visiting cards, 'Ferdinand Dubal, Chairman and Chief Executive, Dubal Trading Enterprises.' They all craved to appear respectable and invented brilliant company names. In a way this offered comfort: respectability must have something going for it, and crookedness was only a path, a stage, like Saul on the road to Damascus. Ferdy had been pointed towards legitimate business by his dad and perhaps this influence stayed with him, although sublimated lately for the sake of collecting a fortune through crack and so on.

It surprised Harpur to come upon cash. In executions it could often be a ploy to take the victim's money and make things look like simple robbery, disguise the true motives. Perhaps that had seemed ludicrous, though: what robber would give a body such thorough car treatment, as Mrs Dubal called it? That would have nothing to do with simple robbery. He rubbed the wallet over and replaced it. One side pocket of the jacket was empty. In the other, his finger closed on an envelope. He brought it out. Dubal's initials appeared at the top right-hand corner in pencil. The seal was broken. Inside, he found three black-and-white photographs. They were poor in composition and light. Possibly they had been taken through a window or windows. All showed sections of a street, possibly the same street, what looked like a main thoroughfare, with shops. Harpur thought that given a couple of seconds and better visibility he would be able to identify it. Not important. What mattered was that Louise Machin appeared in all of them. Harpur did not realize it at once. On the first two he looked at she was part obscured, in one by a couple of elderly women and in the other by traffic. Focus was hazy. Harpur might not have recognized her, especially as the other people in both pictures could have been the subjects.

But the third photograph showed her full face from head on and with nobody else about. Although she had let her fair hair get long, and now wore it flat and pulled back to a couple of short pig-tails, the width from cheekbone to cheekbone and across her forehead was unmistakable. Harpur could almost bear her spouting one of her fucking indomitable arguments or destroying one of his. She had on a three-quarter length dark woollen coat with mock fur collar and cream or white silk scarf, highish black boots and some kind of skirt. It made a complete alteration from her gear and hair-do when undercover with Dubal –

another reason Harpur failed to know her on the other two photographs. With the third as key, though, it grew easy.

He put the pictures back into the envelope and then the envelope into his own breast pocket. He buttoned Ferdy's jacket again and straightened up. That was enough searching. He went and sat in the car, reduced to side lights and switched off the engine. He decided these were recent photographs. He had seen the changed hair length before but not the pig-tails and not the coat. Louise had given herself a new look because she was determined to observe Dubal undetected. That had not worked. Someone noticed her, but probably it was not Dubal himself. Why would he need to take pictures? He'd recognize her from her time with the firm. And he wouldn't forget someone he'd sent off with Perce and Mildly up the hill for elimination after questions. Some of Dubal's people might have seen her hanging around and done the camera work to show him. In one of those pictures you could guess she was on surveillance from the way she stood and her intentness. Louise might be clever and she could act, but she hadn't learned altogether yet how to blank her features. Perhaps in the six months since Jack Lamb on the hillside Dubal had taken on new staff to replace Perce and Mildly, staff unfamiliar with Louise but able to pick out a snoop. They'd tell Dubal and he'd order them to get pictures next time: delivery in an initialled envelope, for Ferd's brown eyes only.

So, what had happened to Louise? Why wasn't she here if she had tailed him? For the second time, he had that lunatic urge to penetrate the darkness. He backed the 106 a bit and changed its angle, then switched to main beam headlights again. Twice more he realigned the Peugeot and stared for a while. Afterwards, he returned to the spot where the car pointed at Ferdy and went back to side lights. He had seen nobody else in the warehouse. Of course he had seen nobody else, for fuck's sake. If Louise were here she would have come out of the blackness and joined him before now, wouldn't she? Why would she hide? This wasn't that multi-storey car-park meeting of Redford and Deep Throat in *All The President's Men*. Harpur knew his carry-on with the lights had been a barmy twitch, nothing better, like walking in the Valencia when she was undercover: just the compulsion to be sure she kept alive. But, if she was not here, where *was* she? A rough anxiety jabbed at him, yet he knew he could not leave to look for her. He had to hand over Ferdy.

The Scenes of Crime squad arrived with their lights and other gear. Not long afterwards, Iles appeared. He had on a dark brown, Afghan-tribesman type hat, woollen with sort of side walls over the ears and a flat summit – the kind rough weather would not blow away in the mountains if you went on patrol. The ACC wore also one of his magnificent dark grey, double-breasted suits, with yellow wellington boots. Over the suit and unbuttoned was a navy bum-freezer overcoat, this too in wool, supreme wool. His skin looked glossy and cared-for under the lights. He might have shaved before coming down here. His shirt gleamed. The tie had insignia but nothing large or garish, possibly signifying some Chief Police Officer grouping or a London club. He and Harpur stood near the 106, a good way from any of the Scenes of Crime party. Iles said: 'I certainly don't see this as answer to every problem on our ground, Col, though most likely positive. The Control Room said an anon call to his mother who then came to your place. That the picture?'

'She'd heard from Ferd that all police are shit but thought I might be slightly less shit than, say, you, sir,' Harpur replied. 'Plus, my address is in the phone book.'

'This eternal dispute, trouser turn-ups or no turn-ups. He wouldn't have them, would he? Did a fashion war kill him?'

'Mrs Dubal thinks you did it, of course.'

'People's mothers – I'm not one to pooh-pooh their instincts. They can suffer overwhelming guilt spasms. If they've produced someone of Ferdy's rottenness they almost *expect* him to finish like this. She would have tried to persuade him towards decency, and now in a tragic, conclusive way she's vindicated. There's a kind of terrible, *Didn't-I-tell-you-dear, Ferdinand*? satisfaction for them.'

'His father wanted him to do patios.'

'That kind of thing,' Iles replied.

'You think she'd see you as a holy moral force, then, sir, bringing due retribution?'

'Possibly without really knowing it, she'd be grateful that even in this new regime a kind of over-arching, natural soundness can prevail,' Iles said.

'She asked quite a bit about your status, stature, under the new Chief.'

'They do worry, these people. It's gratifying in a way, but a responsibility, in fact a burden,' Iles replied. He went nearer to Ferdy and bent over him. 'I expect you had to do a quick, very close examination in case he needed the kiss of life, Col. Explains why there's blood on you.'

'Instinctive.'

'Ah! This is what makes the human race human,' Iles replied. 'To pick up a word of yours, we're all always committed to finding and preserving the least holy tremor of life, aren't we?'

Iles was keen on answers to his questions. Harpur said: 'He doesn't seem to have a vehicle anywhere.'

'You've lifted whatever you wanted from the clothes, have you, you fucking early-bird bandit?' Iles replied.

'I thought it best to wait for the Scenes people, sir.'

'I don't categorize any man just because he clings to his mother, Col.'

'I'm not sure what level his trade was at,' Harpur replied. 'Probably still below a hundred K.'

Iles looked about. 'Do gays use this place? Their jealousies can be appallingly vicious and theatrical. Display's so important to them. They'd like the elaborateness of a death plus disfigurement. Oh, I suppose you'll say *anyone* can become destabilized by jealousy, hetero or homo.' The Assistant Chief's voice grew suddenly edgy and loud, rolled around the warehouse interior and came back as a heavy, heartfelt blurt to where he stood over Ferdy's corpse. 'You'd no doubt argue, Harpur, that occasionally when I refer to, for instance, you and my wife I can become a little less placid than usual, you non-stop, frenzied pussy poacher.' Most of the Scenes of Crime boys and girls seemed to have heard this mode of reflection from Iles before and went on with their duties. 'Me?' Iles yelled. 'You'd accuse *me* of jealousy, Harpur? Oh, really. Why in God's name should I suffer jealousy? Now, when Sarah and I discuss that episode, and we *do* discuss it, in an entirely relaxed, sweet-humoured, measured and –'

Harpur said: 'But someone like Ferdy is probably never going to listen to direct advice from a parent about his line of work, is he, sir? Self-belief was one of Ferd's things. He'd want to make his own selection.'

'In any case, Col, someone close to his mother doesn't *have* to be gay,' Iles replied. 'My own mother had quite considerable streaks of worth and I didn't mind being with her now and then for as much as three-quarters of an hour. The anon call to Mrs Dubal – not with a Bronx accent this time?' The photographer wanted to do shots of Ferdy and Iles moved away.

Harpur said: 'Mrs Dubal doesn't expect anyone will be charged with the Ferdy killing.'

'I see. In that strange, subconscious fashion I spoke of, she needs to regard his death as caused by some abstract yet infallible power of Purity, Col, indeed, of Justice. Listen, when you think of me do you think of me as happy?'

'We'll get quite a bit from tyre tracks in the surface muck here, and they might be able to tell us the weight of the vehicle when they've looked at Ferd's bones,' Harpur replied.

On his way home, he drove to near Louise's flat and parked. Lights burned there and he felt comforted. One window was uncurtained and after about five minutes he saw her cross the room and a little while afterwards all the lights went out. He felt even more comforted. He returned to Arthur Street. There were lights on here, too, although it was after 2 a.m. Nobody seemed to be about. The television had been left on. He assumed the boys had gone and the girls were in bed. He tore up small the photographs of Louise and the envelope and flushed them down the lavatory. He had a couple of drinks, switched off the television and lights, looked in on Hazel and Jill asleep and went to bed on his own. Things could be like this sometimes. Denise would not move in properly, although he and his daughters had asked her to often enough, God knew. They loved it when Denise was here for breakfast. It gave them the sense of full family. Probably Denise had not even told her parents about Harpur: the age business, the daughters business, the freedom business. She could badly hurt him now and then. No, more often than that. Sometimes, in one of his major morose sessions, he could feel really uncared for.

Harpur slept until nine o'clock and was just about to leave for a daylight look at Logan's Warehouse when Louise telephoned. The children must have given themselves breakfast and gone to school. 'I've just heard,' Louise said.

'Dubal? I thought you might have known.'

'On local radio news.'

'Weren't you behind him? You've been watching Dubal since you got better, haven't you? Almost better.'

'Wouldn't I have been in touch if I'd seen something like that?'

'Yes, of course.'

'What's that mean?' she asked.

'Yes, of course.'

'What are you saying, sir?'

'That you'd obviously have been in touch if you'd seen anything.'

'But you don't believe it?' she replied.

'Why say that? You're getting subtle and intellectual, Louise.'

'That's bad?'

'Simplicity's my thing.'

'Bollocks, sir. *Things* are not simple, are they? You're saying, are you, that I wanted Dubal dead because he would have had me killed, and because in any case his people fucked up my head by pistol whipping? I'm Ms Revenge, am I? So, I stay quiet about who did him last night? That your view?'

'He would certainly have had you killed,' Harpur replied.

'You think I've picked up the tone of how things happen here, don't you?'

'There's a tone?' Harpur replied.

'Settle things ourselves, then keep quiet.'

'Mrs Dubal said something like that.'

'She's clever, is she?'

'Which ourselves?'

'You know,' she said. 'But this is an open line.'

'*Were* you behind Dubal last night?'

'He knew how to lose me. What you'd expect, I suppose.'

'No, I wouldn't,' Harpur replied. 'You're a gifted girl.'

'So, you think I saw it but won't say?'

'Lost you where?'

'Oh, not far from his own place. He seemed to spot me at once.'

'Lost you how?'

'You know – roundabouts, one way streets. I'm not trained to all that. Like with Ember and the Hobart. And I'm still a bit slow, not through-and-through fit. There's a medical certificate.'

'Alone?'

'Yes, he was alone.'

'Driving what?'

'An Impreza. Lots of acceleration. Almost it was as if he knew I'd be about.'

'How could that be?'

'Maybe I was seen lurking on previous visits.'

'How often have you watched him before?'

'Three times, since I got my eyes and ears and brain back, more or less.'

'Did he seem to spot you then?'

'No, but I think he's got other people hanging about his places – the offices and his house.'

'People you recognized from your time in the firm?'

'No. But people who looked as if they might belong to him. Not vicars. People who notice.'

'Tailing's an art,' Harpur replied.

'All right, all right. Possibly a camera.'

'Oh, God, snaps of you?'

'You knew that, did you?' she said.

'How could I?'

'I don't know. Things happen here. They're not explained. I've said that already. It's still true. That's what I meant – you think I've become a part of it.'

'Of what?'

'You assume I've absorbed the culture values. Have I?' she asked.

He was not sure whether she wanted him to say he did think it or didn't. 'Part of what?' he replied. 'Tone? Culture values? Your mind's too fast for me.'

'I don't think so,' she said.

Chapter Eight

Ember took E.W. Fenton with him to see the new importer. They drove to North Wales. Things in serious commerce could happen like this: no time ago E.W. was just a no-rank hanger-on, but had become lately more or less vital to the firm and useful in quite large negotiations. It looked to be the same in Manse Shale's outfit. That fucking one-time insolent, loud-mouth chauffeur of his, Denzil, seemed to have moved up to almost boardroom recently. During Ralph's foundation year at university they had studied a novel called *The Great Gatsby,* about the American dream, so-called, showing how someone poor with no breeding could rise in the business and social realm. In the British drugs trade that dream seemed still around, as long as the dream was backed by luck and work. Fenton could show a bit of both. Of course, his clothes had to be a drawback and that heavy-skinned face with the strangely small nose, but Ember would talk to him soon about the clothes. And sitting alongside him in the front of a car you did not have to look at his cheeks and nose too much. Thank God for scenery. In Wales there was plenty.

Ralph still did not know whether Fenton acted for London interests, but if he did he took care not to tout them to Ember. One reason for bringing him to North Wales was to show Fenton that Ralph made this kind of major choice – picking a new importer – entirely solo. Ember would certainly not have feared handling the visit alone. Hinton Quarat was hardly the first big importer he had met and discussed circumstances with. But Ralph decided it might be useful to let E.W. see how several facets of the Ember firm worked, not just its disregard for London. As Number One, you had a general educational, mentoring role, and Ember tried never to slip out of a duty.

Fenton drove part of the way. He did not talk too much and Ember had a chance to do a wide survey in his head of how things looked now. The answer to that was, difficult but all right, he thought. Whenever Ralph counted his assets like this he felt not so much pride as grateful wonderment. Modesty he prized. First and supremely in any inventory of strengths came his family, of course. Margaret had been and remained a superb wife, and there were all kinds of times when he longed to be totally faithful. Loyalty would seem to Ralph then the only right response to someone who gave him so much, helped him so much, and in fact he *was* very often totally faithful. But for his looks – the damn Chuck Heston resemblance – it would have been easy. Despite what he knew he owed Margaret, he suffered from a sort of undodgeable liability to humour other women who craved closeness with him. This liability was only humane, yet it could become a burden. The scar on his jaw fascinated some of these women and they would stroke it excitedly, as if this put them in touch with Ralph's confidential inner being. But to a notable extent his inner being existed for Margaret only. She deserved to know him best.

Ralph's Saab left the motorway and took smaller roads. Mountains were about now. They looked grey and bolshy, not easy for Ralph to feel fond of. He said: 'You're armed, are you?'

'The Walther, as a matter of fact,' Fenton replied.

'A good weapon.'

'I thought about it a lot.'

'Thought about it too long,' Ember replied. Six months ago Fenton had been looking for new armament for Ralph and eventually came up with the Walther. It was *very* eventually, and by the time Fenton moved, of course, Ember had been to the Hobart and supplied himself through Amy and Leyton Harbinger. He trusted this would give a message to Fenton: Get urgent, when it's something for Ralph. The silence resumed for a spell and he could go on with the comforting situation report to himself. Margaret and he had two splendid daughters, the older one, Venetia, aged thirteen, at school in France for the present, to moderate her sexuality after a dicey situation here. She was apparently cooling nicely and getting quite academic: the French understood those things. Then Ember could also think about his home, Low Pastures, a beautiful country house with grounds, many of the inside walls genuine exposed stone going right back through centuries. Finally, he delighted in the glorious potential of the Monty club as a distinguished meeting spot and conference venue, and in his business concerns altogether. What he had achieved conferred stability, brought him rare poise.

'This is a meeting that might give no problems at all,' Ember said. 'Most of what I hear about Hinton is very acceptable. I gather the word "gentlemanly" has been used of him. All right, that could mean only he gets ear hair trimmed by the barber, but I feel sure weaponry won't be needed.'

'I'll condition my behaviour to yours, Ralph,' Fenton replied.

Ralph recognized that qualities like stability and poise, which came to him through unwavering family support, had grown crucial now, at a time of worryingly deep changes on every fucking side of the game. This North Wales trip was part of those changes. Staring ahead at the rough bulk of the mountains, he decided he did not like that last remark from E.W., 'I'll condition my behaviour to yours, Ralph.' He heard a kind of cockiness. It was something that should not have to be said. Of *course* this flunkey had to condition his behaviour to Ralph's as far as gunplay went. They would be delicate talks with Quarat. Did E.W. imagine he could just pull out a Walther if he felt like it and start popping, without any go-ahead from his leader? To say he agreed to condition his behaviour to Ember's suggested he had a choice. The sod didn't. That had better be made clear. Ember said: 'At this level there are large tensions, yes, but very few end in bullets.'

'I understand.'

'Make sure you fucking do, then,' Ralph replied. He considered this a measured and deserved comment to E.W., not in any way rude or extreme. Control he revered as much as modesty. Some men would undoubtedly have lost their equilibrium, hit by all the sudden enormous shifts in conditions affecting sales. It was not just the developments at police headquarters and around the trading area, though these had been grossly unhelpful. Four savage deaths certainly caused disquiet. He would attribute them directly to the commercial nerviness brought on by Mark Lane's departure from the Chiefdom, and the impact this could have on the policy of Desmond Iles. It was true that in the past, even during the most settled spells of peace on the streets, there might be a sudden surge of violence. But this was *all* it would be: a very brief, unexpected dip from the normal. And the normal always soon resumed then, having its own lovely, self-healing power. Now appeared different. Ember could feel a whole, brilliantly unique and constructive police strategy start to splinter: the strategy of wise realism and clever tolerance.

He had often heard it said that British policing had to be by consent. Although Iles was in many ways just a screaming, all-out hooligan with insignia, he had sensitively brought about that consent, not just from Ember and Mansel Shale but people quite low in the firms, and even from the late Dubal. Today, sadly, it was all threatened.

Fenton said: 'Will Quarat be on his own in this house?'

'Mansion, I gather. We assume he's not, even if it looks as if he is.'

'Right.'

'We sit where we can cover all doors, as well as him,' Ralph said.

Ember had met Quarat before, of course, but never in his own property. Although this type of visit always carried risk, it had to happen. The upheaval in police command was not the only anxiety Ralph faced lately. Bulk supply of most trade substances to his businesses had been endangered for a while following grim spells of terrible warfare among importers on the south coast: far away, maybe, but with grave effects for Ralph. Only recently had he managed to establish what he prayed would be a suitable, new, long-term arrangement with this prime freight-master, Quarat. He had one of his homes in North Wales. Ralph was invited there now for a talk on prospects.

Possibly the name Hinton Quarat had been made up or got from an atlas or archaeology news item, but people at high levels of the business might be entitled to their tricks, especially if they had a record. For a while, following the south coast battles among importers, Ember considered going into that side of the trade himself. People had been killed down there, so good chances to replace them suddenly appeared. But the new general uncertainty in the commercial scene because of Lane's removal made Ember reconsider and decide this was not a wise moment for change. He would accept risk, but despised foolhardiness.

'Quarat's probably going to be as worried as we are,' Fenton said. 'To him we're unknown, like he is to us.'

'I'm not *worried,*' Ember replied at once. 'I'm ready, that's all. I won't be unknown to him. He'll have heard of my work. And we've met.'

'Of course. I meant he won't know you thoroughly, over time.'

'I hope I'm able to convey the kind of integrity he'll be looking for, in the same way as I am looking for it in him.'

'This is one of your most remarkable attributes, Ralph –

the ability to convince others of your integrity and steadiness.'

'Because they are real,' Ember replied. 'They are crucial now. Integrity always so, naturally, but steadiness, yes, invaluable, I'll admit.'

The main requirement from Quarat was some trustworthiness, plus bulk prices that allowed a fair retailing take on the streets and in the pubs, seminaries, restaurants, students' unions and rave clubs. For Ralph, the £600,000 profit mark had become a sort of basic requirement, a touchstone, and he grew concerned if it seemed jeopardized: not stupidly frantic but aware. So far Quarat's prices had been tolerable. The trustworthiness was just something you had to hope for and discover or not by testing. Like E.W., Ralph had a full-magazine pistol aboard. He felt very capable, very blessed.

Not, not, not smug, though. He could have sympathized with anyone who, when faced with all these recent uncertainties and readjustments, thought of giving up, or who tumbled into ill-health. Ralph knew it was his wonderfully settled personal situation that propped him, enabled him to cope with the stresses while preserving such fine calm. Once or twice he had even considered bringing Margaret into the business, she was such a consolation. Occasionally, he would remark to her that chaos loomed. She deserved to know the situation. Her replies always dealt with his obligation to show patience, faith in himself, resolution. By suggesting these qualities lay without question available to Ralph she actually *made* them available to him. Her belief in him was understandable, but also an inspiration. This in his view amounted to wifeliness. He knew he could triumph. The geography might be nauseating but he would not collapse.

Up Bala way, Hinton Quarat had bought a former pit owner's baby castle overlooking quite a valley with a proper lake in it, the water dark and very Welsh-looking under low, grey clouds. Now, Fenton took the Saab along a drive lined with trees. Ralph had decided ultimately that perhaps it was better if Margaret stayed apart from the firms, at least immediately, and so he had let E.W. take more power in the office, brought him on this important journey. Despite that doziness with the gun and some streaks of stupid vanity, E.W. had earned a small promotion, and at least his driving seemed reasonable. In any case, Ralph did not have anyone else of even middling calibre around him at present.

Quarat led them into a first-floor drawing room with huge sliding windows offering a view of the lake if that's what you wanted. The windows gave on to a green-painted wooden veranda. A woman of about twenty-eight was already seated in the room, a notebook on her lap. Quarat introduced her as Julia. He went to a sideboard and poured hock for all of them and brought the glasses to each himself. When everyone had sat down he said: 'My feeling, lads, is we'll have to get rid of Mansel Shale.'

Christ, Ember had, of course, considered that way back but to hear someone speak it as a proposal shocked him. 'How do you mean, "get rid", Hinton?' Ember asked. He had a good spot, facing Quarat direct, and with one of the main doors to the room on his half right. That 'lads' amused Ember. It showed jumpiness in Quarat. He wanted to get them diminished from the start, treat them as youngsters. This could be partly on account of E.W.'s kid-size nose and the handed-down look to his clothes.

'Yes, we had quite a lengthy discussion up here on the veranda and so on on a rather warmer day than this, and at the end of it there remained some points of difference, sure, but what we all agreed on, Ralph, was that Shale had to be taken out,' Quarat replied. 'The veranda sold this place to me.'

'I do love a veranda myself,' Ember said.

'A veranda is part of a house and yet also part of the sublime surrounding environment,' Quarat replied. He could get a real glow on his features when speaking of verandas. He was long-faced with a small fair moustache, lieutenant-colonel-looking, able to build Bailey bridges.

His hair was fair, too, and kept long but plastered down. You could imagine him with a UN blue beret on bringing order and reconciliation to some civil war region.

Ember decided to misunderstand for the moment. 'Buy Shale out?' he asked. 'I don't think that, despite all the uncertainties, Manse would be willing to –'

'No, of course he wouldn't sell, Ralph.'

Ember said: 'So, "taken out" to mean –'

'Taken out, Ralph,' Quarat replied. 'Obviously, I'm really happy to have an association with you and your companies, but I find these deaths down there disturbing – in the Press and on television. I wouldn't wish to be connected with that kind of lawlessness in any way. Not to be pious about it, but one has an image to guard.'

Ember really adored this: probably the biggest fucking shipper unhung in the European Union, with a name like Hinton Quarat, and he's got an image to look after! One thing about Ember was he knew how to keep laughter off his face and out of his voice. He said: 'My view, and I know E.W.'s, too, is that these killings are the result of a few very minor realignments, Hinton. Things have settled again. There'll be no repeat.'

'Right,' E.W. said.

Obviously, Quarat would not be Welsh himself, with a name like that, even if it was false. But excellent big places could be picked up as bargains in these far-out spots now mine owners and iron and steel barons didn't exist. Twenty or thirty years ago, the Welsh used to burn down properties taken over by people from outside, especially the English, because it brought a local housing shortage. But something as big as this place would not get that treatment. Your ordinary Welsh worker in the slate quarries or underground power station did not want it, and the veranda would not persuade them. Ember liked the way Quarat spoke only to him, not to E.W. at all. Quarat knew where the stature and power were.

It was a 9 mm Browning Ralph had holstered under his jacket from that Hobart jaunt, although he'd always hated going into someone's house carrying a gun. That invariably struck him as distasteful, something not at all in line with the fine serenities of home life which we all sought. But you could hardly visit a vast fucking den in mountains like this, owned by someone with a fucking name like Quarat, and not be ready to blast back. There were thirteen rounds in the magazine. E.W.'s Walther would hold fifteen, also 9 mm. So, how many people did Quarat have about? When was the environmentally lovely discussion on the veranda? That sounded like more than just himself and Julia. Had the others stayed on somewhere?

'I'm not sure I follow your thinking, Hinton,' Ember said. 'These deaths are very distant from you here in your fine residence. Taint can't come your way.'

'*You're* down there, Ralph. The taint could touch *you*. You come my way, don't you?'

Ember said: 'I'm here today, yes, but –'

'We don't see the death of Ferdinand Dubal as minor,' Quarat replied.

'The general view is he wasn't even up to a hundred K,' Ember said.

'Nowhere near,' E.W. said.

'But improving,' Quarat replied. 'I asked Julia here to do a full study on your area when those things started getting into the media.'

'It was my recommendation to Hinton that Mansel Shale shouldn't be allowed to continue, nor Denzil, his aide, of course,' Julia said. 'Fortunately, Dubal's gone.'

'Julia's been down there, you see, Ralph. I haven't. I'm bound by her advice.'

Ralph had thought Julia was some sort of secretary to do minutes, but he realized now she must be more. She was athletic-looking, tall, a little bony, her smile very cheerful. 'I expect we're only telling you something you already know, Ralph,' she said. 'A business strategist of your experience and grasp would realize instantly that in the new circumstances on your patch only monopoly is a tolerable state or we can expect continual violence and deaths.'

'Julia's done a very thorough analysis, uncontestable in my view,' Quarat said.

'In essence, it's simple,' Julia said. 'The working treaty with Shale – and to a lesser extent with Dubal – this could only function inside the peace conditions created and maintained by Iles. I think I agree with you, incidentally, on Dubal's trading profit, about £80,000 rising.'

'Julia did a lot of work on indicators for Dubal's firm,' Quarat said.

'As it happens, a bit superfluous, given the death,' Julia replied and smiled wider still.

'Yet instructive, surely,' Quarat said.

'Unless you act, Ralph, we'll have a classic business catastrophe in your area,' Julia said. 'But you've probably foreseen this, and E.W. will certainly have foreseen it.'

That enraged Ember. Was this cow saying E.W. spotted things better than he did? Where was E.W. supposed to have picked up such skills? How did she know more about E.W. than Ralph did? Ember said: 'Well, yes, of course, I've done a general overview of possibilities.'

'Anyone au fait with your reputation would expect that, Ralph,' Quarat said.

'A proactive, aggressive police force – the kind you'll get now in the area, Ralph, E.W. – that kind of force has a standard way of blitzing firms like yours and Shale's and Dubal's if he'd lived,' Julia said. 'An attack is made on the dogsbody people of one of the outfits – street dealers, runners, minders. Raids, arrests, all the small-hours terrorism stuff. Takings slowly go down. In a while, rival dealers move in on the trading spots cleared by the police. The targeted firm has to fight back or shrink to where recovery becomes impossible. Open, feverish turf war. The companies do the police's job for them, decimating each other. When the firms have weakened themselves enough, the police go in and annihilate what's left. I've seen it first hand in Liverpool and heard of it in Manchester, half the inner London boroughs and Newcastle. I expect E.W. could give us other examples.'

'All written about in studies. But monopoly means a firm can take losses for a time in one sector, even two or three,' Quarat said. 'It has the reserves to let sectors lie inactive temporarily. And there's no question of other companies getting in and working a takeover during the lull. That's the crux.'

'Monopoly *is* beautiful,' Julia said. 'Well, I'd say is *indispensable* unless you have the kind of sweetly created peace structure that existed in your realm, but which is sure to come apart now.'

'We're not saying you as you to kill Shale and Denzil,' Quarat remarked, laughing.

'Monopoly gives you a projected profit level of £1,280,000. And that's without expansion. A little bit of that could be intelligently spent on contract folk,' Julia said. 'Say the £80,000 coming from Dubal's. A one-off investment. Shale will have his security, especially now things have grown strained. Good people can get around that, though, if the fee's rosy enough.'

Quarat said: 'But a kind of friendship is bound to have developed between you and Shale, and you wouldn't want to be involved yourself in this kind of ploy, Ralph, regardless of how unavoidable, even necessary. This is natural. Admirable. From all I hear he has a decent side. Best leave it to outsiders.'

'And you've gone for some extra security yourself, Ralph, I see,' Julia said. 'That bonny shield in the Monty. An E.W. idea, I imagine.'

'Obviously, Ralph, we approve of any defence measures like that,' Quarat said. 'You are a very promising customer, someone worthy to build monopoly with, capable of running it, nurturing it, developing it, and your skin is precious to us.'

'Thanks, Hinton,' Ember replied.

'Plus, of course, precious to your family and staff,' Quarat said. 'Julia was truly impressed, I know, by the way people spoke of your devotion to your wife and daughters and pushers at all levels of the game.'

'Thanks, Hinton, Julia,' Ember replied.

'This is a real strength,' Quarat said.

'I was thinking of it as we drove here,' Ember said.

'That family backing – the confidence springing from it – that family backing is in fact one of the factors which persuades me you could head-up a monopoly, Ralph, and do justice to the materials we supply,' Quarat said.

'In the car I was actually conscious of the sort of physical . . . physical *entity* of myself produced by the grand trust of my wife and daughters,' Ember replied. 'I hope this doesn't sound vain. I attribute it not to myself but to them.'

Quarat said: 'Certainly. A daughter, well under-age and in danger of shagging around – to remove her to a fine establishment at Poitiers, this is the action of a considerate father, in our view. It signifies more than this one act. It symbolizes wonderful empathy and empathy is always a two-way process.'

'Bilingualism will be such an asset as we draw ever closer to Europe,' Ember said.

'Possibly just provide a setting for these people,' Quarat replied.

'Which?' Ember asked.

'Get Shale lined up for them somewhere. That's the nearest to complicity you should go,' Quarat replied.

'For instance, I gather you have partnership meetings now and then in an hotel,' Julia said.

'That would be perfect,' Quarat said. 'Does he get full of booze, cavorting about in a tuxedo? A bright white shirt front is great for fixing one's sights on.'

'Denzil's never far from him,' Ember replied. 'And Denzil stays sober because of the driving. He still does that, although he helps runs the companies now at exec level. Even wears a chauffeur's cap occasionally to show how mighty Manse is.'

'Denzil will probably have to go as well,' Quarat said.

Fenton said: 'This would put Ralph a bit close to matters, wouldn't it, if it happened at a business meeting, or even on the road to or from? People like Harpur and possibly Iles would know these meetings take place. Harpur gets a lot of whispers. Because he doesn't do anything about the meetings doesn't mean he's unaware. Shale and Denzil wiped out there in the present unrelaxed circumstances and he'll think Ralph, Ralph, Ralph, and probably so will Iles.'

'That's possible,' Quarat replied.

'Yes, perhaps,' Julia said.

Ember hated this – E.W., a damn caddie, talking like Ralph's guardian, as though he lacked a brain bright enough to see hazards. This was the sod so slow getting a gun that Ember had to rush down to the Hobart in person. What sort of guardian was that, then? What kind of brain failed to realize how fast Ember had needed a new piece? 'E.W.'s always alert to tactical snags, Hinton, Julia,' he said. 'I just listen, do what I'm told.' He chuckled for a while, someone big enough to admit his dependence now and then on a small-time artisan, as, say, the pianist Barenboim might be on his page-turner.

And then butlers. Obviously, when there was one of these you watched him hard and as near to non-stop as you could throughout a meal or drink-up. Ralph had been at several places with a butler before. In this kind of house, a butler would know all the dining-room skills, yes, but he might have others, also. When Quarat took them downstairs to lunch, Ember immediately saw a butler, wearing dark coat and striped trousers, like Anthony Hopkins in *The Remains of the Day,* and two waiters. This seemed quite a force to serve four people. Force. Ember would have felt easier if the waiters had been waitresses, or at least one of them.

No, not a sexual or sexist matter but, generally, waitresses would turn out to be genuine waitresses and unarmed. There seemed to be no Mrs Quarat, in this house, at least. Perhaps Julia was Mrs Quarat, or its equivalent for now. She looked loose-limbed. Nobody else joined them at the long, thin table. It was pretty: glass-topped over white material or board decorated with red and blue oblongs. The edges of the glass were trimmed with wood, perhaps cherry. The dining chairs of blue leather had high backs and narrow seats. They presumed slim arses – people who were fit from climbing mountains around the lake. The floor was multicoloured terrazzo and uncovered. Ember thought that in its way this rated as a really tasteful, modern room. Blood could be swabbed off stone no trouble. The butler probably would not do this himself but order some lower servant to see to it. 'The staff are entirely discreet,' Quarat said. 'We simply continue our conversation while we eat.' Ember reckoned this did make them very special staff.

'That's right, isn't it, Ron?' Quarat asked.

'The well-being of guests is our only concern,' the butler replied. He had a great, butler-type voice, slow and no ragged edges. It could be extremely genuine. Too much smiling would have made him creepy when he said this so he stayed grave.

'As if we was not even here – except, as Ron so rightly remarked, to give service,' the smaller waiter said.

'Unnoticed yet noticing, unintrusive and yet attentive,' the other one said. The waiters wore white shirts, dark trousers, black shoes. This was an undoubted show.

'They've worked together for years, Ron, Greville and Kit,' Quarat said. 'They know one another's every move. It's delightful to watch. Ron's pantry is quite a little nerve centre, isn't it, Ron?'

'I tell them – tell Greville and Kit – I tell them we have a role, and a *worthy* role,' Ron replied. 'I believe I've taught them to think of us as a team, yes. I've helped them see that service and dignity are partners.'

There'd be other people in the kitchen, although Ember could not work out how many. Quarat had a real cook and the food was grand: a vegetable soup, lamb and Welsh cheeses with handwritten labels giving the authentic names, bags of Ll's. More wine appeared, white and red, all of it quite a way above OK. Kit did the pouring. Wine must be one of his specialities. The glassware and crockery were brilliant. It did not worry Quarat to show visitors he'd become gorgeously rich from the profits of supplying people like Ember. To be tactful, some of these importers acted hard-up. Ralph felt he was getting looked after here in a style to suit his status. You certainly could not always rely on this from a principal importer. Besides playing poor, some were rude and fucking lordly. Also, Quarat would know Ralph ran a club which after a few adjustments might soon be of towering distinction socially, and was therefore familiar with the best catering.

During the lamb, E.W. said: 'If you're dealing with someone holding a monopoly, Hinton, I take it we could expect a really worthwhile all-round discount on our purchase prices from you. We'd be providing a grand, uncontested market for your freight, and there would, of course, be all the benefits of quantity.'

Christ, who authorized him to talk like that, jumping in like negotiator-in-chief? E.W. kept on munching happily as he spoke, he stayed so comfortable, the fucker. Ember almost snarled at him, but it was best not to look divided in a room with a floor of this kind.

'We would certainly be open to that sort of give-and-take discussion, once dominance is assured,' Julia replied. Ember could see she really believed E.W. mattered. 'We thought close negotiation on terms, that sort of thing, this afternoon, with variables embodied – preferential rates rising as sales rise.'

'Well, yes, we'll want something substantive from the trip,' Fenton said.

Kit, who was giving Quarat some Beaune with quite a professional hold on the base of the bottle, said: 'Economy through scale can, of course, be questioned in some instances, but as to the case Mr E.W. is describing I think it a formidable point.'

'Admittedly we have the so far unknown impact of a

new Chief,' Fenton replied. The words just came, still all relaxed and irresistible. 'It could be that the monopoly would take a bad reverse or two occasionally. But, as Hinton says, it should have the strength to survive this.'

'I don't know no detail, that's as obvious as obvious,' Greville said, 'but what I get the feeling of is that we got a very promising situation here, and one what's going to be run with real sharpness so it can stand up all right in any new system.' He was very square built with a big, round head and big, thick hands. Nothing in his face suggested he'd ever taken a beating. An amiable, thoughtful face. Ember had seen opera stars with faces like this Mozarting on TV.

'My own feeling is Mansel Shale should be done in his home, the old St James's rectory,' Fenton replied.

Greville said: 'With names like that, do you know what I can never, ever sort out? – I can never, ever sort out if it got to be just St James' or St James's.'

'There'd be some security,' Julia said. 'I had a drift around the outside, very cursory, I'll admit.'

'It's tidy to kill someone in their home,' Fenton said. 'Tidy in the sense of *un*tidy.' Quarat had one of his fucking laughs at that, like gratitude in the presence of wit. He was really listening to this bastard and his gibberish, the same as Julia. Fenton would take over if you gave even a bit of an opening, or if you didn't. There might be something about this glass-topped table that made him think he had moved up to a company partnership with Ralph. Later, Fenton could be asked to forget that idea, *really* asked. Most people had plenty of self-belief and conceit, and it only needed some special item mysteriously to set these qualities into play. For E.W. it might be the glass-topped table. Fenton said: 'By untidy, I mean if someone's killed at home there's a whole mix-up of possible motives and suspects – burglary, domestic hates, suicide, a contract. Oh, yes, the contract would be in the list of options, I admit, but only one in a nice untidy cluster. Which makes it *tidy* and safe for us, you see. Whereas, snuff someone at a meeting or on their way to or from a meeting and the first people the police look at is the others at the meeting. Gatherings like that tell a story, or half a story. Did they do it themselves, did they hire a crew? That's how the police think.'

'This is probably a pretty sharp look at things, Hint,' Greville remarked.

'Yet, because the home *is* so suitable, and is known to be so suitable, experienced people like Shale are probably at their most careful and alert there,' Ron said. 'For example, here, in this house, I must say, we keep an eye. Julia, you admit your look at the place was only rudimentary. You wouldn't be able to do a proper check for alarms and so on.'

'Oh, true,' Julia replied.

Ron brought a handsome palely decorated serving dish of sprouts to Ember and replenished his plate with three more. It was beautifully done. You could tell Ron would always have mastery of any sprout he provided, so it would not roll off the plate and especially not into anyone's lap. To regard him as a butler had to be very reasonable in some ways, thick, dark hair brushed almost straight back over his ears. Ralph said: 'I don't feel we've really talked about the sort of . . . sort of *principle* of killing Manse.' There had been a time when, on his own, Ralph accepted that principle, saw Manse's extermination as necessary. Now, it struck him as crude and vicious of people like Quarat, Julia, E.W. and the butler to discuss it so comfortably. Intruders. Outsiders.

'I could see you were a little bothered, Ralph,' Quarat replied, 'leaving most of the talk to E.W.'

E.W. took it, fuck him. Ralph said: 'We've jumped to the methods. Perhaps the major question has been sidetracked.'

'That can happen in discussion,' Kit replied. 'A main factor is taken for granted by some speakers but is deeply problematical for others. I think there may be a term for dealing with this in medieval disputations – rejection of the opponent's major premise, which, of course, destroys also the minor assumptions that follow from it.' He was almost delicate-looking, thin and too tall, skin pulled very tight across his cheekbones, nose and chin, as if only a couple of steps from being transparent. Yet he must be able to shift wine bottle corks that stuck in the neck.

'I hope we don't have to speak of "opponents",' Quarat said. 'I want to believe that as we break bread together here we're all concerned with the same good, basic end, Kit, Ralph. Surely, nobody would question the glowing merits of monopoly in the new setting.'

Ember said: 'Manse can undoubtedly be a lout and a degenerate, the same as anyone with that kind of background, but –'

'Like this,' Fenton replied. He brought three pieces of folded blue paper from an inside pocket and cleared a large space on the glass table-top to spread them. They were about ten inches by fifteen. Fenton put a palm on two sheets in turn: 'The two upper floors in the rectory.' He put a palm on the other: 'Ground floor.' Ember looked at the plans. They were neat and professional. You could have framed them to decorate a wall, the way some people did with machine drawings. Good God, when had he done all this and how? And another how – how did he know these plans would be wanted here today? 'The main security is Denzil, who has a flat on the top floor.' E.W. indicated one of the sheets which showed second-storey rooms. 'There's a communication system with him, of course.' He pointed a finger at several small circles drawn on all the plans. 'Internal phones. Plus, naturally, they're both carrying mobiles most of the time. I don't know if Denzil shoots all right, but he likes guns and he could do damage if he's close. No alarms, for the usual reasons. Shale doesn't want anything flashy or noisy that might bring the police into his place poking about. Best quality locks on doors and windows, but locks are only locks, and windows are always glass.'

'Wife? Live-in woman?' Kit asked.

'His wife, Sybil, left him,' Fenton replied, 'and is shacked up somewhere here in Wales with her new man, as a matter of fact. Off and on Shale does have a bird sleeping in for short spells – a few days, or couple of weeks, maximum – yes. There are three main names.' He did some recall and held up one finger at a time as he gave the list: 'Patricia, Lowri, Carmel. Never more than one at a time. He's fussy about appearances and despises promiscuity.'

'Women of that sort, women housed on even a temporary basis, can show terrific loyalty,' Kit said. 'Might attempt to save him, or would be willing to give evidence subsequently.'

Ember said: 'Plus – and this is important – his children live with him. Let's see all the . . . all the implications of this, shall we? Kids of school age, Laurent and Matilda. He's devoted.'

'Yes, probably easiest in the day when the kids are not present,' Fenton said. 'There's a chance the woman would be out, too – supposing it was a time when he had a woman staying there. Carmel works at an estate agent's. Patricia has sick parents and visits them quite a bit, usually afternoons.'

Ron came down the room and stood behind Fenton, studying the plans of the rectory interior. He leaned over and pointed to a large sitting room on the ground-floor plan. The white cuff of his shirt gleamed. 'That would seem to be the ideal spot, Hinton,' he said. His voice was more chatty now and quicker. 'This communication box could be knocked out as a first move. Enter via the house side door here.' He pointed again. His cuff-links were leaf-shaped, tasteful and not too big, in dull, muted gold. 'As E.W. says, a lock's a lock regardless and can be coped with. Broken glass is no good because of the warning din. All right, Denzil is upstairs in his flat and hears the shots, supposing it's done with guns. This is a point – does it have to be? Do all hirable people use guns only? If Shale were slaughtered silently and very fast it might be possible to get up to Denzil while he's still unaware. That would be a knife to do Shale but probably a bullet for Denzil, when there'd no longer be need for silence. But, let's suppose not, suppose it has to be guns throughout. All right, Denzil comes down this staircase here, I take it, at a rush, pistol ready, and it would be only a matter of waiting for him inside a ground-floor room with the door open. Then pop out and finish him before he reached the bottom steps, possibly. Exit through the same door, which is *so* beautifully adjacent. Perhaps, in fact, we wouldn't need to hire. It looks straightforward. Possibly, Hinton, one or two of us hereabouts could handle it and qualify for the fee. Julia's glass is empty, Kit.'

Ember said: 'And Manse's kids come home from school and find –'

'Whichever way we pick there got to be pluses, there got to be minuses,' Greville replied.

Chapter Nine

'Thanks for coming all this way, Mr Harpur.'

'If this is where you feel most relaxed, I –'

'Most relaxed.' Acidity coated the words now, as if she'd found the phrase in the back of a drawer like a forgotten garment and was shaking it out and holding it up to get a good look. This was mockery, nearly a sneer. 'Most relaxed, yeah, and safest. Safest, this is the thing. I wouldn't feel like that at home. I wouldn't feel like that if you came to Oxford, suppose you would. And we're almost finished for Christmas, anyway. People know I'm at Oxford, don't they? They can locate me. I've had phone calls. In London – yes, I feel *relaxed*. It's nice and big and anonymous and crowded.'

'What phone calls? Safe from what?' Harpur said.

'Need Des Iles know you've come here to meet me?' Fay-Alice replied. 'He's your boss, isn't he? Does he know everything you do?'

'I –'

'No, of course he doesn't.'

'I can cook up a cover tale if necessary. Is this about Mr Iles, then?'

'I needed to see someone. I can't go to my college personal tutor with a problem like this, can I? Nor friends or my mother. You're used to it.'

'What?'

'Death. Threats,' she said. 'Sort of threats.'

They were in a huge DVD and CD music shop off Piccadilly Circus. She had suggested the spot when she rang Harpur from Oxford. This seemed to be the one place she knew in London, and not a bad choice. The temple of Youth was all right for a sightseeing visit. They could sit privately in a booth and talk while listening to discs. She'd have to buy something to justify the time. Fay-Alice seemed on a retrospective jaunt and was playing sixties soul from Stax, with vocals by Otis Redding, Carla Thomas, William Bell. Harpur liked the verve and swoop and ingenuity in this stuff, might even think of taking the one with Thomas's 'Gee Whiz' on it. In their large-minded way, his daughters did not object to historical music, would sometimes allow that the past had its riches. Jill even listened to the Beatles once when she was running a temperature.

'Look,' Fay-Alice said, 'did Iles kill for me?'

There weren't many girls who could ask a question like that. He felt something theatrical to it: the scale of the inquiry, the short, snappy, dramatic words, the marvellous, sharp distinction of her profile as she gazed towards the sound system, like speaking to the back row of the stalls. Always there had been more to Fay-Alice than her long back. 'Do you want to believe he'd kill for you?' Harpur replied.

'Not *would*. Did. Do you think I'm vain?' She stood, hit a goofily arrogant, eye-bright, self-satirizing pose and spoke like a melodrama: 'Look at me, look at me, men do murder for me.' She sat down again. 'I'm not the only one who wonders about Iles. But, all right, yes, I'm vain, vain and scared.'

Harpur said: 'An appalling death like Dubal's – people start all kinds of steamy, wild theories when such things happen.'

'His mother's been on the phone.'

'She and Ferdy were close. Yes, she's disorientated by his death.'

'I'd say orientated. Can do the tracking needed to locate me. When she rings me she's ringing the right persons, isn't she?'

'Persons, plural?'

'She rings me and it's meant also for someone else.'

'Rang you to say what?' Harpur replied.

'Rang and still rings.'

'Rang and still rings to say what?'

'It *is* frightening, isn't it?'

'What?'

'What she's asking. What she believes,' Fay-Alice said. 'Yes, you're right, there's plainly a thrill element, even a thankful element if someone sees off your father's murderer for you and trashes the corpse as bonus, but –'

'We don't know Dubal killed your father.'

'Iles knows.'

'Don't you think we'd act if any of us were *actually* sure?' Harpur replied.

She stared at him for a moment, baffled possibly. Or maybe it was irony. Universities taught a lot of irony. 'Act? Haven't you noticed? Somebody *has* acted: Dubal flattened in a warehouse. That's one reason I'm nervous as well as pleased. He had colleagues. And a mother. They might think retaliation.'

'You don't *look* nervous.'

'How do I look?'

'Well –'

'No fucking chat-up lines, Harpur, OK?' she said. 'I know about my features and back and boobs.'

'What other reason – for being frightened?' he replied. 'Others?'

'Oh, Iles, of course.'

Fay-Alice had come on a lot since the prize-giving at Taldamon school. She'd learned how to be terrified. She still had that long back and serene, magically symmetrical face – still had the elegance and grace that went with them. But some jauntiness had shrivelled. This was more than simply growing up. People close to the Assistant Chief often did learn how to be terrified, and Harpur assumed she had become close to him. Harpur felt saddened that she could not be relaxed – meaning safe – about seeing him in Oxford or back home. Getting to full womanhood had become a trip of dark tangles for Fay-Alice, and, of course, she was bright enough to know it and resent it and wonder if she'd ever recover ordinary, half-baked, lovely, youthful happiness and confidence. He would have liked to help her with them, but 'no fucking chat-up lines, Harpur, OK?' She knew about her appearance. She'd hear of it from admirers all the time. Harpur kept a description of her in his mind, terse like an art gallery caption: 'Girl with long back.'

Otis Redding's 'Mr Pitiful' came up on the CD. Harpur adored the music, even with a bum title like that. He could already hear Jill's deepest puke noises if he bought it and she read the contents list.

'"This is Agnes Dubal, as I expect you've guessed. You're shagging Desmond Iles, aren't you, dear?"' Across the gorgeous CD din Fay-Alice did a not-bad imitation of the voice, giving the sha syllable of shagging real sparkle and duration. 'That's what she comes on the phone with, this as a start.'

'Which phone?' Harpur replied.

'What? Why? "I don't deny he's attractive, despite everything," Mrs D tells me. "Have you seen the red scarf with the leather bomber jacket? Like a svelte, First War German air ace, full of smart evil. But you had to open up to him, anyway, didn't you?" A college residences phone. Three stuck on a wall in the vestibule, cheaper than mobiles. No glass between. The numbers are in the book under the college name. I get called down from my room to speak and that's how she begins. There are people all round – on the other phones, going out, coming in.'

'How would she know?'

'I told you: the numbers are in the book.'

'No, not that,' Harpur replied.

'What?'

'That you're shagging Iles.'

'Who said I *was*?' she asked.

'Mrs Dubal.'

'She assumes a quid pro quo for killing her boy. Or a quim pro quo, doesn't she? She thinks I couldn't be more obligated, couldn't be more loving, more won. Do Ferdy equals get to do Fay-Alice.'

Had Harpur ever heard a woman use the term 'quim' before, and about herself? He laughed at the impact. That must be what Oxford did for a girl, or a prime private school. Active vocabs were extended. 'So, what did you say to her on this extremely public public telephone?'

'I said, "You fucking crone – talk more shit like that and I ring off." '

'The people around heard this?'

'I don't think it would shock everyone. You catch quite a lot of blurts like that on those phones – to stalkers, hangers on, dons sniffing for more than essays.'

'But the "fucking crone" bit is extra, isn't it?' Harpur replied.

'Some of the stalkers, hangers on, dons sniffing for more than essays *are* fucking crones. Or they'd like to be fucking.'

'I might ask my daughters to sidestep university.'

'Some do all right, don't they? Your occasional live-in friend, for example. Anyway, the rough warning quietened Mrs Dubal. As if I'm going to discuss Des with her! I asked what she meant by "attractive despite everything", as applied to Iles – I said, "Despite *which* everything, Mrs Dubal?" "Everything," she answered. "You sound joyous." I remember that – not joy*ful*, joy*ous*. That's up a notch, isn't it? "Joyous at Ferdinand's death and so on." "And so on," I took to mean the car ploughing.'

'That's so brutal of her. Joyous? My God, Fay-Alice – to think you'd take pleasure in someone's death and defacement.'

'Oh, I had to tell her I was naturally *somewhat* joyous,' she replied. 'I don't think I'd ever used the word "somewhat" before. Just right, though. It would have been incredible, otherwise. She said that even when I was cursing her I sounded joyous, and more than a bit. So I said,

"Possibly." There have been several calls. Perhaps I'm mixing things from a few.'

'Do you mean, you're summoned from your room in the residences each time and go down to the phone to answer?'

'That's it.'

'How exactly?'

'What?'

'How does it work?' Harpur asked. 'Is it that someone's passing near the phones, hears the bell, answers, is asked to fetch you and has to come up to your room?'

'Right.'

'The phones take incoming calls? Unusual.'

'They take incoming direct dial calls. Not through the operator – no reversed charges, no collect. Is this important? Don't you believe I had the calls? Why would I say I did? Why do you want the detail?'

'And then you trek all the way down to answer,' Harpur replied. 'I say "all the way". How far are you from the phone?'

'I'm on the second floor.'

'So, a trek.'

'Sort of.'

'And has Mrs Dubal told the messenger who comes for you her name?'

'Of course.'

'You go down, even though you know the kind of muck she's likely to say?'

'If someone has climbed all those stairs to get me, I can't say I don't want to take the call, can I?'

'And that's why you go down?'

Fay-Alice put her head back and, looking at the booth's padded ceiling, said: 'Part of it. But, also, I suppose, yes, there must be an enjoyable side. I really like it that the old bitch is in pain and wearing herself gaunt trying to find out who killed her murdering, shithead son. If you produce someone like that you deserve the lot. Or, she knows who killed her shithead son but looks for proof. But why, when the proof would go to Des Iles? Doesn't she know? Can someone still be naive at her age, and with a son like Ferdy, about how the law works, or doesn't? Perhaps proof for the Press or TV. A moral stink. Anyway, I do my honest best to give her a bit more agony. OK, frown and frown, but I shouldn't think you've had a father murdered, Mr Harpur. Just me and Hamlet.'

'I can understand your –'

'Even a father like mine.'

'You come down again from your room and she just starts as before, does she?' Harpur replied.

Fay-Alice began her imitation again: ' "Has Iles said anything to you about it? Like, did he promise you the killing, as other men might promise a bird jewellery or the Seychelles, as sex bait? Ferdinand told me he'd heard Iles was really obsessed by you, Fay-Alice, even more for now than with his whore at the Valencia, although he'd never give *her* up, clearly." That kind of wholesome chat. I'm supposed to pass it on to Des, I expect – show she's digging and that she knows some things. Bother him. Make him do something stupid and panicky and give-away.'

'Her thinking is poisoned for the present, you see,' Harpur replied.

'This is the number I like best of anything.' she said. 'Respect Yourself', by the Staple Singers started. 'It's a fair message.' Delight in the tune flashed over Fay-Alice's face. Her eyes were a warm blue, her hair short and as near blonde as was realistic. It had hung down, clean and lively, off her neck when she put her head back just now to think and stare up. Harpur could see how the ACC would be captivated by her: that combination of sweet calm with moments of glorious vividness. The Assistant Chief loved that – thought life itself should be this way. 'Des Iles would never get so crude or explicit as to give a death promise, would he?' she said. 'The idea might be around, sort of perfuming the air, but to frame it in words he'd regard as vulgar, degrading – to himself, that is.'

'Which idea?'

'Which d'you think? Besides which, Iles would have another reason for doing Dubal, wouldn't he? My father was his favourite grass. Now, Iles faces an information drought. Dubal has to suffer. Isn't there something mystical between a police officer and his fink?'

'He liked Wayne. We all did.'

'My father was his favourite grass, and Dubal killed him.'

'We have no evidence for that,' Harpur replied.

'Which?'

'Which what?'

'That dad was Iles's grass or that Dubal killed him.'

'Either.'

'Or Dubal's people,' she replied. 'Like the one at the school.'

'We get a blank there.'

'What sort of stuff did dad give him?' she asked.

'Officers don't always discuss with colleagues material received from outside sources, even supposing your father *did* inform.' Jesus, the pomp.

'I thought it was all supposed to be regulated and organized now to prevent corruption.'

'What?'

'Grassing. I read in the Press how it had been systematized after some kicked-out cases that involved grasses – so no policeman could claim any informant was his and his only. All belonged to the whole force.'

'That's certainly so,' Harpur replied.

'But really it isn't?'

'Informants and their handlers are very carefully supervised.'

'Are yours? Was Desmond's?'

Harpur remembered Wayne Ridout commenting on her educated ability to ask questions, unacceptable, grossly clever questions. 'The way things operate now is much healthier,' he replied.

Fay-Alice said: 'I should think dad told him about anything in the drug firms that might make one of them too powerful and upset the peace. Or a new one getting on faster than he should, like Dubal. It was all to do with balance, wasn't it? Like the arms race in international affairs – OK as long as everyone's round about equal. Dad must have been really valuable. Think of the Taldamon fees.'

'I hear nothing but good of the school,' Harpur replied. 'It's odd when you call him Desmond. I think of only the old Chief doing that.'

'His wife? You know his wife, don't you? But perhaps the two of you didn't talk about him much.'

'I suppose I don't see him as a first name person.'

She looked for another way around the wall: 'Mrs Dubal said her son thought he had a tail.'

'Someone from one of the firms?' Harpur asked. 'They do that. Like industrial espionage.'

'A woman, youngish. In fact, she asked was it me.'

'Absurd. Her mind's knocked sideways, poor creature.'

'She thought I could have been helping Des Iles – locating Ferdy for him to slaughter.'

'God, absurd twice.'

'It's unnerving. *Did* you have someone behind him?' Fay-Alice asked.

'Tailing Dubal?'

'If you had a girl tailing Ferdy, she might have seen what happened to him, in the warehouse and before.' She seemed to concentrate on the music for a little while. 'But she'd have told you by now, wouldn't she? Would she? Do police always tell each other everything?'

'Tailing's an art,' Harpur replied. 'I haven't any women officers trained to it. Certainly not young ones.'

'Can you see now why I'm a bit uneasy – why I wouldn't want this meeting back home or in Oxford? Probably silly to be spotted with you. There's Mrs Dubal, there's Des Iles. I don't in fact fuck him, you know.'

'Wise,' Harpur said. 'He's had crabs. I'd hate to spoil anything between you two, but at least crabs. He might be clear now. He hasn't talked about them lately or shown me. Where don't you fuck him?'

'Yes, we meet.'

'Conversation?'

'A drink.'

'You go openly to bars together?' Harpur asked.

'A drink in the car.'

'He admires you, I know.'

'Obviously, he *wants* to.'

'What?'

'Fuck.'

'Iles can be like that. I expect he whimpers about harsh deprivation, does he?'

'But we don't,' she said.

'He'd be frustrated yet certainly respect your attitude – like in this disc. I know how highly he regards you.'

'You mean he must think something of me if he keeps meeting me even without a fuck?' she asked.

It was the sort of blunt, amazingly perceptive question you could get from the young. Harpur said: 'Your interest in French poetry captured him. And I can understand this. Denise – the undergraduate friend of mine – is the same. She recites a French poem about a wolf who never complains, just accepts. Stoical? She thinks I should be like that when she goes off now and then for a while.'

'With?'

'Oh, yes, with.'

'With?'

'Lads of her own age. Or intellectuals,' Harpur said.

'But you do make love in between times? It's not *all* French poetry?'

'Not all, no. Admitted.'

'Did Iles tell you he was fucking me?' she asked.

'He would never talk like that, even if he was.'

'But I heard he often tells you you were fucking his wife,' Fay-Alice replied.

'He can get edgy, like all of us.'

'In any case, you'd already know. Obviously.'

'What?'

'That you'd been fucking his wife. Of course, there was a time when Des was off me, anyway.'

'Because you offered too much gratitude for what he did at the school. He's always uneasy about thanks. He has a kind of humility. It's unlike other people's humility. Not much in Iles resembles what's in the rest of us. Have you noticed his Adam's apple?'

'He changed again.'

'Well, he would. He does admire you.'

She grimaced for a second, creasing the fine skin. Harpur wanted to forbid it, as if this were a lovely, proud kid who should not have to fret and get troubled yet, just enjoy old music and the glam and privilege of Oxford. Stupid: hadn't he already noticed she'd needed to mature fast since Taldamon, and it would take an idiot *not* to notice? She wasn't dressed student but had on a long, tan cashmere-wool overcoat which she'd unbuttoned in the shop to show a quite formal turquoise silk-style suit. This was a girl you wouldn't mind being seen with on a brewery tour or in the hospitality suite of a Premier League soccer club. 'It's worrying that a man would kill to please me, Mr Harpur. Exciting, as I said, but . . . oh, I don't know, eerie.'

'It would be if it had happened.'

She smirked. 'You have to lower the portcullis. Fortress culture. But he kills to please me and I still don't take him to bed, do I? Look, I know I mentioned all that stuff about girls in school saying how lucky I was and how they'd love to shag Des Iles. Actually, they said bonk – like a one-off. It's a word so right for now, my generation, isn't it – typical – to suggest jolly pleasure without commitment, without irksomeness. No real harm.'

'My father told me they said "bonk" when he was a schoolboy in the war.'

'Oh?'

' "On the bonk" meant with a hard on. They used to go

to the pictures to see Betty Grable and, as a matter of fact, Alice Faye, to get on the bonk in the cheap front seats.'

'Really?' She coloured for a second.

'They'd joke about fly buttons bursting and crackling on the screen like bullets. The Odeon had an educational role those days and trouser flies had buttons.'

'Yes, like that with the Sixth at my school as well – just talk and fantasy, wasn't it? But Ferdy Dubal spread over a warehouse floor . . . it's a bit different. This is . . . concrete? This is *real* bullets.' She shook for a moment. It didn't seem an act. 'And I mean, there *is* Des Iles's age, isn't there, and the greyness? *Was* someone watching Dubal when Des killed him and drove over him?'

'Fay-Alice, you keep talking as if this is fact.'

'Yes, I do.'

'Crazy,' Harpur said.

'All right, all right, is there information that says it *wasn't* Des Iles? I don't want to blame him wrongly.'

'Someone like Dubal would spot and shake off a tail.'

'Mrs Dubal said Ferd told her you had someone undercover in his firm originally, a girl, but he asked her to leave. He wondered if the tail was the same girl. There was even a name – Machin, Louise Machin? Out-of-town cop.'

'I thought you said she suspected *you*.'

'That's Mrs Dubal, not Ferdy. She's primitive and bright – theorizes about Iles and me, believes everything comes down to sex.'

'So much does.'

'For you, too?'

'Ferdy *asked* the undercover girl to leave, did he?' Harpur replied.

'What he told his mother.'

'Just asked?' Harpur said.

'Yes, it seemed . . . it seemed a bit gentle and unlikely to me, as well. Simply requested a snoop to withdraw? Toned down for Mrs Dubal? Do you know about it? Did you have a girl in there? Was she killed or something, like that Raymond Street? Oh, God, she was rumbled?'

'Mr Iles doesn't permit undercover, because of Street,' Harpur said.

'Yes, but did *you* have a girl in there, you as you? *Was* she following him? I want to know Des didn't do it, that's all. I don't have to know who did. As long as Dubal's dead and it's settled somehow for dad, I don't care. Except I think I hope it wasn't Des Iles, although it would be such a fancy tribute from him. Would he get all cold about gratitude again?'

'You mean you don't want to go to bed with a man you know has killed?' Harpur replied.

'Des is great, not just the scarf and bomber jacket and total swagger, but it's . . . well . . . it's an *unusual* idea.'

'He's an Assistant Chief Constable, for heaven's sake.'

'An Assistant Chief Constable with former crabs. Anyway, what does Assistant Chief Constable signify?'

'Where's law and order if you believe an Assistant Chief could –'

'He was an Assistant Chief when those men were killed after the Ray Street acquittals, wasn't he?'

'What does Street have to do with –'

'This means you don't *know* – I mean know as *know* – you don't *know* Iles didn't finish Ferdy, does it? You really didn't have a tail on him?'

'You're talking guilty until proved innocent,' Harpur replied.

'Certainly. But this is Desmond Iles.'

'Aren't you a bit jumbled, Fay-Alice? You seem scared if you're thankful he'll back off, but also scared that, if he's tried to please you with some proxy vengeance and you still rebuff him, he –'

'I once heard dad say at home to my mother that Iles was no joke. I'm not sure I even knew properly who Iles was at the time but I could see dad worried, and the comment stuck. "No joke" in dad's language meant a full-time, blood-on-the-teeth savage.'

True, Iles was no joke. Or he could be one of those jokes composed only to piss on normal taste. 'It's all preposterous, Fay-Alice,' he said, 'the whole concoction.'

'No, he does want me. He does.' She said it instantly and sounded hurt, desperate to be believed. Harpur still felt unsure what she wanted. Unsure whether she knew. Did she intend to get clear of Iles? Or would she like to sanitize him if she could – if Harpur could *for* her, now – and bring him closer? *He wants me*. And did *she* want *him*, despite the age matter and general worries, like was he a killer?

Harpur still hoped, half-hoped, she *did*. Hazel might be safer then, to use Fay-Alice's word. Hazel made him anxious. Single-parenting brought frets. Did he exaggerate the ACC's interest in her? Was it just pleasant friendliness? Possibly. Did he exaggerate Hazel's interest in Iles? Possibly. A similar uncertainty as with Fay-Alice. At the base of these confusions lay Harpur's wonder that any woman or girl could see anything in the ACC, and Harpur's knowledge that some women and girls somehow did.

When Iles was around back there, Harpur disliked being far from home too long, like this London episode. And he would ensure he returned in decent time this evening, no matter how friendly and so on Fay-Alice might get, opened up by the music and general West End stimulation. He could not rely on Denise to look in to check the girls were all right. Harpur had rung her earlier to say he was called away, though not what for, but Denise could get preoccupied with her dopey academic load and/or social opportunities at the university, and might not manage a visit to Arthur Street today. Understandable enough. She was a student, not his wife, not the girls' mother. He had to be reasonable, didn't he, didn't he, and accept in tolerant fucking spirit how she so fucking selfishly decided to timetable herself? In any case, Iles might not discover Harpur's absence, and, if he did, would have no idea when he might abruptly reappear, this righteous and protective daddy. A man had a lot of sides.

'Are you missing tutorials and gaudies and supervisions

and all that sort of thing, Fay-Alice?' Harpur asked. 'Will you be rusticated, gated and caned at high table?'

'Like that.'

Of course, Harpur saw why Fay-Alice had wanted this meeting, had persuaded him to London. She hoped he'd say something – hint at something – which would give her the truth – a bit of the truth – about the death of her father and of Dubal, and about the possible tailing and witnessing, and about Iles. Above all about Iles. He'd wormed far into her mentality, as the tireless, impossible roughneck mysteriously but undoubtedly could sometimes with women. In her academic way, she needed Iles defined. The ACC would have been a difficult commodity for a girl of Fay-Alice's age even in ordinary conditions, despite her being bright enough for Oxford and cool enough for the quim pun. And these were not ordinary conditions. Not really: as Fay-Alice had said, Dubal dead then car-carved on the warehouse floor introduced quite bleak elements.

Harpur could not offer her any hints or disclosures or slices of truth. Instead, he dished out tranquillizers. Plainly, the most insolently ludicrous of these was: how could anyone who had faith in law and order believe a British Assistant Chief Constable might be behind the display vengeance-killing of Dubal? It was one of those questions spoken as if it needed no answer. Fay-Alice would have liked an answer. So would anyone else who knew the details of Dubal's death. Harpur decided the question must do on its own, though.

'All right,' he said, 'the only true bit in the whole bag of flimflam might be that Iles wants you.'

'The rest of it starts from there,' she said.

'There isn't a rest of it.'

Harpur bought himself the 'Gee Whiz' CD and a box of all four for Fay-Alice at £42.99. Student budgets were tight and Nora Ridout a widow, although the cashmere-wool coat must have cost. Harpur did not think Fay-Alice had expected his gift of the discs or fished for it. She looked surprised and charmed, but failed to kiss him or anything like that. Perhaps he shouldn't have spoken about Iles's hatred of gratitude. She might imagine it a police characteristic. Perhaps she felt Harpur hadn't delivered at this meeting. He knew he hadn't, or only the discs, thank God. He had carefully listened to himself not talk too much.

Just the same, now and then when Denise neglected him, shelved him, Harpur could get distraught and would be affectionate with someone else, as antidote. Of course, Hazel and Jill despised him for these occasional promiscuities. They considered that with his looks and age he should realize how lucky he was to get a girl like Denise, and stay patient and faithful. That might be sensible, but Harpur felt you did not sojourn to London, spend half a day listening to hormonal music with a magnificent girl, then expect decorously to shake hands, say Cheerio and return home. He decorously shook hands with Fay-Alice, said Cheerio and set about returning home.

The boxed CDs had to be paid for from his own money. It would have upset him to make Fay-Alice an official charge on the informant fund, because this could suggest a very grim slice of determinism: father a grass, daughter a grass. Fay-Alice had to escape the dismal shadow of Wayne, and Harpur took it as a duty to help. Grasses were admittedly vital and precious, but he did not see Fay-Alice as one. In any case, he would loathe to make a formal item from talk that kept suggesting Iles was a cock-driven and driving killer, even though he might be. It came back, didn't it, to the question which received no answer because the answer seemed built in: where would law and order be, for heaven's sake, if one believed that of an ACC, even an ACC who had or had had crabs?

Iles wanted another visit to Ralph Ember's club, the Monty, just he and Harpur. The ACC loved to make this kind of call now and then. At the Monty, he could throw his weight about and nose into all sorts. And he had a kind of time-blessed liking for Ralph, enjoyed talking to him, reassuring him, insulting him, terrifying him. Iles sometimes told Harpur that the welfare and community sides of policing were as vital as any other – 'traffic direction, lost dogs, bicycle theft'. The Assistant Chief drove. It was dark. He said: 'While it's still possible, we should make the most of fine local institutions like Ralph and the Monty. I expect you'll recall the lines from a Walter de la Mare poem.'

'It's odd you should mention that,' Harpur replied.

> ' "Look thy last on all things lovely,
> Every hour,"

Col.'

'One of Mare's snappiest, sir.'

' "Look thy last" because such treasured items might be gone soon. For example, even before applying those lines to the Monty, I felt like that about the old Grill downstairs at the Ritz in Piccadilly. Undoubtedly you did, too, Col.'

'An oasis, sir.'

'I imagine that like me you frequented the Grill, knowing it could not continue as it was in such a cheapskate age as ours.'

'Many a time I told myself that while hurrying urgently there, sir.'

'And now the same about Ralph and the Monty,' Iles replied. 'Yes, yes, "all things lovely".'

For a couple of moments, Harpur thought Iles somehow knew he had been up to London to see Fay-Alice and, in the slimy, roundabout way he'd use sometimes, was saying so. Piccadilly, Piccadilly, Piccadilly. But now Harpur saw that Iles intended something wider, a theme. He was one for themes.

'He could go, Col. The club could go.'

'Go?'

'Just go.'

'Ralph sell up? I always understood he had big, long-term ambitions for the Monty. Of course, he knows they're mad but they still bring him hope.'

'Removed, Col. Destroyed. Ralph's certain to be a target in any hostilities, and if Ralph is, so is the Monty.' Instead of driving into the club car park, Iles stopped a little distance away in Shield Terrace. 'We'll watch a while.' The big Ford was fairly new and conceivably might not be recognized worldwide as the ACC's yet. Yes, conceivably. Iles switched off his lights. 'Change everywhere, Col. People, things, disappear. Think of Wayne Ridout. A great, great informant, Col. Removed.'

> ' "Look thy last on all things lovely,
> Every hour,"

sir.'

'But change can also be positive. Thank God there are other informants.'

'None registered by you, sir. I'd know. I'm Controller.'

'Fuck off, Col. Who registers all their grasses? Do you?' Again Harpur wondered if he had spoken to Fay-Alice about the London trip. This more or less echoed segments of the talk with her. 'Obviously, I had to register Wayne because funding was needed to place his daughter in Taldamon school.'

'That's the girl with the long back, isn't it, and the nearly-name of some old film star – Alice Gable? Related to Clark?'

'From a considerable source, I get in-depth profile information on E.W. Fenton, Col,' Iles replied.

'Which considerable, unregistered source would this be, sir?'

'This is what I was saying about Ralph.'

'What, sir?'

'He's beginning to falter. He takes on someone like Fenton. Slack of Ralph. Dozy. Suicidal. Ember can't manage him. Ralph has to be in peril.'

'Ralph knows how to keep subordinates subordinate,' Harpur said.

'Here he is now,' Iles replied. Fenton, wearing a dark

suit and black patent shoes, came out of the club and walked to a Citroën in the car park. He looked buoyant. Ember appeared at the door and waved him off. Fenton climbed into the vehicle and drove away from them down the Terrace.

'He's around Ralph such a lot now,' Iles said.

'Bodyguarding. Ralph and Shale are naturally more edgy since the new regime.'

'My information says more than minding.'

'Information from where, sir?'

'And the profile suggests Fenton would not settle for a mere heavy's job,' Iles replied.

'Profile from where, sir?'

'You'll say someone with a baby nose like that hardly deserves a profile at all.'

'Will I, sir?'

'This boy's some strategist, Col. He knows organization. In fact, his forte has been to organize, reorganize, commodity trade in one or other main city, take his whack, move on. I'm talking about Hull, Sheffield, Birmingham, Preston. No overstaying. No form. Just inspired consultancy.'

'So, how is this known?'

'My whisperer says Fenton's changing, though. Yes, change, change. We all do, don't we, Col? He's getting older. Perhaps he's slowing. Very feasible. Natural. The way someone like you might slow, for instance.' He started to shout. 'I ask myself, would you have the verve and disgusting appetite these days to go after the wife of a colleague and friend such as, let's imagine, Sarah, my –'

'Fenton slowing in what way, sir?' Harpur replied.

'The wish to establish himself, stop nomadding even though it's been profitable. His suit looked like shit on him, but it's £1500 shit. He desires a permanency somewhere. Ambition. That eternal yearning in all serious villains to get respectable, almost respectable. The fierce wish to be a real businessman, with an impeccable front trade to conceal the rest. Does this square with what you've discovered about Fenton, Col?'

'I –'

'You've discovered fuck all, have you?'

'Your grass is a bit of a psychologist, is he, sir?'

'Informing is about more than what time the greengrocer will be burgled, Harpur.'

'Oh, I don't mind a bit of guess and character drawing. Think what they did for that TV programme, *Cracker.*'

'Don't despise TV, Col. I understand there've been two or three quite good things on over the last forty years and I've definitely considered getting a set. Anyway, the profiling of Fenton by my contact stops at about this point. But I can apply it, extend it, Col. Even you might be able to. Fenton crosses the outback, rides into our town and sees Ember's firm. There's Ralph at the top, not much senior management support. My reading of E.W., based on the profile, says he'll wriggle his way in there – do a favour or two for Ralph like fixing the Monty bullet shield and maybe knocking down a troublesome up-and-comer like Ferdy Dubal.'

'You really believe that, sir?'

'You, also, thought me for Ferd, did you, Col?'

'There was an artistic aspect.'

'Thanks.'

'And if you wanted to get among Wayne Ridout's daughter.'

'Fay-Alice?'

'That's the one, sir. It might be a winning gesture to waste the man who wasted her father.'

'I can see that, Col. But I'd hate to have a girl crawling over me, long back and so on or not, just because I saw off an enemy. That would be so damn thank-you-very-much. Abject. Repulsive. Fucking should be much nobler. I can't forgive adoration.'

'That a quote?'

'Which?'

' "Fucking should be much nobler." '

'St Augustine.'

'You're always radiantly sensitive, sir.'

'I am, I am, Harpur. My mother said it would give me a painful yet extremely worthwhile life. They always talk a lot of bollocks, don't they, mothers?' Iles drove down to the Monty car park. 'There's something vague in my information that says E.W. is already involved with Ralph on quite major transactions, possibly with an importer. No names to date, though. No locales. Fenton, as I see it, will get to number two in Ralph's outfit, then go for the elimination of Shale. Fenton's the kind who will want monopoly. Until that, he won't feel fireproof in our new conditions. He's got to make himself strong enough to take on the new warrior Chief and the rest of us. This is a very pragmatic, one-step-at-a-time, cautious operator. But as soon as there's monopoly he annihilates Ember one night. Goodbye, Ralph, goodbye, the Monty as we know it, and as Ralph wants it:

"Look thy last on all things lovely,
Every hour,"

Col. Why, Ralph!' Iles called as they entered the club. 'Didn't I see another letter in the Press from you about the need for better control of space station traffic in the heavens? This was an argument that went to the very nub, the very stellar nub.'

'Mine's a small voice,' Ember replied. 'I felt a duty, that's all.'

'Harpur thought the letter could be published in separate form, as a kind of tract, and handed out on the streets. He's from a Bible-punching background and used to do that sort of thing with the Gospel. You wouldn't think so now, looking at him, and hearing about his lech obsessed way of –'

'The bullet screen is fine, Ralph,' Harpur said, 'but it might be an idea not to stay as much as you used to at one special part of the bar. I know it's your trademark, to be at that desk – proclaims instantly the marvellous, co-identity of the club and yourself – something that members and visitors appreciate so much – but predictabilities are something to be avoided for a while now, don't you think?'

It was fairly early evening and only a few members occupied the club. Iles gazed around. Ember put a port and lemon for the ACC on to the bar and Harpur's one-third, two-thirds gin and cider mix in a half-pint glass. Ember poured himself an Armagnac. 'Harpur does worry over you, Ralph. The company you keep.'

'I feel the same about him,' Ember replied.

'How do you see it now?' Iles asked.

'What?' Ember said.

'The politics of things,' Iles replied.

'Which politics?' Ember said.

'Well, we've had four deaths,' Iles said.

'The politics being why nobody's arrested?' Ember asked.

'We're working on all of them,' Harpur said.

'That right?' Ember replied. 'Some stuff seems to be coming out after all this time. I heard of maybe two men climbing the hill by the anti-aircraft site where Mildly Sedated and Perce were shot.'

'Yes, we've heard of that, too,' Harpur said. 'But possibly Sedated and Percy themselves.'

'One of the two men very big, maybe 250–260 pounds,' Ember replied. 'That's not Mildly or Perce.'

'In the dark, of course, something like physical qualities – difficult,' Harpur said.

'The second one pretty big, also, but nothing like the other,' Ember said.

'*How* big?' Iles asked.

'Not as big as the other.'

'No, you said that. But how big?' Iles said.

'As Mr Harpur said, in the dark it's tricky,' Ember replied.

'All right,' Iles said. 'But a general guess. For instance, Col's size? Is that the idea you get from what you hear?'

'It could be that region,' Ember said.

'Yes, we've had this sort of report,' Harpur replied. 'Very tricky to take further. Who's your witness, Ralph?'

'This is general talk in the club,' Ember said.

'But starting from where?' Iles asked.

'This is general talk in the club,' Ember replied. 'And possibly a vehicle.'

'Car?' Iles asked.

'Might be a car. Perhaps a van,' Ember said.

'Yes, we heard of a vehicle,' Harpur replied.

'Perhaps the information comes to both of you from the same source,' Iles said.

'But we don't know Mr Harpur's source,' Ember replied.

'Nor yours, Ralph,' Harpur said.

'This is general talk in the club,' Ember said.

'We're having to stay with our original view that Mildly and Perce had crossed Dubal somehow and were taken up there for execution,' Harpur replied. 'Garland's trying to identify the vehicle, the possible vehicle, and trace it to Dubal.'

'In a way it's a pity Dubal's dead,' Ember said.

'Which way's that then, Ralph?' Iles asked.

'He could have been questioned,' Ember said.

'People like Dubal usually haven't very much to say,' Iles replied.

'Especially now,' Ember said.

'What's the general talk in the club about Dubal, Ralph?' Iles asked.

'Oh, obviously, that you killed him,' Ember replied.

'Yes, I was just asking Harpur if he thought that.'

'That you developed the taste, following what happened after Street's death. It must be embarrassing for you,' Ember said. 'You've got a new Chief, Mr Iles, so I imagine you wouldn't want to get off on that kind of footing.'

'Which?' Iles replied.

'Suspected of the Dubal extinction, no matter how unbelievable it might seem to many,' Ember said.

'Thanks, Ralph.'

'Wayne Ridout's daughter is quite a piece,' Ember replied.

'I hate to hear any woman described like that,' Iles said.

'This is the girl whose schooling you paid for,' Ember said.

'School fees these days are a load – as you'd know, Ralph, a daughter in Poitiers and the other one at a private place here,' Iles said.

'Lovely chin and arse,' Ember said.

'I hate to hear a woman described like that,' Iles said.

'This is general talk in the club,' Ember replied. 'This is the kind of girl a man might kill for. I hear you're out with her in your car when she's home for a weekend, Mr Iles, having winter picnics, that sort of thing. You visit Oxford? That sort of thing. Pleasant. Considerate. I feel you're the kind who'd want to offer a young girl proper preparation, not just plunge. That kind of girl. This closeness could be awkward if it got about, even for someone with such a wholesome reputation as yours, taking into account the Ferd death and the extras done to him. Could that be seen as wooing? Might it strike a new Chief so, a new Chief out to get you, remove you? This is a girl who needs to keep her mind functioning nicely for university tasks, not get the back of her head banged about on big Ford rear seat upholstery.'

'Harpur's very concerned about your relationship with E.W., Ralph,' Iles replied.

'Relationship?' Ember said.

'Right-hand-manning in your outfit,' Iles said.

'E.W. does some little tasks for me,' Ember replied. 'Ad hoc.'

'I've heard of ad hoc,' Iles said. 'But have you got E.W.'s background – sort of profile? I think that's what people like Harpur would call it. Harpur frets that you might not have E.W.'s profile, know his mind, his scale.'

'I don't feel I need to pry,' Ember said. 'His work is satisfactory. At its level. No substantive tasks, obviously.'

'This is generous of you, Ralph, and typical of you, if I may say.'

'One takes people as one finds them,' Ember replied.

'Ah. You subscribe to the same phrase emporium as the old Chief and Harpur, do you?' Iles asked. 'Carry anything these days, Ralphy?'

'Carry?' Ember replied.

'That suit – of such fabled cut one can't make out if there's a shooter on your tit.'

Ember said: 'Happily, I can envisage no situation where –'

'Does E.W. want to knock Manse over, Ralph?' Iles replied. 'This is what troubles Harpur – that you could be led into such a head-on, crude type of thing. Possibly you'd considered it yourself, even without E.W. In one way, it would make sense. But where are your ambitions for the Monty as our new Athenaeum club if you get tied into something of that sort?'

'What profile? What background?' Ember asked.

'E.W.'s? His character history,' Iles said. 'That's what we'd all wish to discover, Ralph. *We're* used to being ignorant, I'm afraid, but what upsets Harpur is that *you* might be ignorant, too.'

'So why doesn't Mr Harpur say something about it now?' Ember asked.

'Anxiety, I imagine. Tension,' Iles replied. 'Anxiety on your behalf.'

'I don't need it,' Ember said.

'I tell him this,' Iles said. 'But you know Col. The mothering side of him. I tell Harpur and tell him that you're fond of Manse Shale and would never wish to provoke a trade war with him which might leave Manse, or even you, dead, Ralph. To kill someone in what was once a rectory, for instance! Monstrous. I assure Harpur you could never be persuaded into that kind of set-to, no matter how E.W.'s influence has grown and will continue to grow. But will Col accept this? Sorry, Ralph.'

'What influence?' Ember said.

'I say to Harpur, don't I, Harpur, when he begins to fret: Am I mistaking two people? We're talking about Ralph Ember, aren't we, about Ralph W. Ember, who writes letters on universal topics that are pubished in the Press? Is he going to be dragooned by some damn employee, some fly-by-night?'

'Or then another aspect,' Ember replied. 'There were those tales of a police girl planted in Dubal's little firm.'

'Which tales are those?' Iles asked.

'Suppose Dubal found out and sent Mildly and Perce up the hill with her to get rid, and this is discovered somehow and there's a rescue party, a rescue duo,' Ember replied. 'Big lads. One *very* big lad.'

'Which rescue duo?' Iles said.

'Some kind of conflict between the firms or even within Dubal's own firm,' Harpur said. 'These have to remain our most likelies.'

'What sort of rescue duo?' Iles asked.

'I find I can think of the future with a certain serenity,' Ember replied. 'Of course I am aware of changes. But so much has been achieved here by intelligent self-regulation. I can't believe it would be deliberately endangered, no matter by what regime.'

'Sure you can believe it, you sanctimonious, gabbling prick,' Iles said. 'Everyone wants peace on the streets, but not everyone wants it the way we've been getting it. Even Col's dubious. You're good at early sightings of disaster, Ralph. And at avoidance measures. Use them. You could get hit from outside and in.'

'But couldn't all of us, Mr Iles?' Ember replied.

Jack Lamb rang Arthur Street to arrange a meeting. These days, if one of Harpur's daughters took Jack's call, she was quite passably civil. He'd come to the house one night on an emergency visit unlinked to any of the present turmoil and they'd met him, approved of him, found Jack nothing like what they'd imagined: not slimy or furtive or fawning, not like a caricature grass. Now, Jill didn't yell out to Harpur without covering the mouthpiece that a fink was on the phone. A fink *was* on the phone, but she found sweeter ways to say so.

Harpur and Lamb met tonight at the old foreshore blockhouse, put up all those years ago to throw the Nazis back into the sea. It was stocky and square and might have done that if they'd ever shown up. Now, it was what was described and prized as 'war architecture': slab cement with gun-slits. For this spot, also, Jack would usually put on army surplus. Tonight he wore a green beret from the Second World War and a bum freezer overcoat that had its real moment when officers rode horses in the First. Jack did what he usually did and stared out for a while at the darkness on the face of the deep to check no invaders loomed, and to ensure the tide still knew its damn limits.

'I worry about Ralph Ember, Colin. I worry about Manse Shale,' he said, turning. It was black in the blockhouse but Harpur could make out his frame and the outline of those hefty features. 'This lad Fenton.'

'I've heard of him,' Harpur replied.

'He's been on an absolutely major deal trip with Ralph.'

'That right?'

'You know this?'

'This is the lad who put the Monty shield up?'

'Are you pissing me about, Col?'

'Not much is known of Fenton,' Harpur replied.

'I've arranged for a profile.'

'That right?' Harpur replied.

'It seemed important. Col, there are whole areas I'd never grass about.'

'Definitely.'

'But this – this could involve the general peace.'

Here was Jack's justification of grassing again. And Harpur listened, again.

'Commerce – yours truly's as much as anyone's –

requires that peace, Col,' Lamb said. 'And mine is the great and lovely cause of Art.'

'Right.'

'This is Ralphy and Fenton with a super-importer. The name's Quarat. Their meeting – like cementing things, perfecting the business plan?'

'Where did this happen, Jack?'

'You've got at least three people present in that gathering, Quarat, Fenton, a lady called Julia, who are all directed towards outright, uncompromising monopoly. That's plain in Fenton's profile. Quarat will be the same. I've had tabs on him from far back. The lady advises. This trio are sure to have reached total rapport in any policy session. Possibly they already knew each other, though they might not let Ralph see that. They'll run him. Do you understand the peril for him and Shale? Can you see the prospect of a bad, unbreakable empire, with manageable villains like Shale and Ember eliminated?'

'How many other people at this meeting, Jack? Where and when? Quarat? Is Quarat big enough to have domestic staff, aides?'

'Does the Home Office or whoever realize what they do to this patch by removing Mark Lane and neutering Iles?' Lamb replied.

'Someone else at this meeting is your source, right, Jack?' Harpur said. 'Servants present? That kind of thing?'

'I expect you heard there's a buzz around about two people up the hill,' Lamb said.

'Well, clearly, two people up the hill, Mildly Sedated and Perce.'

'Are you pissing me about?' Lamb replied. 'Plus a query van.'

'Which buzz?' Harpur asked. 'Who?'

'You've heard this, have you?' He moved towards the blockhouse door. 'The saving or not of this domain is on you, Col.' Lamb saluted with huge gravity and smartness and withdrew into the night, like a commando off to cut sentries' throats.

Chapter Ten

Trade strategy meetings between the boards of Ralph Ember's firm and Mansel Shale's always took place in a hotel-restaurant called the Agincourt on the edge of the town. Most times Ralph went armed, and especially now, obviously. He had gone through some bad scares at the Agincourt. These were two firms in alliance, yes, but alliances might get shaky: Britain and America friends with Russia against Hitler, Britain and America enemies of Russia in the Cold War. You could never be sure about Manse, and especially now, obviously. This was why, at the start – before Fenton and Quarat and Julia – why, at the start, unprompted Ralph had thought about removing him.

As well as Manse himself there was Denzil, apparently deputy chairman of the company these days, although he still chauffered Manse and did general heaviness. Denzil had never been known for tact or discretion but increased responsibilities might bring these out in him, the way they said Truman produced all sorts of surprising qualities once he unexpectedly became President.

Most nights the Agincourt put on medieval banquets with wench waitresses breast flashing like Nell Gwyn and plastic halberds and boars' heads stuck on the walls. The firms had an arrangement for a business dinner there every few months on a Monday, when the Agincourt would normally be shut. The waitresses were asked to wear modest clothes in keeping with business discussion. Ember took the Walther. He would humour E.W. Nothing else had been said about the detail and timing of how to blow holes in Manse, but Ember had a feeling that E.W. could have been privately in touch with Quarat and Julia and Ron, the butler. In fact, Ralph had a feeling, too, that they or people hired might try it this night, after the meeting, when Manse went home to the rectory. Ember could not have explained where these feelings came from, but always respected his instincts. Quarat had seemed to want some hurry. He might have discarded E.W.'s recommendation that daytime would be best.

Of course, targeting tonight assumed Manse and Denzil did not attempt something themselves at the Agincourt. After a drink Denzil could get excited by the trappings of war and field sports. At times Denzil was just a sick prick. Or Manse might actually have carefully schemed a blitz. Possibly he wouldn't think of the objections E.W. and Quarat had made to the Agincourt as killing site, or he'd perhaps ignore them. People did go at problems in different styles. This illustrated free will, and Ember more or less favoured that.

Clearly, if Manse did start shooting here Ralph would have to shoot back, regardless of the difficulties this might cause with the police later. In view of all the anxiety around, Ralph's main concern had to be not an investigation later, but whether he would in fact be capable of getting the Walther out, placing a finger round the trigger and firing. All that deep breathing stuff to offset panics did not really do much for Ralph when the panic became major, and in the Agincourt tonight it could be major. He was accustomed to worrying about Manse, but this evening he had to worry about someone on his own payroll, Fenton. E.W. had what figured in the current commercial claptrap as his 'own agenda', the shit. During massive panics Ember's fingers sometimes refused to bend.

He and E.W. went in separate cars to the Agincourt and, driving there alone, Ralph could do what he loved doing, direct his mind to larger matters than the merely tactical, and the undignified prospect of bowel-squeezing panic.

With his kind of mind, he felt an obligation to seek the overall view. Questions of family, for instance, preoccupied him. Not just his own family, though the uncertainties there were serious. Suppose all the indicators turned out right and E.W. hoped eventually, or sooner than eventually, to overtake Ralph, shove him out and set up a cosy link with Quarat. Even if they let Ralph live, they wouldn't let him earn from the core business. What happened then to his home and the club and his daughters and Margaret? Would the girls have to be taken out of their fine schools and put into some state place? Ember certainly did not despise state education. Once or twice he had thought of writing to the Press to discuss aspects of it, such as the importance of uniform, though caps for older boys might not be acceptable in the twenty-first century. Many children could profit from such schools. Think of William Hague, ex-leader of the Conservative Party. But, simply, Ralph's daughters were not used to that system and it would be heartless and irresponsible to throw them into a sink. Such crudity would be poor for his social reputation.

Pre-dinner the firms' leaders always had drinks at the Agincourt's small bar. Ralph had asked them to stock Kressmann's Armagnac but, obviously, he did not drink this *before* a meal, it was what the French called a *digestif.* He took a Campari. This he felt helped liberate his palate for the dishes to come. Mansel had gin and Italian vermouth, which Ember considered sweet for an aperitif, but this again was that free will matter. Most probably Mansel had heard someone talking about gin and It, or read a mention in some class magazine, and he'd think it sounded sophisticated. He loved the idea of sophistication – fair enough for someone like Manse with his little face and ferrety eyes.

Denzil sometimes had stout, sometimes Coca Cola. It was not worthwhile to think for long about *his* tastes. He had something stuffed in his trousers belt. Even if it hadn't bulged there you could have guessed by the way he fussed over keeping his jacket done up, like trying to hide a baby bump. To Ember it looked at least a .38 and possibly a .44 or .45. A gun of that calibre fired from as near as across a dining table would really tear at someone's physique. It made Ember emotional to think of himself hit in the throat or chest by a bullet of this size. Tragic was the only word for how he would lie on the floor or be sprawled back in his chair after an attack like that. Even if it were E.W. who was broken open point blank tonight, Ember knew he himself would feel bad, regardless of E.W.'s shitty scheming. There were comic, distorting mirrors in the Agincourt and Ember tried to visualize how E.W. would come across in one of them if he got shot, which, obviously, God forbid. These mirrors would sometimes put a look of agony and lostness on to someone when they were in their ordinary state, so if a person were shot with a thick bullet their appearance in the glass might be notably touching. Nobody could have spotted anything in E.W.'s face as it was now, without the mirror, about secret stuff with Quarat or Julia or Ron.

'My view re the general scene?' Shale said. 'My view is our enterprises hold up regardless of the new environment, by which I mean a changed Chief and supposed change of policy. As I see it, some of us rushed too fast to battle stations. I mean, we *expected* changes so we *imagined* they was taking place.'

'Which some of us?' Ember replied.

'Oh, Ralph, I'm in this as much as you, of course, of course,' Shale said. 'I don't accuse. Always we have known deep in our minds that it all depended on Mark Lane. It looked like it depended on Iles, but in what's referred to by many as the subconscious we was aware, Ralph, you and myself – let's call it the directorate, without undue vanity, I feel – we was aware that what Iles could do for peace operated because he had a Chief like Mr Lane. I don't know if I'm right and you can be *aware* of something in what's referred to as the subconscious, because if it's in the subconscious many would say we was not *aware* of it, it was just there, lurking there, like a mugger, ready to come out and yell its message at that other part of the mind, known as the conscious part.'

Denzil said: 'Christ, Manse, you been reading again?'

'So, the old Chief goes and we're ready for terrible change,' Shale replied. 'Even if it don't come we find it because we've made ourselves scared there *will* be terrible change. This don't add up, not at all. We got a nice settled way of doing things here full of the best decorum, and because it's settled nobody can mess it about. They know this. Of course they know it. This way of doing things is the *normal* way of doing things in this domain. This is the point, surely. Definitely. We have built our own conditions here, our own culture. It would be just mad for anyone to try and upset these. Vandalism. They can't fight what time has done for us. I mean, consider America.'

'America's always a consideration one way or the other,' Denzil said. Last time Ember could recall, Shale was using a 9 mm Beretta which would probably have a fifteen round box. Maybe Manse went for the gin and Italian to match it.

'Most likely some of you know America used to belong to Britain,' Shale replied. 'This is factual. Then America gets to go on its own after a big change way back. I mean way, way back, before Eisenhower. Now, in this twenty-first century, they've clearly got their own life over there. No question. They got their own leaders and government. Not pounds, it's dollars, isn't it? Not petrol, gas. For them this is normal over there. They have *made* it normal. It wouldn't be no good at all one of our people from the government going over there and saying, "Look, you used to belong to us, so stop calling arse fanny because only fanny is fanny." They wouldn't listen because they believe in Yank ways now. And we would not have the rudeness and cheek to tell them they was wrong. It's the same here with trade. What we got is something that is *our* way of working, and it works beautiful. It has took over from them other crude ways, like street slaughter in London or

Manchester or Liverpool. This is a system. It can't be fucked about with now in this twenty-first century.'

'The accounts are good, Manse, that's a fact,' Ember replied.

'Confirmed,' Shale said.

Obviously, the *real*, deep accounts were never produced at Agincourt meetings. For that, Ralph and Manse had a confidential session one-to-one, different place, different day. This was not because the authentic figures were poor and might discourage staff. It was because Ralph and Manse realized an unpleasant envy could be caused if their incomes got known by followers. Tell Denzil Manse's yearly take was £600,000, rising? Fucking indelicate. *Still* rising, as Manse said. Now, Shale began to outline the doctored accounts for Denzil and E.W.

Because Ralph knew these figures meant nothing, he let his mind slip back to the thoughts that had occupied him en route in the car. As well as concern for his own wife and daughters, he felt troubled, in a different style, about Iles's family also. But why should he worry over possible destruction of that arrogant prick's home? Perhaps because family was family, even Iles's. Or perhaps because, as a result, Fay-Alice would be permanently lost to the area and therefore to Ralph's attractive plans for her. As he saw it, if Fenton brought off what he wanted and achieved a monopoly too powerful for even Iles to control and contain, the ACC would regard his function here as closed. Possibly it was already closing, under the new Chief. But E.W.'s blatant sovereignty would make Iles's defeat utter and intolerable. Might he then decide to go – perhaps quit everything, his work, his home, his daughter, his wife, and disappear with Fay-Alice? This was not an alarmist forecast. Iles already had Fay-Alice Ridout on the side, didn't he? Some observers said it might be far *more* than on the side – that it seemed disgustingly deep, meaningful, unfleshly. He'd heard almost incredible gossip that Iles might not even have fucked her yet. People who'd done some surveillance had seen only the picnics, genuine, hamper-supplied, in-car picnics, all clothes on, occupying both front seats throughout, non-tilted. Yet Iles did not appear sick or prematurely ageing. Rumour said he'd had crabs. Might he still have them and be putting on the gentleman until they cleared? He could be like that, acting out sly, phoney humaneness.

But Ember felt more inclined to believe Iles was behaving with honest, decent restraint, sinisterly respecting the young girl's wish to govern the pace. It seemed unlikely for a sex wretch like Iles, yet possible. In fact, here might be a cruelly significant relationship with a non-lust element, even if it *was* Iles. This would seem to go beyond what he did with girls from the Valencia. Fay-Alice's Oxford side and poetry and so on would intrigue the snob bastard, bring substitute satisfaction.

It really distressed Ralph to think that Iles, desperate, broken, humiliated, might on a terrible impulse destroy his fine home. And this would be vastly worse if he went off with Fay-Alice. Everyone knew Iles adored his child, called Fanny, as a matter of fact. Why couldn't the rampant slob content himself with looking after her and his wife? Ember found it agonizing to think of Fay-Alice, with that lovely frame, taken right out of circulation by an egomaniac like Desmond Iles, who should be tending his domestic role, the scheming swine.

Ralph felt Fay-Alice was certainly a girl intelligent enough to appreciate and delight in the Heston resemblance, but also to see there was so much more to Ralph W. Ember than a flukey star-match status. It would be appalling if a destroyed Iles decided to retire and set up house in Oxford with her until she graduated. Given a degree and that arse she would, of course, be able to get a great job in the media, charity administration or some top Whitehall Think Tank, and help keep him. Iles would look at salary tables and calculate how much she could add to what was left of his pension after he decently paid the Rougement Place bills. Ember thought it despicable for a man to depend on his wife's or woman's earnings. If he, personally, could get something going with Fay-Alice, he would not object to her being away at Oxford to finish her course or taking a job in London. He could visit. Hotels. A flat, even. Cost he would never let become a hindrance. He did not always like love interest too close geographically. That kind of relationship might turn demanding and awkward. This day and age, women were often off on their own for a while and within reason he did not mind.

Ember switched his brain and ears back to Manse's Agincourt survey: 'We got something we're entitled to be proud of here,' Shale said. 'Without blasphemy, I hope, we got like a Creation. What we done is bring a good way of life for many out of what used to be chaos. Compare the Bible. *Let there be light*, it says there. Here, it's *Let there be sweet trading conditions*. Some might want to destroy this, just as Satan wanted to destroy that other Creation, through spite. They can't do it because what has been created is bigger and stronger than they are.'

'Absolutely, Mansel,' E.W. replied. When Ember had arrived at the Agincourt E.W. was already here, smiling a really good time with Manse and Denz, doing a prime socializing job, Ralph would concede. Naturally, Fenton would be carrying something, perhaps another Walther. That made a comfortable chunk of fire power, unless Manse had additional people hidden around the building. This was always the trouble at the Agincourt, a big place with some sections locked off, or supposed to be locked off, when the Monday meetings happened. It would take an hour to do a worthwhile search and, in any case, Ralph would have felt it rude to Manse to demand a look-around. After all, Manse could be regarded as a treasured, even loved, business associate. Yes, Ralph had thought about killing him, and he brought a gun tonight in case Manse tried get pre-emptive with the Beretta in a business sense. But some politeness was still vital. Yes, also, Fenton might know how Manse would be put an end to later on tonight away from the Agincourt, and possibly Denzil as well, but for the present the approved rules of a friendly gathering applied, and you would not suggest another guest might have a regiment on the premises ready to blast to nothing the fire power of two Walthers.

Ember felt delighted he could go over all these points without even the beginning of a panic. If he had needed to pull the Walther out now and start making a point he felt almost sure he could, and hit Manse and Denzil where it really counted. One thing Ember hated – gun-play that did not do itself justice. In fact, he hated the term 'gun-play'. It should not be *play*. He loathed shooting only meant to 'wing' people, as it was idiotically known. If you had to fire – and he always prayed and prayed it would be unnecessary – but if you had to fire you fired to kill. No, not some dim game.

They went in to dinner. A medieval banquet used to be swan but impossible these days, and not just because the length of neck was too much for the smaller kitchens and dining rooms of modern buildings. Swans had become an officially protected species. Not even the Queen and so on killed them. At the medieval banquet they served goose instead. There were real wines that came in unopened bottles, not the mead slurp they served in jugs at skin-you prices the rest of the week to Dumbo coach parties. Shale and Ember took it turns year by year to pay, Manse this year.

'Me, I always look for the positives,' Shale said.

'I'll back you on that, Manse,' E.W. replied. This was the kind of thing you could expect from E.W. He did not really know Mansel Shale, yet he would call him Manse at quite a formal dinner with poultry and various stuffings which Manse was paying for.

'When I say positives I'm talking about indicators, for example,' Manse said. 'Oh, I know when we speak of the accounts that these accounts have a big slice in them from the time of the previous regime, before Mark Lane went. You could say distorted, too favourable. This is why I ask, get some concentration on indicators. In my firm we got month by month and in fact week by week indicators in certain particular spots, such as Dring Street, the My Pip nightclub, the Poratha hotel and bars. They're *like* typical, like one result in the General Election can tell you the whole picture. Well, in all these places, lads, sales are up this last three months and, what is more, this last week.'

'Hear, hear!' Fenton cried.

'The new regime's in place, am I fucking right, and yet commerce is as commerce should always be, expanding,' Shale said.

'Brilliant, Manse,' E.W. replied. Ember became even more certain Shale would be killed tonight and most probably Denzil. Fenton was really doing a soothe on Manse, agreeing with every damn thing, like a valet, acting like the horseshit about America made sense. Of course, Manse had a brain and he might see E.W.'s carry-on. Even Denz might see it. This was what Ember meant about something pre-emptive. Now, he did experience the early outlines of a panic sweat. Moisture formed on the back of his fork hand as he ate the goose and good veg. His eyes seemed fine, though – able to focus all right on Manse and Denzil. Ralph tried to keep his gaze off the funny mirrors because if your eyes went bad the sort of picture you'd get from those mirrors would be twice as awful.

'Another positive as I hear in the wind is Ralph's got a new importer,' Shale said.

'I was going to mention that in my report,' Ember replied.

'It must be a real good relief to know you're fixed up like that again after earlier troubles,' Shale said.

'This is Hinton Quarat,' Denzil said.

'Yes, a grand relief,' Ember replied.

'How does he see things, Ralph?' Shale asked.

'See?' Ember said.

'Like, his thinking,' Shale replied.

'About which aspects?' Ember asked.

'The, like, general future, I believe Manse means,' Denzil said.

'Don't fucking tell me what I mean, you jumped-up fucking Wheels,' Shale replied.

'Piss off, Manse,' Denzil said. 'I was only trying to damp down your verbiage.'

'Don't,' Shale replied. He took a bare, gnawed goose bone from his own plate and flung it on to Denzil's. 'Pick at that, you assistant fucking baggage man.'

'What's Quarat's view of the general future, Ralphy?' Denzil asked.

'Yes, what's his view of the general future, Ralph?' Shale said.

'Fortunate to have a beautifully established market with two major firms in civilized cooperation,' Fenton said.

'You know him, this Quarat?' Denzil asked.

'As a business link, through Ralph,' Fenton replied.

'Plus this woman who works with him – Julia, as we hear?' Denzil asked.

'Julia, that's it,' Fenton replied.

'This is a woman yet someone in her own right,' Shale said.

'Considerable personality,' Ember replied.

'A thinker, as I'm told,' Shale said.

'She's famous at that,' Denzil said.

'If she's fucking famous at it we don't need you to fucking tell us, do we?' Shale replied. 'You ever heard of a fucking tautology?'

'I got one in the car if you're short, Manse,' Denzil said.

'What Julia is famous at is being a thinker,' Shale said.

'Ah,' Denzil replied. 'Why don't I ever see things as clear as you, Manse?'

'A thinker in a commercial way,' Shale said.

'Hinton Quarat values her,' E.W. said.

'You know that, do you?' Shale replied.

'It was very apparent,' E.W. said.

Denzil leaned in friendly style across his plate and the bone from Manse and said to E.W.: 'I never know with "apparent" whether it means it *seems* to be like this or that but might be something else, or if it's *apparent* because it is obvious and true, such as "It was apparent he had joined the army because he had the uniform on." Strange double meaning, wouldn't you say?'

'Sod off,' Shale replied.

'Yes, Quarat clearly esteemed her,' E.W. said.

'I'm in favour of esteem for women,' Shale replied. 'They've had a big struggle. Suffragettes.'

'This was quite an episode in history,' Denzil said. 'Many have heard of it.'

'Economics,' Shale replied.

'Now, here really *is* a topic,' Denzil said.

'What, Manse?' Ember asked.

'Her thinking – it's Economics,' Shale replied. 'Degrees in it. You could call her a round peg in a round hole.'

'The best,' Denzil said.

'I done inquiries,' Shale replied.

Flan came in next. Manse told the girls they could go. He would see to the coffees and run the bar. It was all in the price. He gave them a twenty each, no big show about that.

'What Economics is about is what's referred to as the market and competition,' Shale said. He did not touch flan himself, although not slim. 'By the market I mean the Stock Market and general trade.'

'What she hates – competition,' Denzil said.

'I think *I'm* fucking telling this,' Shale replied. 'Didn't you fucking notice? I've had inquiries made, character guides.'

Denzil said: 'You can get people in Economics who love competition, such as making everyone really work at things because they're scared the other side will do better. But some in Economics are different.'

'What Julia hates is competition,' Shale said. 'How she sees it – competition is a waste. It don't work.'

'This is this different view in Economics,' Denzil said.

'You're going to ask, why don't it work, as they think,' Shale said.

'No, we're too busy with the flan, Manse, to ask why it don't work, but you can tell us, anyway,' Denzil replied.

'This is how some people in Economics look at things, not just Julia,' Shale said. 'What's called in the Economics world, "a school of thought".'

'All kinds of schools in Economics,' Ember replied.

'You at the college – I expect you bumped into them, Ralph,' Shale said.

'Many arguments,' Ember said.

'So, obviously, this got to affect us as us,' Denzil replied.

'They think – this "school of thought" – they think that when you got competition what you got is outfits so scared of one another they spend all their time and all their money and all their strength fighting one another instead of just getting on with things, getting on with things meaning selling stuff to people at a nice price,' Shale said. 'This is what they mean when they say competition is a waste.'

'I got to admit this is a point of view,' Denzil replied. 'If I was in Economics I would not kick this point of view out of the door.'

'They think competition is a phoney, people like Julia,' Shale said. 'And, like E.W. noted, Quarat listens respectful to her. She advises. Why is it a phoney? It's a phoney because all the outfits fighting one another are fighting one another because they want to knock the others right out of things. They want to smash them, finish them. When a shop cuts its prices what's that for? It's so it pulls all the customers and forces the others to go bust. The customers are laughing because things are so cheap. But what's it like when the other shops go bust? Then there isn't no competition is there, because there's just the one left who's the winner? So, the one who's left puts all the prices back up again, higher and higher because people got to go to them because there isn't nobody else. What people like Julia say is what competition is about is getting rid of the competition so you can carry on after without no competition.'

Ralph watched Denzil slap the table near his flan plate and really laugh, he was so surprised at Shale's speech. It seemed a true revelation for him, the thick shit, this slab of basic, basic stuff. 'What, like you and Ralphy trying to get rid of each other?' Denzil replied.

E.W. said: 'Oh, I –'

'Well, this is a woman who looks at our domain because now Hinton Quarat got a concern with this domain because he's going to supply Ralph and Hinton Quarat is her boss,' Shale said. 'All right, she sees commerce going on more or less as usual, so peaceful, don't she, as I said? That's lovely – good for trade. But, of course, she've heard things could change any day. There's already a sign things are unmellow, such as Dubal minced, and maybe the other deaths, also. All right, Dubal might really have got it only because he upset Iles by killing his grass, Wayne Ridout, who was a pal –'

'And also upset the grass's daughter who Iles is knocking off or would like to,' Denzil remarked.

'Do we have to be so fucking coarse?' Shale replied. 'This is a young girl of no known slagging as yet even though a student.'

'Well, it's a factor,' Denzil said.

'And, yes, Dubal also naturally upset Wayne's daughter Fay-Alice – some fucking name,' Shale said. 'And, yes again, this is a girl the Assistant Chief admires considerable and would like to get across, if not already, though this is not proved, the already part, I mean. But Julia don't think like that, even if she heard about Iles getting so ratty. These elements are just friendship or sex. This girl, Julia, is Economics. She thinks things got a proper cause, not vengeance for a snitching mate, not just dick. Oh, no, how she sees them killings is they're a sign things have gone unstable. She thinks Dubal got killed and maybe his two people, Mildly and Perce, because we in this domain was on the fast track back to trade war. So, someone gets rid of a bit of the opposition, I mean Dubal. And she's the kind who would think the next move in the new system under the new Chief is a three-way war on the streets – Ralph, us, the police. And that's the kind of competition she thinks is so crazy, such a waste, so expensive, so uncommercial.'

'Do you know what this is, Manse?' Denzil asked.

'What?' Shale replied.

'What you just said,' Denzil said.

'What?' Shale asked.

'An analysis,' Denzil replied. 'Has to be. I never heard something that was more like an analysis than that, looking right into things. Someone good had been giving you the info about all that – Julia, Quarat, maybe from inside – but it's you that's come up with the analysis, Manse. Don't you other lads think so?'

'This is certainly one interpretation of how things might be,' E.W. said.

'You know this woman, this Julia?' Denzil asked.

'A conference in North Wales,' E.W. replied.

'Someone there broadcasts?' Denzil said.

'You don't ask questions like that,' Shale replied.

'Why?' Denzil said.

'Think, you fucking serf,' Shale replied.

'Is this leak all around?' Denzil said.

'Information got its own life,' Shale said.

'But, E.W., did you know her before? Did you know Quarat before?' Denzil said. 'Why I'm asking, E.W., is, if you knew them before, it would tell you if this analysis carried out by Manse is a good analysis – whether this is the way she would most likely regard things.'

'Manse has done a lot of thinking here,' E.W. replied.

'When you said "one interpretation" did you mean this was *only* one, for instance, and there could be so many others and Manse's interpretation might be bollocks?' Denzil asked.

Ember said: 'Manse is certainly entitled to his own reading of things.'

'What I got to ask is what advice this Julia would give

Hinton Quarat if I got it right and she sees the situation like I think she sees the situation,' Shale replied.

'This would be her job, would it, Manse, an adviser, confidential, like myself in that respect?' Denzil asked.

'She got training. This woman's an expert,' Shale said.

'What could be known as a guru,' Denzil said. 'It wouldn't worry me if people called me your guru, Manse.'

'Advice?' Ember replied. 'Clearly, Manse, if she's opposed to inefficient competition she'd want us to continue the peace here, regardless of the changes.'

'Exactly that,' E.W. said.

'Or maybe she believes in monopoly,' Shale replied. 'Monopoly is how they are sometimes in Economics.'

'Monopoly?' Denzil said. 'That's just one having the lot?'

'Just one,' Shale replied.

Denzil pushed his plate away, like needing more space to think. 'Implications, yes?'

'Hinton Quarat's customer is Ralph, isn't it?' Shale said.

'Oh, God,' Denzil said. 'He's the one?'

Ember was glad he'd finished most of his meal because his hands had become a bit weak and runny. Christ, you would think these two sods, Manse and Denz, had been at the Quarat meeting, not just a voice from inside, say that wine waiter, Kit, or the other one. Ember spoke to himself forbidding any hand movement to his scar. He would keep right out of *actual* speaking for a while. He might not be able to manage words, anyway, especially hard-consonant words. The gun nudged his chest and should have brought a bit of consolation but he knew it was useless to him.

'It's here I would depart from Manse's analysis,' E.W. said. He gave it moderation, reasonableness, yet also a bit of now-hear-this. Ember would never have thought until E.W. that someone dressed in clothes like that could be so cocky. Ralph should have spoken to him about these garments by now but had put it off. People sometimes grew offended if you told them their style was crap.

'What, Manse, you saying Quarat and this Julia want to get rid of you and me?' Denzil asked.

'Best I ask for discussion,' Shale replied.

E.W. gave a really good laugh. Even though Ember felt so bad and knew the realities, this laugh sounded to him honest and wholesome and full of abiding love and endless respect for Manse and Denzil. Many fools and decent folk would have believed this laugh right through. E.W. had so much flair he might not need honesty as well. Perhaps he could even get away with clothes like that. 'It's why I said *one* interpretation,' E.W. remarked.

Things stayed quiet for nearly half a minute and Ember got his tongue going and achieved, 'Absolutely.'

'If I might give you my own assessment of what Julia meant,' E.W. said.

'Did you know her already – the way her mind goes?' Denzil asked.

'We must not do what Manse warned us against at the beginning – fall into imagining certain developments simply because we have been told those developments are imminent,' E.W. replied. 'I'm speaking about monopoly.'

'Such as only one running the total thing?' Denzil said.

'Perhaps we've sort of conditioned ourselves to believing that if the peace breaks up someone is bound to try to rise above the turmoil by securing monopoly,' E.W. said. 'It's more or less formula.'

'That fucking butler there when you was at North Wales?' Shale asked.

'We know *him*, don't we, Manse?' Denzil said.

'Ronaldo, if you can believe it,' Shale said. 'Like the footballer.'

'What about if Manse and I went about calling ourself Mansello and Denzillo? Would people wear it? Or you as Ralpho.'

'But we must not become obsessed by the spectre of

monopoly,' E.W. replied. 'And I do not believe Julia thinks of nothing but monopoly, nor Hinton Quarat. Certainly not of *killings* in the interests of monopoly.' E.W. gave them another pally guffaw. Ember found it free more or less totally from the reek of cordite. 'Cartel, that's her thinking, not monopoly,' E.W. said. 'This was obvious to Ralph and myself. Cartel – that agreement between favoured companies for the sake of controlling all trade. In some mouths this is an abusive word. Cartels can be regarded as anti-public, like monopoly. But they have their positive aspects, too, their benign function, as the economist, Julia, would appreciate.'

'You knew her before all this?' Denzil asked.

Ember said: 'Benign cartels were obviously her favoured form.'

'Now, of course, this type of cooperation already exists between your firm, Manse, and Ralph's,' E.W. replied. 'We wouldn't be here at this beautiful occasion if not. But I could see – and I know Ralph shares this – I could see that what she wanted was a *strengthening* of the connection, not its abolition. A formalizing – more than at present. I sensed, for instance, she'd like joint boardroom meetings made routine, not our dinners only, like tonight. She's a serious one, office-centred, doesn't *really* think work can be done over a good meal! I know she wants more integration, more systematic exchange of information. She – like Manse – believes the alliance is so brilliantly established that it has become the norm in this area. It can be, and urgently should be, fortified, made even better. This was very much her view, and therefore Quarat's.'

'Anyone would have felt this,' Ember said. He gave it heartiness. 'It amounted to an accolade for how things have run here and continue to run, despite upheavals.' He felt easier now. The murk had risen from his mind. He began to see how he would behave, how he *had* to behave.

'As far as Denzil can find out, which is not usually very

fucking far, that butler got no criminal record,' Shale said. 'And they call this a fucking law and order country! What else he got to do?'

Manse served coffee and brought the Kressmann. They all had a drop. In the bar earlier, Manse had given only a summary of the accounts but now did a full, formal presentation, though with fake figures agreed by him and Ember, of course. It was as Manse had said: good increase, even in the last month or two which were after Lane's departure and the beginning of the supposed new conditions. If Manse had produced the true accounts the percentage rise would have been greater still. Ralph and Shale had agreed a £20,000 bonus for Denz and E.W., plus a maximum-jewelled Centido watch each from a platter of them Manse had luckily come into from somewhere. It made Ember queasy to see such a refined piece of machinery on a wrist like Denzil's. Ember had the notion that if Denzil only lay dead somewhere, the watch slightly exposed by a pulled-back sleeve, it would not be so bad, not sickening, but the Centido seemed wrong when Denzil could still swallow drinks and move about and be fully Denzil.

Listening to the fine fiction as Manse detailed their past trading year, Ralph felt unbreakably bonded to him. This was what he had meant a few minutes ago when he decided how he should and must behave from now on. That episode when Ralph had thought about killing him – had even prepared for killing him – it seemed so distant now. Possibly to have heard others, newcomers, discuss how to wipe him out had revealed to Ember his real affection for Shale.

In a way, the agreed lies that Manse offered so sincerely in his special grammar increased Ember's regard for him. If the figures Shale declared now *had* been the real ones, they would still show a sweet achievement, and would have made Ralph sure that here was a business associate worthy of trust and total fellow-feeling. But Ember knew the grand, authentic figures were vastly ahead of these and therefore his liking for Shale must be so much higher. Manse looked naff, talked like anti-education, yet existed as part of a good local fabric. Ember existed as another part, and it would endure, as Manse had said. These people who wanted him removed were not completely evil and not completely foolish: Quarat, Julia, E.W. Definitely not foolish. Some of their arguments impressed Ember off and on in North Wales. But *only* off and on. There had been moments of revulsion and moments of doubt over E.W.'s role.

As Ralph watched and listened to Manse give the phoney accounts such a beautiful glow, he knew he could not side with the three who schemed his death, or perhaps more than three if Ronaldo and one of the waiters were counted. Probably not both the waiters. Kit or Greville did some treacherous mouthing. None of these folk enjoyed any true acquaintance with the history of the domain, its traditions, the sinews of community. At present, Ralph truly and fully felt for Manse what E.W. had only pretended to feel. And Ralph remained troubled, also, about what would happen to Iles and his family, and therefore to the possible availability of Fay-Alice, should monopoly really dawn. He felt it would be immoral to assist in any development which delivered a fine girl like that to a maniac like Iles.

Mansel finished his coffee and carrying a glass of Armagnac went and posed in front of one of the distorting mirrors. He stared for a while, did not seem to laugh. Perhaps he liked the image, as some politicians were flattered by those foul caricature dolls mocking them in the TV satire show, *Spitting Image*. He said: 'Makes you realize what jumped-up, comical, fucking flash-in-the-pans we are.'

'Many would consider you're hard on yourself, Manse, but I don't know,' Denz replied, from where he sat at the table still.

Ember went and stood alongside Shale. It seemed important. Christ, they did both look unbelievably freakish but Manse definitely more. Shale muttered to Ralph: 'They'll come to my place for me, won't they? I got it right?'

'It could be tonight.'

'That fucking Ronaldo?'

'I'll return with you,' Ember replied.

'Will you be all right?'

'Of course I'll be fucking all right,' Ember said.

'Of course you will. If Quarat's there, too, and we kill him you're going to need a new importer again.'

'These are details,' Ember replied.

'And E.W. might be with them.'

'Naturally he'll be with them. He's central.'

'Could you kill him if it came to it, a colleague?' Shale replied.

'These are details. We keep you alive. They might have a plan of the house.'

'You know they have?' Shale replied.

'It's the sort of thing E.W. would supply. Thorough.'

'You know he's done one?'

'They'll use the side door for entry,' Ember said.

'Denzil can be useful now and then in a shoot-out.'

'Christ, Denzil.'

'And then if it comes to disposal – the more bearers we got the better.' Now he did giggle for a while: 'I've never seen anyone look so fucking gross and barmy in one of these mirrors as you, Ralph.'

Ember said: 'E.W.'s carrying a Walther. That's fifteen rounds.'

'Ronaldo's the one to watch for.'

Chapter Eleven

'You can talk in front of us, it will be quite all right,' Jill said. 'We're used to it.'

'I'm not really sure Louise wants that,' Harpur replied.

'Well, you see, it's a –'

'We don't mind a bit people calling here, Louise,' Jill said. 'Now and then Denise will get stroppy and hurt if it's a girl, such as yourself, won't you, Denise, but not if it's obviously a police matter. Is this a police matter?'

'Louise is a detective in the force,' Harpur said.

'So, is it a police matter?' Hazel said.

'Of course it's a police matter, isn't it, dad?' Jill said. 'Denise can tell it's a police matter and doesn't look at all ratty tonight, even though Louise is youngish. Honestly, you don't, Denise. Are you, like, undercover, Louise?'

'There's no need for "like",' Harpur replied.

'Are you undercover, Louise?' Jill said.

'There isn't any undercover,' Harpur said.

'I mean, calling to see dad at home, sort of on the quiet, not at the nick,' Jill said.

'There's no need for "sort of",' Harpur said.

'On the quiet,' Jill said. 'Denise doesn't live here but she's here quite often. Obviously, she's not our mother.'

'No, she's too young,' Louise Machin replied.

'That's one reason,' Jill said.

'We love her,' Hazel said. 'Dad loves her, of course. But we love her also. She's an undergrad. Full of learning as well as all the rest of it. You might not have expected his daughters would love his girlfriend. But why not, I would ask. She keeps dad happy, very happy. Most of the time. This is important to us. Our mother was murdered, you know, a while back.'*

'Yes,' Louise said, 'terrible.'

Hazel said: 'They both had relationships with someone else, mum and dad – dad with Denise and so on – and mum also going her own way, but I think it could have really depressed dad, I mean, your full clinical depression, if Denise had not been around to give him good love and some cohabitation after that.'

'Many girls of Denise's age would have got scared,' Jill said. 'I don't mean just getting sort of involved . . . just getting involved in a murder like that. They might have been scared that suddenly the married man they were going out with, a fling, was not married any more, which might scare a girl because she could think he might want to marry her instead, not just go out with her and the lovey-dovey side, whereas there's a big age gap, and a girl like Denise might be afraid she'd be forced into some forever thing with him with that hair and his clothes and music, plus taking over two kids, one of them being Hazel and all her niggles.'

'The other being Jill and all her blab,' Hazel replied.

'Sometimes his music's not too bad,' Jill said. 'Do you know Stax, Louise? It's soul. "Gee Whiz". Ancient but it moves all right.'

'Can you three go into the kitchen briefly and continue the game?' Harpur asked. They had been playing poker, 10p minimum call, when Louise arrived at just after 11 p.m. The children should have been in bed but Harpur was losing at the poker and had insisted on trying to win his money back.

'Is this urgent, Louise?' Jill asked. 'I suppose it must be, coming here. Have you unearthed something vital?'

'Routine,' Louise replied.

* *Roses, Roses*

'But coming here late at night,' Jill said.
'Not very late,' Louise replied.
'It must be difficult being a detective on this patch,' Hazel said.
'What's referred to as grey areas,' Jill said.
'I expect that's so in all police districts,' Louise replied.
'Hard for you to know what people like dad and Desmond Iles *want* unearthed and what they want left alone,' Jill said. 'Hazel's quite interested in Des Iles, but of course he's here, there and everywhere. Have you seen his red scarf?'
'Let's go then, shall we?' Denise said, gathering up the cards and money.
'We'll make some tea and sandwiches for when you've finished your little talk, Louise,' Jill said.
'The girls are right, aren't they?' Louise said, as soon as they'd gone.
'On what?'
'Grey areas.'
'Jill picks up phrases. Hazel's boyfriend's mother's not keen on the police, and he repeats stuff she says in front of the girls. "Grey areas", "wheels within wheels", "canteen culture", "institutional favouritism".'
'As you know, I try to adjust to it,' Louise replied.
'What?'
'The grey areas thinking.'
'No such thing,' Harpur said. 'Not here. Even if there had been, would a new Chief tolerate that?'
'Perhaps the new Chief won't – ultimately. But the new Chief's still casing the domain.'
They were in the big sitting room at Arthur Street, on separate settees facing each other. Harpur said: 'Try to adjust to it how?'
'When I see things. Do I blow a whistle, do I stay quiet?'
'Which things?' he asked.
'I'm following Dubal. Dubal is killed.'

'You *did* see that?' Harpur asked.

'I told you, I lost him.'

'Did you?'

'Did I tell you? You know I did.'

'I know you told me, but did you lose him?' Harpur replied.

'So, he's killed, I've lost him, I switch,' she said.

'To?'

'I want to know what goes on. That's detection, isn't it?'

'Switch to what, who?'

'I need to know about the trade here. It's . . . oh, it's weak, it's irresponsible not to know.'

'Switch to what, who?' He felt nervous about this girl. Her wide, large-featured face always looked serene enough, but that's not how she was. He would not have picked someone serene. So now he had to put up with what he did pick.

'I thought someone like Ember. He just sails on and on, rich, self-satisfied, increasing. We need some depth on him.'

'You followed Ember?'

'It seemed . . . necessary.'

'We know a huge amount about Ember. We'll act when it's time.'

'Yes?'

'Certainly,' Harpur replied. This appallingly conscientious, intrusive, gifted kid. She'd make a wonderful detective, but he wished she'd make a wonderful detective somewhere else. 'Followed him where?'

'Miles. And miles. He went with his sidekick, Fenton, to a mansion type place in North Wales, near Bala. But maybe you know this.'

'I'd have to look at the Collator reports,' Harpur replied. He'd seen all the Collator reports. Nothing about North Wales. He was not sure they collated Ralph these days. Did you collate stuff on the local, grey area scenery?

'I couldn't get very close, but I asked around.'

'Asked around where?'

'The locals. They'll speak English.'

'It's the kind of thing that gets known about – someone digging like that,' Harpur said.

'How else do I find out?'

Yes, how else.

'The owner's loaded, obviously,' she said. 'This is a place with twenty, twenty-five rooms. Mid-Victorian. Big chimneys, big gables, a few acres of roof. Someone called Hinton Quarat. I'm on sick leave, so I can't ask the computer about him. But living in style – a staff, including a butler who shops in Bala occasionally. Someone pointed him out. Wiry, hard-looking. And at least two other flunkeys. So what's Ralphy Ember doing there? Is Mr Quarat some sort of big supplier? An importer, even?'

'Ember did lose an importer a while ago. Perhaps this was to fix new arrangements, yes.' He felt he owed her some truth. He felt she owed him some. 'Listen, Louise, you're able to follow someone as experienced and wily as Ember and Fenton all those miles to North Wales and not get spotted.'

'Much luck.'

'Possibly. Yet you say Dubal was able to drop you on a tiny trip in town. Is that right? Is it? Were you still behind him when he was killed et cetera? You think we don't talk about ticklish matters like that? You're teaching yourself selected silence? You consider this as learning the urban job?'

She gazed at him for a bit. He wasn't sure whether she gave a millimetre nod. 'And then, tonight, they have a meeting in the Agincourt – Ralph, Fenton, Manse Shale and Shale's chauffeur, Denzil,' Louise replied.

'We know about these get-togethers. They're regular.'

'So, you watch?'

'Not always.'

'No, not always,' she said. 'Not tonight. Shale and Denzil leave at the end of their evening and I assume return to the rectory. Ember and Fenton are in separate vehicles and Ember seems to set off home, to Low Pastures. I stay with him, know the route by now. But he gets out of town and then circles the motorway roundabout and comes back the way he's just gone. I realize after a while he's making for Shale's place.'

'Christ, he's going to try to do Manse? Something preemptive, before the war starts? You witnessed this as well?'

'As well as what?'

'As well as Dubal's death.'

'Dubal lost me. No, I don't think Ralph went gunning for Manse. Well, I know he didn't. I couldn't see it, but I'd say he was welcomed in. I'm looking from a distance. The door opened. A rush of light from the hall. The door closed. No stealth, no violence. I park a way off and walk back. The rectory grounds are nice and big and bushy. I can find cover.'

'I've done it myself.' But, God, this girl took risks.

'I'm there a couple of hours and then the lights go out in the rectory, attic floor first where, maybe, Denzil has a flat. Then the rest. I decide I'm on to nothing at all. Ralph's staying the night for some reason – maybe after private talks with Shale, no Fenton and Denzil. They'd probably need that, wouldn't they – the private accounts? I'll give it another half-hour max. I'm feeling stupid. But, then, after twenty minutes I'm suddenly aware of other people in the grounds, making for a side door. Though it's pretty dark, I can make out one as a certainty from his build as E.W. Fenton. And I think – I *think* – Hinton Quarat's butler, the right sort of springy body. Sorry, you don't like "sort of", do you? The right springy body. They might be blacked up and Fenton has a dark woollen hat on, like SAS. I think – again, I *think* – they were carrying pistols, held down against their leg most of the time, hard to spot. All right, I suppose I should have used the mobile, got to you at once. But this is what I mean when I say grey areas. Am I supposed to do anything about what's going on, or do I just let it resolve itself? It's how villain wars are handled here, isn't it – get them to annihilate one another? Peace on the streets or pieces on the streets, pieces of *them*. I can see it might be sensible.'

'No, not like that at all,' Harpur said.

'Yes, I can see the sense and have to conform.'

'And that's why you stay quiet about Dubal?'

'I don't stay quiet: I keep saying I lost him.'

'All right. Anyway, you were wise not to phone-speak in the rectory grounds,' Harpur replied. 'Voices carry in enclosed terrain. Mobiles are never secure.'

'Yes, well I suppose I thought of some of that, too, but mainly – mainly I wanted to fit in with the philosophy here.'

'Yes, we're all philosophers on this patch.'

'Mr Iles is a philosopher.'

'Mr Iles is a great policeman,' Harpur said. And there were times when Harpur thought this might be true.

Louise said: 'Then, immediately, comes shooting from inside the house. The guns aren't silenced, as far as I can make out, but this is a house standing apart. There's still a bit of traffic noise. Nobody from around there hears.'

'How much shooting?'

'I thought eleven rounds, not all from the same weapon.'

'Not ten, not a dozen, eleven?' Harpur said.

'Right. I'm supposed to count, aren't I?'

'Not everyone would, in those conditions.'

'Which?'

'Dicey.'

'I didn't have anything to do but count,' Louise replied. 'I thought it would be stupid to go in.'

Thank God for this much, anyway. 'Good.'

'Do you mean that? Should I have?' she asked. Now, the large, genial face had lost its blandness. She thought she'd failed, longed to be told she hadn't, wouldn't believe it when reassured. She was bright enough to define the domain's philosophy, not bright enough or strong enough to be certain how to react to it. Should she adopt it, and opt out of incidents like the one at the rectory? *Had* she adopted it about Dubal's death? Or should she have intervened – tried to intervene? Harpur could understand her confusion.

'No, you were right not to go in,' he said. 'You'd already done phenomenally.'

'Would you have gone in?'

'No,' Harpur said.

'Curiosity?'

'No. You were unarmed. Probably five guns in there.'

'You'd have risked it? Scared them by yelling?'

'These aren't people who get scared by yelling. You did right. A protective foliage job.'

She gazed at him again, trying for a read of his eyes. OK: Harpur knew how to make his eyes non-communicative. He recalled very early on trying to read *her* face and eyes. Not easy. In any case, he did consider she'd have been mad to go into the house. One near squeak was enough.

She seemed to pick up his thought. 'Do you think I've been for ever disabled by that episode on the hill?'

'You couldn't have done better.'

'Say ten minutes and Denzil comes out of the front door. He brings the Jaguar up close. They don't put any lights on in the hall. Denzil opens the Jaguar boot and then goes back into the house. In a while, three of them come out carrying what's no question a body.'

'Which three?'

'Ember, Shale, Denzil.'

'Also no question?'

'Enough light for that. My eyes are used to the dark, very used to the dark by then.'

'Do you think Ember knew they were coming?' Harpur said. 'Was he there to help with the trap? You said firing started immediately. Ralph must have beaten the panic, or Manse and Denzil did it all.'

'The three load the body into the Jaguar boot and go back inside. They reappear with another body and push this one into the boot as well, though there's some messing about with legs and arranging. The three get into the car, Denzil driving, Shale alongside him. They don't put the headlights on until they reach the road, luckily, or they might have swept the grounds. I couldn't go with them. My car was too far away.'

'You'd done enough.'

'Had I?'

'I'd leave things like this, Louise,' Harpur replied.

'You mean, Stay quiet? *Please keep noise levels down in this grey area.*'

'I'll pop in on Manse tomorrow for a bit of a conversation and a look around. There won't be anything.'

'How will Mr Quarat manage without a butler?' Louise replied.

Somebody knocked on the front door and Harpur heard one of the children go at a scamper from the kitchen to open it. After a minute, Jill brought Iles into the sitting room. He had on the bomber jacket and red scarf. Mrs Dubal was right. He did look as if he had just strafed something over Flanders. 'Col,' he said, 'saw lights as I was on the way home and thought I must call.'

'On the way home from where, sir?' Harpur replied. 'An Oxford trip? Or is it their Christmas vacation? Oxbridge finish early, don't they?'

'This is Louise,' Jill said. 'She's a detective. One of yours, but I don't suppose you know them all.'

'Ah,' Iles replied.

'I thought maybe undercover,' Jill said.

'Ah,' Iles replied.

Denise and Hazel came in from the kitchen. Hazel was carrying a tray with the large teapot and sandwiches on it. Iles at once went to her and took the tray, maybe getting some finger to finger contact. Harpur could put up with that. Iles said: 'Oh, but this is wonderful. Grand that everyone should be up so late.'

'The girls have school tomorrow,' Harpur said. 'They're going to bed now.'

'Oh?' Iles replied.

'Now,' Harpur said.

'Poor Haze,' Jill said.

'Wart,' Hazel replied.

'What's it mean, an Oxford trip?' Jill asked.

'Mr Iles likes Oxford. It's the spires and so on,' Harpur said.

'What trip?' Hazel asked.

'Mr Iles has a friend there,' Harpur said. It was fair to warn her off, if she needed it, and he was afraid she might need it.

'What friend?' Hazel asked.

'Yes, a friend,' Harpur replied.

'What friend?' Hazel asked.

'She won't let it go,' Jill said. 'Is this a student friend, like dad and Denise?'

'One has so many friends,' Iles replied.

'Too many?' Harpur said.

'What's that mean?' Jill replied.

'Bed now,' Harpur said.

When they had gone, Iles said to Louise: 'I suppose you were just checking in for a little advice on this or that from Colin?'

'Very minor, sir,' she replied.

'Burglary?'

'Supermarket trolley theft,' Louise replied.

'A scourge,' Iles said. He munched and drank.

'We're getting there,' Louise replied.

'Grand,' Iles said. 'I know it's particularly bad around this kind of area, the kind of area Harpur chooses to live and bring up children.'

'Fierce,' Louise replied. 'People keep their coal in the trolleys, not the bath, these days. They've learned about bathing even in this kind of street.'

'Harpur might move you on to something yet more crucial in due course,' Iles said.

'Mustn't run before we can walk,' Louise said.

'My God, if they hear you phrasing like that they'll rush you up to Chief rank,' Iles replied.

In bed later Denise said: 'Some vast secret between you and that Louise?'

'A work secret.'

'Excluding Iles?'

'Oh, of course excluding Iles.'

'I don't feel so bad about it then,' Denise said. 'It *must* be work. That's how work works, isn't it, *your* work? Cut colleagues out.'

'Why should you even start to feel bad?'

'There are times when I seem on the side,' she said.

'There are times when *I* seem on the side.'

'There are times when you *are* on the side. I've told you that,' she replied. 'It's because of my entitlement to see an unrestricted chunk of life and because of my youthfulness.'

'Fuck your youthfulness.'

'Well, you do, you do, you will.'

'Anyway, *you're* never on the side, Denise.'

'It doesn't feel like that sometimes. Tonight.'

'All of that other business is on the side,' he replied. 'You, you're the centre.'

'It doesn't feel like that sometimes.'

'It's unreasonable,' Harpur said. 'You ask for more from me than you're willing to give.'

'I *can* be unreasonable. It's my youthfulness.'

'Fuck your youthfulness.'

'Yes.'